HERE'S WALDO

HERE'S
WALDO

Nick Olson

atmosphere press

This book is in your hands thanks to the love and support of Harmony, CJ, Sean, Wendy, Linda, Joan, Dustin, Matt, Yuriy, Marcos, and Brian, and all the folks who gave notes and encouragement as I worked on and talked about this thing for the better part of six years. Thanks also to Nick Courtright, Kyle McCord, and everyone over at Atmosphere Press for believing in my dream and making it a reality.

Here's to all the non-belongers out there.

PART I

1. The Prodigal Son

The old prodigal son story came to mind as I drove down 294 and watched Bay Colony's apartment buildings rise up over the flatness of the Illinois earth. And it's fitting, because you can't get more biblical than good old Des Plaines, IL.

We've got locust plagues in the form of summertime cicadas that sap the will to live with their cries before attaching themselves to shirt backs, the car seats of those foolish enough to crack the windows of their AC-less beaters. Yearly deluges from the Des Plaines River, to the point where canoe is viable transport. Wailing and gnashing of teeth in the unincorporated part of town (where I'm from), where the primary forms of entertainment are drug use and drag racing on roads that are more pothole than street. The city's claims to fame include being the site of the Flight 191 crash back in '79 (still the deadliest aviation accident to occur on U.S. soil); the hunting grounds of killer clown John Wayne Gacy; and the hometown of the world's first Mickey D's. Yet with all of that said, here I am anyway. The prodigal son returned.

While I respect Jesus' skills as a storyteller, I'm going to have to rewrite a couple of his parable's plot points for the

3

sake of my story. So go ahead and swap out the archetype of the extravagant son who loses it all with the one scraping by with internet writing gigs and unrealistic literary ambitions. Substitute the forgiving father with the estranged mother, the hypochondriac mother who finally got the terminal cancer she always wanted.

But maybe I'm getting ahead of myself.

Better to start at the beginning.

2. The Beginning

In the beginning, there was the bowl cut. The OshKosh B'Gosh overalls and repeat three-peat Chicago Bulls shirt. Drew propping me up awkwardly with hands under armpits and me crying in every damn picture. In the background of a few of those polaroids, there's Mom with poofy '90s hair, smile all teeth and crinkled eyes, unaware of the glioblastoma that would one day eat away at her brain. Dad behind the camera, before the divorce and all the rest. Drew blissful in his ignorance that in another decade he'd be shipped off to prove himself once and for all in the sands of Afghanistan. All of us oblivious to the fact that in those moments we were as close as we'd ever be to being a real family.

I spent my formative years on the Space-Jam-blanketed floor of a two-bedroom apartment in Bay Colony, splitting my hours between Nintendo 64 and cartoons. Bay Colony's a quaint (read: ghetto) little collection of condos tucked away in the cupboard underneath unincorporated Des Plaines' stairs. Its apartment buildings are arranged in U shapes that surround a pond in the center, each of the U-tips pointing toward water like cups that'll never be filled. A moat of blacktop surrounds the buildings, becoming more like a traditional moat whenever it rains hard enough to fill the potholes. The local interstate, 294, swipes a diagonal line to the west and provides a zoolike view for the motorists who pass through. To the south, you have townhomes being swallowed up by a wave of McMansions. To the north is a defunct fisherman's lagoon that now functions as a marijuana hideaway, and the east end of the place is cordoned off by a creek that trickles into a lake just off Good Avenue, where McMansionitis has already been diagnosed.

In short: The place is purgatorial. Part of a city, but not at the same time. A blasted twilight realm that can't be charted or fathomed. Both here and not, acknowledged only when necessary or else forgotten entirely. And looking back on it, the place couldn't have been more fitting for a non-belonger like me.

3. The Non-Belonger

First time I ran away from home, I was eight, and chubby, and still decked out in my little league uniform, and I actually thought I needed to carry a bindle. I couldn't find a polka-dotted blanket to make it proper, so I settled for the *Space Jam* one. Got as far as Bay Colony's pond before heading back home.

A couple blocks from Bay Colony, there's a wreck of a rec area known as Dee Park. Baseball diamonds more weed and mud than grass and dirt. Basketball courts as boxing rings. Gujarati Thugs duking it out in between games of cricket. Kids jumping from trees just to see what'll happen. And yes, I suppose there were little league games too.

We were the Manta Rays. Dad was head coach, Drew assistant. We were up against the D-Backs that day. Head coach: Mario Scalveretti, Jr. (AKA Chooch). Star player: Mario Scalveretti III (AKA Li'l Chooch).

Chooch was all sharp lines and angles, like someone ordered him out of a catalog or something. He'd do things like make his whole team run bases in the middle of the game if they were scored on. Pepper his coaching tips with "goddamn"s and "like a girl"s. We were down by double digits, and Chooch was letting us know it by encouraging a chanting eight-year-old chorus of "You suck!"

The chants would switch over to "Where's Waldo?" once I got up to bat. Li'l Chooch was playing catcher, embellishing the Waldo chorus with "fag," careful to say it just loud enough where only I could hear him. Neither of us knew what the words meant, all we knew was that the big kids said them. All I knew was that it hurt.

Dad pitched, forehead vein throbbing as he arced me an easy one. I swung and missed. Struck on the next one too, and so I figured I'd just stop swinging. After a couple minutes (and more than a few "good eye"s), the crowd started booing. And not just Chooch's section—the whole damn bleachers joined in. My mom included. Granted, she was looking in her compact and hadn't looked to see where her boos were being directed, but still.

Chooch marched out of his dugout, legs like John Wayne. Put his hands up to quiet the crowd. Crouched down so he was at eye-level. His beer breath made my eyes water. I didn't want to be, but I was always afraid of him.

"Gotta choke up, kid. C'mere."

Chooch grabbed my hands and slid them up the bat's handle, tapped against my insteps to widen my stance. I looked into the middle distance, to my dad at the pitcher's mound. He looked away.

I struck out anyway. I'm sure you can guess how LC responded.

And what did I do? Well, what any scared, pissed off eight-year-old would do. I turned around, choked up, and swung for the little bastard's head.

4. Aftermath

The thing about catcher's masks is they're fairly good at keeping objects away from their wearer's face. So I should've expected it when the bat rebounded and split my lip, when it knocked me on my ass. But I didn't.

LC wasn't hurt at all, but we both cried in the way that only startled kids can, silent till we knew it actually hurt, till we were sure people were watching, before bawling our eyes out. And parents ran over, and words were exchanged, and arms grabbed, and then Dad was on the ground, hand to mouth. Seeing him like that and knowing that I was the cause of it felt worse than the split lip did.

Then parents' feet and children's feet and the feet of park employees, and threats of calls to be made and lawyers to be hired, and LC and I sitting in the dirt like human weeds, crying and staring at each other, willing the other to stop first. The game was cancelled; prospect of any future games in doubt. My stomach dropped as Drew lifted me back up.

We went away, all of us, to the car. The seat belt was molten on my skin as I buckled myself in. I remembered to breathe.

And the look my dad gave me in the rearview as he pulled into our Bay Colony parking space. Eyes trailing over my split lip, his own blooming into something purple, something red. And the way his eyes couldn't meet mine as he turned the ignition off, engine fading into silence.

5. Swan and the Pond

Dad held frozen peas to his mouth while he fought off Mom's verbal volley. I was in my room, head swirling, packing my bindle for the long journey ahead. Only the essentials, of course. Holographic Pokémon cards. N64 games. Pogs.

I silently said my goodbyes and snuck out the back door when no one was looking.

The lightning bugs were out and hovering over the pond, little warped reflections in the fading light, taking the place of the stars usually covered up by Chicago's gift of light pollution. The willows that lined the pond's edge hung low and commiserated with my eight-year-old problems. They didn't judge me when I sat under them and cried like a baby.

I quieted down after a while and got that hiccupy breathing kids get when they've stopped crying abruptly. Sat and looked out at the water. The image of my dad, on the ground in front of me, his lip split just like mine. I squeezed out tears. My breath started coming out ragged, pained. I held my breath to stop the noise, but it kept up. That's when I noticed the swan.

He lay there, beaten and broken on the rocks, neck bent like PVC pipe. His breath came out half honk, half whimper. He lifted his wing, put it back down.

We stared at each other, my breath hiccupy and his coming out of PVC pipe lined with broken glass. The willows' branches danced over our heads. Lightning bugs dipped and sought a moon they'd never catch. Cicadas droned in the distance. And we stared and waited.

I crouched down in front of him. Lifted his head and held it up. I wanted him to be comfortable. He opened his beak as if he might bite. Closed it again. Still stared.

I leaned down and kissed him on the cheek, right under his ever-staring eye.

And he died peacefully, in my arms, just like that.

I set him down gently, picked up my bindle, and headed back home.

6. Back Home

I snuck in as stealthily as I snuck out, parents none the wiser. They kept themselves busy by arguing while I was gone. Drew was playing *Turok* in our room, which kind of ruined my stealthy entrance into same.

"How far'd you go?"

"A mile. Ten miles. I walked a lot."

Drew looked at me. A raptor tore Turok to pieces.

"I went to the pond."

Back to his game.

"There was a swan there. And somebody beat him up and I kissed him and he died."

"Cool story."

"Why would somebody beat up a swan?"

The tick-tick of pressed buttons.

"Good on you for swinging at the little prick's head today. You shouldn't have cried, though. Looked like a little bitch."

Another death, this time to a T-Rex. Drew took out the game and blew on *Mario Kart*'s contacts. Docked it.

I knew what was coming, so I didn't bother sharing anything else, even though I wanted to. Drew was about to beat my ass in *Mario Kart,* and I was to face the impending defeat like a little man. Drew pumped up the volume to drown out M & D, but good luck with that.

Mom had this way of locking the word "divorce" into place like a gun being cocked in a satisfying tchick-*tchick*. Duh-*vorce*. Many nights I fell asleep to that lullaby coming through the paper-thin walls. First the whisper so as not to wake Drew and I up. The inevitable outside-voice version. Then the grand finale, the I-don't-care-if-the-whole-world-hears scream. It's messed up, I know, but I'd snuggle up with my plush Taz and get right to sleep every time. Like someone whose apartment grazes train tracks, unable to fall asleep without the driving squeal of steel on steel.

"Wanna play?" Drew asked me.

I made sure my controller was plugged in before I said yes. I was too old for pretend multiplayer.

7. Mark Twain Elementary

During weekdays, us tiny humans peddled our wares, and mingled, and played, and yes I suppose learned a thing or two at Mark Twain Elementary. Being a K-6 institution, the sixth graders were the primary dealers. Us lowly third graders scraped by with Warhead and Wonder Ball exchanges for authentic Duncan yo-yos, maybe the odd pog if we were really lucky.

Our bazaar was a stretch of blacktop that hugged the school. We'd stick to the high, wall ball-friendly walls and keep under the security cameras they had sprouting there: badasses evading Big Brother's surveillance. The younger kids stuck around the island of a trailer in the center of the blacktop (where my classes were held), while the older kids ran the playground with impunity.

I dealt in Pokémon cards, and only holographics to boot. My little corner of blacktop became a veritable hub of activity. The Baby Bottle Pop to card exchange rate was debated, offers of homework to be done considered, deals made. And then LC and his crew came over.

His "crew" at that time was him, Chaz Billington, and Fernando de la Paz. Chaz was a ten-year-old third grader and Fernando already had a mustache, so shit tended to not be taken by them. A couple of my potential clients collected their merchandise and took their business elsewhere. LC greeted me first:

"Whatchu got?"

Fernando snatched the cards out of my hand, handed them to LC. Chaz looked constipated.

"Mine."

LC pocketed my holo Blastoise.

"Mine."

Shadowless Mewtwo.

"Hmm."

He pulled out the greatest treasure of them all. The card of cards. Dark Charizard. Team Rocket. Holographic, of course. Sun glistening against the foil like it was put in the sky specifically for that purpose. I felt dizzy.

No one moved. No one made a sound. LC's face unreadable.

He lifted up the card like he was Link holding the Triforce.

Paused, waited, considered.

Ripped the card in fucking half.

Fernando leveled me in the gut immediately. I doubled over, hit the ground. I wanted to cry, but I knew I couldn't. I wouldn't give them that. I considered detention, the very real possibility of a worse beating should I fight back. I caught my breath and got up to face them anyway. But by then the bell had rung, and everyone was already inside.

8. Lunchtime with Rodhi

I always sat next to Rodhi Boshi, at our table. When I say our table, I mean ours. Like, population: 2, ours. I sponged off pizza grease with my napkin while Rodhi dipped his chapati, dabbed at his mouth after each bite. He handed over little bits of it without my having to ask: a ritual of ours. Pulled out some biology homework that was several grade levels higher than the norm for his age, started up conversation while filling out a gene table:

"How was recess?"

This was necessary to ask, as Rodhi never recessed. Rodhi crammed.

"It was good."

"Good?"

"Yeah. I played pogs and went on the swing and there was a bird that came and took a dump on Mario so it looked like ice cream melting on his head and we all laughed. Even Mario."

"Really?"

"Yep. And I played football with the older kids and they had me as quarterback and this one time I threw a perfect spiral but the other times it flopped like a pancake in the air but they still caught it and ran it in for a touchdown and then

17

it was time to go 'cause the bell rang."

"Who'd you play with?"

"The older kids. I told you."

"Which older kids?"

"I don't know, just the older kids."

Rodhi adjusted his glasses. Buried himself back in his homework. I didn't know why I couldn't tell him the truth.

"Uh, there was Robby the sixth grader. And Mario. And—"

"Mario's not older."

"Yeah. I know. But he was there."

"I thought the bird dumped on him?"

"It did."

"So he played with a bird dump like ice cream on his head?"

"It went away by then. It washed away. In the rain."

"It wasn't raining."

"It was for a little while. Like two whole minutes, then it went away."

"Was not."

"Was too."

"Was not. I would've seen it. The classroom has windows."

"Whatever."

"You're making S up."

"What?"

"You're making S up. Shit."

Both of us instinctively peeked around for authorities, but we were safe.

"Am not."

"Are too and you know it. What'd you really do at recess?"

"I already told you."

Rodhi stared at me a while, waiting for a confession that wouldn't come. I shook my head, shrugged my shoulders. To him or myself, I'm not sure. I felt stupid, and my face was hot.

We ate in silence for the rest of lunch.

9. Mother-Son Bonding

She'd always wait till everyone else was asleep. Open my door as quietly as she could. No matter how quiet she was, though, there was always a creak. When the door creaked, it was time for movie night. On the night I'm thinking of, the feature was *The Shining*.

I had this thing where I'd look at Mom for moral support at all the scary parts. And *every* time, without fail, she'd twist her face into the scariest fucking visage of terror and anguish you've ever seen. Not like a funny, ha-ha fake scary face, either. Like scar you for life scary. Even though I knew she'd do it, I'd still look over every time.

Her dialogue during the feature:

"Come on, open your eyes."

Blood rushing out of the elevator.

"There's nothing even scary on now."

Scatman Crothers takes an axe to the chest.

"It's fine, she's gone."

Decomposing lady gets out of the bathtub, laughing.

I watched, eyes half open, petrified, stuck between the lady on the screen and my mother sitting next to me on the couch.

When it was over, Mom put the VHS back in its

Blockbuster case—a rental forever marooned on the shores of our apartment. Led me back to my room, whispering "redrum" and then feigning ignorance when I'd get spooked and turn around.

She stood in the doorway, head tilted to one side, clawed fingers reaching out to me as I lay down. The bookending creak as the door closed and I shut my eyes tight.

10. Father-Son Bonding

We always went out at night—cloudy conditions ideal. That's when the fish in the pond were most active. That and Dad would have less chance of getting caught without a fisherman's permit that way.

Dad would start in the mud at water's edge, a minefield of goose shit, hunting for nightcrawlers. Beer belly power-lifting a Bulls shirt. White New Balance collecting mud at the toes. Standard dad-issue sunglasses, the ones that reflect like a puddle of oil. Mustache rivaling Super Mario's. World's Best Dad hat intersected by ancient sweat stain.

He'd huff and puff trying to launch himself at these poor worms that, I'll admit, were pretty elusive when they needed to be. And he'd light a cig, and the cherry would glow in the faint wind of the night, and I'd stoop over with a Maglite half the size of me, ostensibly trying but really just getting my fingers dirty and looking up at the stars.

He'd eventually catch the bait, though, and crack open a PBR, and we'd sit and wait with poles stretching lines into the night, the cicadas eerily quiet. You could actually hear yourself think. So I'd always break the silence, because I was eight years old.

"When do you think the aliens will come, Dad?"

"They're already here. At Groom Lake."

No response from me.

"Dreamland."

Nothing.

"Area 51."

"Oh, cool!"

Dad nodded, took a swig of PBR. I did the same with my coke. A worm wriggled ineffectually in my hand. I dropped him on the ground, let him return to his worm family.

"How'd they catch 'em?"

"Some were crash survivors. Some went willingly. Diplomats and all that."

"Dipplemats."

A lonely cicada woke up, droned for a few seconds, went back to sleep. It was a full moon; the second moon in the pond indistinct, not fully formed. Not many men could handle a cigarette, can of beer, and fishing pole with as much grace and dexterity as my father.

"They've infiltrated every aspect of our government. Military, politics, you name it."

Swig.

"C'mere."

I hated leaning in when Dad was drinking: His beer breath reminded me of Chooch. But I did anyway.

"Every star you see out there..."

He pointed at the sky for effect, hic-burped into my face.

"Every damn one of 'em's a sun for some other poor bastards out there."

"Really?"

Stubble undulated on Dad's neck as he nodded.

"Every damn one of 'em."

"Wow."

"Yeah. So you can't tell me— Oh shit. Oh shit!"

Dad jumped to his feet and yanked the pole back as hard

as he could, almost hit me in the face in the process. He still had the beer in his hand, which spilled down his shirt and splashed onto mine too, soaked our nightcrawler hunting grounds. The cig went next, down his chest cherry-first, started burning a belly button hole in his shirt. Dad flicked it into the water, sizzling out as he reeled so fast the line caught in the reel and he had to pull it out of the water with his hands.

He pulled, one arm length after another, grunting. The cicadas were all crying. And there's the catch, breaking water, flying into my father, then bouncing off, hooks catching his shirt before tearing free. Dad catching his breath.

On the first hook: a bluegill, about the size of my eight-year-old hand.

On the second: enough seaweed to choke a whale.

11. Now I'm Eleven

I think you've got a handle on eight-year-old me, so for your convenience I'm skipping ahead to my eleventh birthday: March 11, 2001.

The festivities were held at the local Laser Quest, as was Midwestern norm at the time. In attendance were LC and crew (my mom drew up the RSVP list), some third graders, and Rodhi. I smiled when appropriate and told myself I'd have a good time no matter what.

It was Rodhi and I versus the world. I mean, on paper we were evenly distributed, with LC and I as generals of our laser armies, but all of my recruits defected once LC insisted that those who fought with me were gay. I still didn't know what that even meant. We stood shoulder to shoulder for most of it, Rodhi and I, eyes half-closed to strobe light. Feet dodging snuck-in-pizza, throw up. Glimpses of shirts and shorts against glow-painted wall. The robotic screeches of registered hits. Dance music that hadn't been swapped out since '96 at least, CD occasionally skipping on a track, over and over, like we were being lulled into hypnosis. I was just happy to be there with Rodhi.

LC came around a corner during one of the skips, holding

some other kid's equipment in front of his own, letting it take the shots for him. He came down on us midway through my "that's not fair," snatched Rodhi's rifle, and broke it over his knee, plastic shards skittering across the floor as he lobbed the remains over a wall and ran off. Rodhi gave chase, yelled for me to hang back when I tried to join in.

Then some weird shallow breathing, like one of the laser shots actually wounded a kid or something. Strobe lights turning everything to stop motion. The whole world coming to me, not the other way around.

I approached a corner, the breathing even heavier.

Hugged the wall and held my gun barrel-up, close to my face, like all the cool guys do in the movies.

Rounded the corner.

And here's my thought process at eleven:

There's a dude sitting up against the wall. Older—*way* older. Like high school older. His pants are down, and there's a girl next to him trying, for some God-forsaken reason, to pull his wiener *off*. Like full amputation. The poor dude in a semiconscious state, just trying to hang on, the pain is so great.

Just as I was mustering up the courage to step in and prevent the impending manhood removal, he saw me. And he lost it. The girl screamed once she saw me, too. The guy got up off of the wall, wiener still out and dangling. Pushed me so hard I toppled back and fell to the floor, against my laser equipment. Heard it crack but was too shocked to care as I got back up and scurried away, back to the front, just in time for the buzzer to signal round's end.

12. Monkey See, Monkey Do

Aside from having to open up a gift of underwear in front of everyone, the rest of the party went pretty well, actually.

I ended up getting exactly what I wanted: the Handheld of Handhelds, the one I'd clipped any and all news articles out of *Nintendo Power* for—the Gameboy Advance. Not from my parents—they couldn't afford it. Drew saved up summer lawn mowing money and got it for me. In the color I wanted, too (glacier). He even included the launch title I'd been dying to play: *Super Mario Advance*.

A little brotherly hug from me. An "okay, okay, don't be a bitch about it" from him.

I had a decent chunk of the game beaten on the car ride home, continued on my top bunk once we got back. I wanted to continue in the bath that night but decided I'd rather not get beaten to death by my older brother if I could help it.

I kept going back to that moment in Laser Quest as I lay in the tub. The thwarted wiener amputation. The vicious attack.

The curiosity got to me.

I'll admit I was surprised when replicating the girl's technique wasn't met with excruciating pain. When the old metamorphosis happened. The one that made no sense to me

27

at all. Ripples spread out in soapy water. Drops dripped from the faucet. I'd stop at the slightest sound outside the bathroom, then start up again when the coast was clear. I thought of the GBA. Of Pokémon cards. Of Britney Spears.

When the stuff came out, it floated there, at the surface. Started making its way for me. I splashed it away and jumped out of the tub. Regarded it the way you would a cockroach scurrying out of a cereal box. I stood there, dripping on the tile, shivering in the air, a vague sense of shame welling up.

I pulled the plug. Opened the drain. Watched it all whirlpool away and remembered to grab my towel.

13. CCD

Tuesday nights were reserved for "preparing for my personal faith journey in Christ." Our catechist was Mr. Grissel—ex-military, older than hell, and hell-bent on convincing us we'd go there if we didn't shape up right this instant, mister.

Grissel gravitated toward Bible passages that emphasized punishment, or killing, or punishment by killing. Cool at first, yes, but it got old after a while.

I was assigned a seat next to none other than Mario Scalveretti III. Yep. He just had to be Catholic too. Fernando sat in the other seat, tried on the constipated face since Chaz wasn't there to do it. I knew they were just trying to scare me, but knowing that didn't prevent it from happening anyway.

After class, we'd wait outside in the dark, on the blacktop, surrounded by foggy field as we waited for pickup. Grissel was supposed to wait until the last kid was picked up before leaving, but he had a habit of mysteriously disappearing right at the end of class.

LC and Fernando would walk behind me as we all marched down the hallway—a prisoner being led to his execution. Usually, I'd get a couple muttered insults, maybe a punch to the gut before Dad picked me up. This night was

29

different. This night, LC wanted to show me something.

"Hey Waldo."

Sneakers on pavement, faster.

"Waldo!"

I turned around. Everything seemed either too fast or too slow, the product of a faulty projector.

"C'mere. I wanna show you something."

Fernando grabbed me. LC lifted up his shirt, proffered his right side to me. A jagged, mangled scar went nearly from navel to back. Not fresh, but not exactly faded either. I didn't know whether to feel pity or fear, so I settled for something between the two.

"That's from knife fighting."

I took a step back. Fernando shoved me forward again. Grabbed hold of my right hand before LC said:

"Touch it."

I pulled my hand back, tried to retract my fingers into a fist.

That's when LC pulled out the knife.

The moon glinted against its blade, caught in the pockets of rust like dirt dumped back into a hole. The look on his face was defined not by what it was, but by what it wasn't. Not victorious, or excited. Not even angry. There were tears in his eyes. His lips traced inaudible words. My stomach turned over, and everything went hazy. I felt like even if I wanted to, I couldn't complete a thought.

So I touched his scar. Brushed against every groove and bump. Felt how the skin crisscrossed and collapsed into ridges and valleys of flesh. Stared into his eyes as his tears started to fall. As mine nearly did too.

Fernando pinned me to the ground, LC and the cool moon both above and staring down at me. That reflection on the blade as LC brought my shirt up and touched knifepoint to skin. The sharp, bright pain, and the yell that sounded like it came from outside of me as he pushed down and drew blood. The animal fear and fight inside my body.

I'm not sure what stopped him. All I know is that at some point, he pulled the knife out of me and disappeared into the dark with Fernando, into the fog of the field.

14. Waldo Collins, Paramedic

The rest of the kids on the blacktop were far off, closer to the double doors as they joked and talked and played. The cars on the street behind them dopplered past in the light drizzle, headlights cutting through fog. My brain was just as foggy.

I reached into my backpack, shaky fingers trailing blood on the zipper. Pulled out the first things I could find: a "Jesus is my Friend" worksheet packet and roll of Scotch tape.

On the sheet, there were word banks with things like, "confession," "excommunication," and "original sin." A connect-the-dots rendition of Jesus, pretty impressive considering the limitations of the medium. Multiple choice questions with answers that were only slight variations of the same theme. I tried not to panic. I remembered a line from an old VHS I played once: "Fear is the mind-killer." It didn't really help, but I said it to myself anyway.

I crumpled up the page and pressed it against my side, because I didn't know what else to do. Tried not to cry out from the sting as I soaked the blood with connect-the-dots Jesus. By the end, I had the whole packet Scotch-taped to my side. I staggered to my feet and ringed out the side of my shirt until I was sure the blood wouldn't stain our car. I didn't want to get in trouble.

About a minute later, my dad showed up. I covered my side with my backpack as I walked to the car. Told him nothing when I got in. Still haven't, even now.

15. September 11, 2001

We were working on a project in the library. Poster boards strewn over all available table space. Lines drawn against ruler edge. Index cards hastily memorized. Sharpies covertly huffed in the corner.

I super-glued the cut shut. It worked wonders for stopping the bleeding, but my skin took on a reddish, almost purple hue that even at eleven I knew couldn't be good. I didn't inform M & D. We barely had money for food, let alone stab wounds. It was something I knew they'd argue about, and if they were going to argue anyway, I at least didn't want to be the cause of it.

When the itching got too bad, I scratched, and the blood oozed past flaked-off super glue and onto my *Courage the Cowardly Dog* tee. I stood there, awkwardly, holding the shirt several inches away from my skin with one hand as the other applied pressure with some tissue, because I thought I remembered something about applying pressure. Part of my brain screamed at me to tell someone, to go to the nurse, do something, but in the end, I didn't want to be a bother.

That's when I noticed all of the teachers and librarians crowded around a rolling-carted TV.

The first thing I saw were flames and smoke as they

spewed out of the North Tower and skyward, the camera zoomed in a little too close to see the whole picture. I figured it was nothing more than a building fire.

I watched with them, unseen and unheard. Saw an explosion billow out of 2 WTC, just beneath the gaping wound in its twin's side, and it was suddenly as if I were outside of myself, watching myself watch this happen. I listened as Katie Couric and Matt Lauer and every teacher and librarian collectively gasped.

Hands covered mouths. Grown men and women suddenly seemed as scared as I was, tears in their eyes. A stack of papers fell to the ground as a teacher with family in NYC rushed the librarian's phone and started dialing.

*

"Why'd they bomb the towers?"

"They weren't bombed, I don't think. The planes flew into them."

"Did anybody get hurt?"

"Yes. Yes, people got hurt."

"Are there more planes gonna crash?"

"I'm not sure. Right now they know of the two that hit the towers, and one other plane that hit the Pentagon. You all remember our lesson about the Pentagon?"

Urgent nods.

"Are there planes gonna crash into the Sears Tower? 'Cause my mom works in the Sears Tower..."

"No, it's, it's okay, we're, don't cry. Now everyone, everyone, calm down."

It went on like that, our sixth grade social studies teacher Mr. Bilker the only trusted source of information. We were a conference room of the press asking questions, most of them centered around the possibility of Chicago, Des Plaines, and even our school being hit by a plane.

Everything else in our social studies class was just a story, a series of dates and occurrences to be memorized and regurgitated for standardized tests. But this was real to us. This happened.

After school, I stood out on the blacktop in Bay Colony, with Rodhi and some other neighborhood kids, looking up at the sky, searching for planes. Talking urgently about what the government would do once they found whoever did it. Blood seeped from the wound in my side. Not enough to hurt, but enough to let me know it was there.

Interlude: Rodhi

Baba is on the couch. Mama says he's resting, but I know what that means. His breath reeks, even across the room, and I tiptoe as if I might wake a sleeping giant. Mama tells me I'm not to drink when I grow up, that it's against our religion. She tells me this as if she has to. The air is thick with the stink of paint, and I breathe in gasps before holding my breath again, a diver getting ready to enter the deep.

There's a canvas sitting on the floor next to the couch, half-completed, the scene a sunset with a willow weeping its fronds over a little boy who's looking out over a pond. You can almost see the swan at the farthest edge of the pond, but just barely. Only a dab of its gleaming white in the fading light. Even when he's drunk, Baba can paint the most beautiful pictures. He always tells me he could've been a master. If he'd just gotten his chance, he could've been a master.

Mama hands me my shoes, the ones with velcro that light up every time you take a step. I have this thing where every time I put the shoes on and velcro the straps, I take a stomping jump to watch them light up, but I know not to do that this time. This is our competition, between Mama and me, to see who can be the quietest. We're like sneaky robbers making off with our own safety.

I lose this competition.

I trip over a toy I left out, one that Mama told me to pick up earlier. I nearly fall but don't quite, right foot coming down hard, stomping, loud enough to wake Baba, my only consolation being that the shoe finally lights up like I wanted it to.

Baba asks what's going on, as if he has to. As if he doesn't know that Mama's taking me away from all of this, taking me away from the paint stink and the beer stink and his drunken stupors. It was always only for a couple hours, just staying at Nani's till it was safe to go back, but everything seems different this time around. So I don't know. So Mama, I think, doesn't know.

Mama instinctively hugs her arm around my neck, motions me over to the door. Baba tells us to wait, but we don't. He gets up, holds his arms out to regain balance, and staggers to the side. Knocks over his canvas with his ankle, then steps right through it. Sunset reds gather at his ankle where his foot pushed through, giving him the illusion of a serious injury, blues mingling with the reds as he pulls the foot back out, then steps onto the carpet, spreading the paint as he finally gets his feet underneath himself.

Baba does that yell he does sometimes, the one where spittle goes flying from his lips and he looks like a rabid dog. He yells at Mama with such rage that you can hardly make out the words. He says it's all her fault, that she's ruined it. Mama tells Baba he's been drinking, and the way Baba looks at her after she says that, you'd think that this was news to him. He takes a step toward us, cracking one of the corners of the canvas in the process. He reaches down and grabs the canvas. Whips it at the wall, where it makes contact and sends paint flying to the left and right of the hit, as if this is the supernova of a painted star. That's all Mama needs, apparently, because she takes me by the hand and opens the door, shuts it on Baba's words right as he's making his way over.

Mama doesn't cry until she realizes she didn't grab the car keys, and even then, it's that silent cry she does, the one where she looks away and doesn't make a sound. She takes me by the hand, and we make our way down to the pond at the center of Bay Colony, sit on the grass by the water's edge and take a second to catch our breath, to figure out what to do next.

After five minutes or so, Mama looks at me. She opens her mouth to say something, the lightning bugs flashing behind her, but nothing comes out. But then, finally:

"Bus."

Des Plaines doesn't have many bus routes, not like Chicago, so we have to walk about a mile down Potter to the nearest one. I ask Mama if we're going to Nani's, and she says that we aren't. I ask her where we're going, then, and she says nothing.

We finally make our way to the stop, and we sit on the bench next to each other. At least I sit, anyway. Mama gets up after a minute and paces back and forth. Five minutes pass, maybe ten, before Mama tells me to stand up. The bus isn't coming, she says. The bus isn't coming. Except it is, down the street a bit, LCD screen on top announcing the next stop. I tell Mama. Look, I say. Look. She does, then looks back at me.

"We have to go."

I start to cry as we walk back home, but that doesn't work, so I tell Mama that my feet hurt from all the walking. Without hesitating, she picks me up into her arms and cradles me. I actually drift in and out of sleep in her arms, sometimes looking up to see her calm face, eyes ahead, tears running their course down, leaving her chin and making contact with my face.

16. Junior Red Devils

I was out in the park, playing GBA, and I realized that there were American flags all around me. I paused my game and looked around, counted them all. On and on down the complex, hanging on the insides of windows, little bumper stickers on cars. It wasn't a conscious thought at the time, but it sat there, in the back of my mind, waiting to come out: Everything had permanently changed.

Drew came up to me, interrupted the thought. He told me I'd been signed up for the local junior football team. That the season had already started, but the coach (same one Drew had had back in the day) insisted that of course Drew's little brother could start late. That yes, Mom and Dad were okay with it. That no, I shouldn't just "sit this one out" and wait till next season started. That my first practice was today—in an hour. That it didn't matter if I didn't know how to get there. That Drew would drive me.

My excuses exhausted, I hopped into Drew's rusty old Camaro. On the way over, we passed more American flags than I could count.

They were doing suicides on a yellowed football field when we got there. I didn't know at the time that sprinting to a line, touching the line, and sprinting back to touch the line you started at in full football pads was called suicides. But I would learn.

Coach Dumas and Drew caught up with each other for a few minutes, and I stood there as they did, staring at the grass, wishing I was home. Everything took on the quality of static as they talked for a while and then grabbed me some pads before Drew had to go. Everything came back into sharp focus once Drew left, and I was stuck with kids I didn't know and a coach who made me uncomfortable.

No matter which size we tried, none of the pads seemed to fit right. I did the best I could with what was available, but my thigh pads still sagged around my kneecaps. I had to pull my helmet up by the facemask to see properly.

Coach Dumas didn't waste any time. He had me immediately square off against the linemen for Oklahoma, a drill where two players get into position inches from each other and slam into their opponent at the blow of the whistle till one's on the ground.

He started me off against a kid who was a full foot taller than me. The coach could tell I had no idea what I was in for:

"Just drive your feet at the whistle. Hands up, on the front of his pads, but don't grab them. Okay? Drive through him and knock him out like we're gonna do to those ragheads, huh kid?"

Coach laughed, and all I saw was LC. Saying something I didn't know the meaning of, but which I knew was meant to hurt. We got into position, and Dumas blew the whistle, and the other kid ran me over. Laughter from the team, stifled by Dumas.

I felt like I wanted to cry, but not because I was hurt. There was some anger I couldn't place, a confused rage inside of me, and I didn't know what to do with it. A couple more of the kids laughed when they saw this on my face, on my shaking lip. And the look on the coach's face. Like he was holding back laughter himself. I couldn't take it.

I turned and sprinted down the field, cleats sending up tiny cylinders of mud. Didn't look back the whole way home.

17. The Fight to End All Fights (Until the Next One)

I got home feeling like I might throw up, head throbbing, sweat dripping off of my uniform. My family sat on the couch, oblivious to my presence, watching MTV: Eiffel 65's "Blue (Da Ba Dee)." I wanted to yell out, to throw something, but I decided I'd just go to my room instead. Drew noticed me before I could.

"The hell? Why are you back?"

The words just came out, and I couldn't (or wouldn't) stop them.

"The coach is a stupid dumbass asshole with a dumb name who I hate and I'm not going back there ever again."

Drew was actually stunned for a second, but he was never one to back down from a fight.

"So you're just gonna bitch out the second you get there?"

Dad:

"Stop it, Drew."

"What, so he can just sit around and do jack shit like you? I knew I shouldn't have gotten him that fucking video game."

"Watch your goddamn language."

44

"Or else what, you gonna fucking ground me, Dad? Or should I say Waldo's dad."

Mom tensed up, looked at Drew with ice in her eyes. And there I was, pulling out of myself again, the room hazy, indistinct. I'd seen Roger and Drew fight before. I heard myself say stop it.

"No, I'm not gonna fucking stop it. The dumbass never told me, so I don't care if he knows that I know."

Dad got to his feet. Drew too, both of them with that regretful look on their faces—the look that said that what they were about to do was enforced by a code they couldn't control.

"I knew you couldn't be my dad. My dad wouldn't be such a pansy."

Dad clocked Drew in the jaw, sent him to the floor against the techno chorus of "Blue." I was in a place beyond thought—stuck in observation. Drew clawed at Dad's ankles and pulled him down to the ground. The two of them rolled around, red in the face, grabbing and punching and yelling. Mom pounded on their backs whenever she could make contact, and I howled in my saggy football pads, covered up their fight with my voice. Mom:

"Rog, stop it! Roger!"

Little cuts dotted the landscape of my father's neck from where Drew's nails had latched on and slipped away. Rivulets of blood threatened the collar of Dad's tee. I didn't know what to do except pick up the cordless and call the cops. I waited for the wail of the sirens, until I could see the red and blue flashing outside our window, past my puffy eyes. When they came, I ran off, still crying, to my little hideaway.

18. My Hideaway

Neighboring Meadow Lane has a storm drain that some teenager pried the bolts off of long ago. It feeds into a forking, snaking, town-wide tunnel system. He used it to covertly get high, and I used it as a hideaway for times like these. I didn't tell his mom, and he didn't tell mine, so we coexisted well enough.

I wiped my face and slipped one padded shoulder through the manhole, then the other, the sweetly stubborn scent of pot that clung to everything down there wafting in. I didn't need a flashlight.

I could never get used to the spooky sound of rushing water in the distance, the hollow "pinks" of condensed droplets hitting ground, getting louder the closer you got to my room. My room was a ten-by-ten hollowed-out cube of concrete, lit dimly by the jars of lightning bugs I kept down there. My pens and notebooks were right where I left them. Everything here had an order, and that alone started to make me feel a little better. I started writing by bug light.

It was a story about molemen and aliens and The End of the World as We Know It. You know, the usual.

To wit:

And then Walgar the Magniterrible One descended and
went down ~~into the dark~~ into the depths with his ^really awesome sword
in his hand and then and then he smited the evil dragon
Doomar as he shot fiery ~~fire~~ flames over at him. But to
Walgar's surprise, the battle was not done just yet. There was
another from the upper relms who ~~would~~ dared to defy him.
It was his brother, Drune the Popular! And he said to Drune,
"But Drune, we're brothers!" he said. But Drune ~~laughed~~
cakled in his face really loudly and unleashed his team of
infinity aliens, and he said to Walgar, "No we're not, silly
Walgar. My father isn't the same as yours, but is actually an
alien!" he replied coolly as he smiled and cakled.

It didn't really matter what I was writing. Just the act of
putting something down helped to ease the buzzing in my
head. But I knew that they'd eventually start looking for me,
and I didn't want my hideaway to be found. So I put my
stories away, and I headed back home.

19. No Man's Land

It was dead silent when I got home. I mean not a sound. That's when you knew there was something wrong in my household—when we'd gotten beyond yelling and lapsed into a furious silence instead, like a severe burn that starts to feel cold. TV off. N64 unplugged preemptively. All doors shut. I sat in the living room for the rest of the day in silence, hoping no one would come in, a weight in my chest, and I waited for night to appear in the view past the slits in our patio's blinds, where long ago indoor ball playing had claimed its victims. The moon peeked up over Bay Colony's apartment buildings; its rippled twin danced in the man-made pond at complex's center. I don't remember how long it took me to fall asleep, but that's how it happened.

*

Dad had been locked up for the night on a domestic charge, and he was pissed and ready to continue the fight once Mom picked him up from the county jail. But he wouldn't be able to—Drew wasn't there, either. Being fifteen, the cops must've let him off the hook.

I knew there was only one place my older brother could've run away to. He'd gone there before, and he'd go there again—to PGN's house. Before Mom and Dad could see me as they tiptoed and staggered in respectively, I scurried around the corner and snuck out through the patio door.

20. To PGN's House

You could say that PGN was our maternal grandfather. But that wouldn't even begin to scratch the surface of the man, this person who commanded both attention and (it seemed to me at the time) the life force of the universe itself. Made Walgar the Magniterrible One look like a chump. Did shit like read a dense history book before lunch. Sent shivers down your spine with a word. Or a look. Or just by being in the same room as you. Had a laugh (incredibly rare, mind you) that you could feel the bass of in your own chest. He had three names, but I was pretty sure he lost them in the war. And don't ask him what those names are. Trust me.

If I had a central goal back then, something to aspire to, something I wanted to become, it was to be half as tough as PGN. Half as manly, half as strong. I wanted to be free of LC's bullshit, to be able to kick the ass of anyone who'd mess with me. But no matter what I tried, I was still just Waldo.

I caught a bus to neighboring Evanston, IL—the town where PGN lived. Made it to Colfax Street, to the imposing haunted-house-in-the-making that was my grandpa's place. As I walked up the steps of his patio, there was the faded old smell of pipe tobacco and match sulphur that clung to everything PGN owned. I thought I'd skip the doorbell and slip in unannounced.

Bad idea.

As the door opened, I watched through the crack as PGN jolted out of his easy chair and reached behind it, to where he kept his gun. I shut the door back up and called out to him that it was me. That I was sorry. He told me to enter, then:

"You raised in a barn? Never heard of knocking?"

"Sorry, Grandpa."

"Sorry wouldn't put your head back together, would it? Use your brain, boy, that's why God gave it to you."

"Yes sir."

He adjusted his neck brace and led me in, past stairs worn down by pillow races Drew and I used to have on holidays, past the creepy owl painting that stared into your soul above the easy chair, past pictures of PGN's leatherhead college football days, and into the dining room with its long dining table, which Drew happened to be sitting at one head of at that moment, eyes red and puffy. He hid his face, and I remember wishing that he wouldn't. I wished he'd show how he was really feeling so that I could finally do the same.

"The hell are you doing here?"

Drew noticed the look on PGN's face.

"Heck. Sorry, heck."

"I don't know. It was just stupid and boring there."

"Yeah, okay. They know I'm here?"

I shook my head.

"Good. At least you did one thing right."

PGN stepped in:

"All right, enough chitchat. Since I've got you men here, I might as well put you to work."

PGN stationed us out in the backyard, to rake and weed and till 'til he said we'd had enough. The way he operated was to bring a pitcher of lemonade outside (for him, mind

51

you, none of it for us) and let us go only after the pitcher was empty.

I wiped dandelion fuzz from my eyes and looked up at Drew as I worked. As I looked, I noticed every facial feature we didn't share. Our noses didn't match. Neither did our eyes. All the things I never saw before.

"Hey, you know when you said all that stuff about how Dad was a pansy and how he wasn't your real dad and all that?"

"Yeah?"

"You were just kidding, right? I mean, you were just trying to make him mad, right?"

He kept pulling weeds, tossed them into his garbage bag with a renewed fervor. I could feel something inside of me closing up for good.

"Drew?"

"What?"

"That was all a joke, right? What you said?"

"What do you think?"

"No."

"Then why'd you ask?"

"I don't know. It was stupid. I'm sorry."

I cried quietly to myself, the weeds' sharp leaves in my hand cutting flesh as I clamped down. It was so bad that Drew actually put his arm around me. He never did that.

PGN was coming over, so I acted like I'd come across a patch of wild onions as I wiped my eyes. Drew and I didn't say a word until we were done, we just let the silence float there between us. He didn't put up a fight when I suggested going home, just scrounged up fare for the both of us and played punch buggy with me at the bus stop till our route showed up.

Interlude:
Mona

It's a quarter to two, and Waldo gets home at three. Roger's not back till six, and who knows when Drew will come home. There's still time. The soaps are on, and there's a funny word. Soap, like days when PGN would catch me swearing and wash my mouth out, it turning everything to itself the way tofu does, only soap milk or soap bread or soap orange juice. And the nights when PGN had to lock Mommy in her room when she Went Away, always going away in her mind and launching herself at us like a wild animal, snarling and telling us she wished we were dead. PGN locking her in her room and the way her fists would slam the door till well past midnight, PGN sleeping on the living room couch and me on the floor, his snores almost drowning out the pounding, comforting, and I'd get to sleep just as the first light of dawn sliced through the window.

But we're here now. It's a quarter past two, and Waldo gets home at three. I turn the soaps off. Reach into my robe's pocket and pull out the prescription bottle, light coming through its bright orange, coating the pills inside. The pain stopped months ago, but I still get them filled. There are

53

other kinds of pain. I take three—the father, the son, and the holy spirit.

And there's another one.

Sunday school let out at a quarter past two. It was three, and PGN still hadn't shown up. Father Felter took me to the back of the church and brought out a bottle of wine. He drank from it once, twice, three times. The sign of the cross. He gave me the bottle. I was to drink. I did, and he took me even farther back, to a closet. He turned the light on so I wouldn't be scared. I was still scared. He told me to come in, that it would be our little secret. I said okay.

I blink, and I am here. It's quiet out. Too quiet. Not even the rushing of cars down 294. If I listen close, I can hear a faraway freight train blare on its horn and trundle down the tracks. A train.

I was out on my own. In my pockets a razor and some sleeping pills. The el tracks sliced through Evanston greenery the same way I'd slice through my arms. PGN was at work, and Mommy was luded out on the couch, eyelids fluttering. I had time. I didn't have enough to pay for fare, so I hopped over the turnstile when the attendant wasn't looking. I waited till the coast was clear and got down onto the tracks, avoided the third rail. I didn't want to fuck this up by half-electrocuting myself. I walked the tracks that stretched out over my city, vertigo every time I looked over the edge. No driving squeal of steel on steel. I was alone. My hand shook as I pulled the pill bottle out of my pocket. It shook so bad that I dropped half of the bottle's pills when I opened it, the only word I knew then being fuck. I tossed the rest of the pills out and screamed at the sky. Produced the razor. Lifted my sleeves, skin like porcelain shining in the sun. Touched my forearm's skin. Cold. Looked away. Scratched at it, but not too deep. Blood just barely surfacing, peeking its head out. I went to scratch the other arm but cried so hard that the tears blotted my vision. I tossed the razor away. Located a staircase meant for maintenance. Train whistle as I got off the tracks. Doppler sounds as the whistle went past.

Whistling. The kettle's ready. Forgot I even put it on. I take it off the fire and turn the burner off. Grab the mug on the counter. Listen. Cars down 294, a departure from O'Hare flying overhead. There's burning in my head, but there's no way to get it out. No way to stop the noise. I tip the kettle over my hand and watch the water touch my skin, listen to the sizzle as I retract my hand out of instinct. Instantly red, splotched like an unusual birthmark. I listen some more. Waldo talking with one of his friends. Making his way to the door. I cross over to the bathroom and lock the door behind me. Turn on the faucet nice and loud. Go to look at myself in the mirror but don't. I bring hand to mouth, enter finger inside and feel the contours of my palate, the place where gums meet teeth. I stick the finger all the way down and let everything come out. I rinse the sink till there's nothing left, gargle and spit. Look up at myself. Past myself.

Freshening up.

21. Bailing Out Rodhi

When Rodhi and I were bored, we'd take a walk through the overgrown woods to the east of Bay Colony, make like we were intrepid explorers on a fresh continent. We'd grab our walking sticks and pick through the detritus that accumulated back there—old VHS tapes, AOL trial discs, and wafer-thin beer cans that'd been crushed and bleached clean by the sun. We were talking about the football team I'd been signed up for.

"And you're gonna go back to practice after all of that?"

"I mean, what else can I do?"

"Not go. Tell your family you don't want to play."

"It's not that easy."

"Pretty sure it is."

Until Rodhi said it, it didn't seem possible to me. We crossed through the woods the rest of the way in silence, wisely avoided the nearby nesting geese who had their run of the place. I pictured what my family might say if I quit football. An intoxicating excitement as I allowed myself to not care, if only for a moment. Rodhi and I made our way over to neighboring Meadow Lane. Someone had shot holes clean through the stop sign. They couldn't be positively IDed as to whether they came from a pellet gun or something of a higher caliber.

We made our way past skaters as they did kickflips (the *Tony Hawk's Pro Skater* games were in full swing then, as were gelled, spiked hairdos); past the house with a caged-up German shepherd in the backyard; past little kids trying out wrestling moves they just saw on TV on each other in front lawns; to the End of the Block, where few dared to roam.

A hush when we got there. The skaters stopped skating. The wrestlers stopped wrestling. Their eyes were no longer on the two of us, but on a spot slightly above us. Standing on top of one of the townhome's carports was a kid who looked like one of the Columbine shooters. The rifle in his hands completed the picture. One of his wastoid friends was with him, bending the tab on a beer can back and forth, back and forth. It snapped. The kid with the rifle:

"What the fuck are you doing here?"

I couldn't think of anything useful to say, so I said nothing. I was observing myself again, pulling away from what was happening. The kid with the rifle looked Rodhi over.

"Where are you from? Afghanistan? Pakistan?"

"I was born here."

"Yeah, but where are you from?"

"I'm an American. What does it matter?"

"It matters 'cause I say it matters. Where are you from?"

Silence, but only for a moment.

I heard the words "go fuck yourself," but it took a second for me to realize that I was the person who said them. The kids on the roof were stunned too, and I took advantage. I grabbed Rodhi by the arm and whipped him around. Kept myself between them and Rodhi as we ran. I was within my body enough to feel the absolute animal fear of the situation.

Then the shot came. And with it the pain. The loss of consciousness.

22. Bailing Out Waldo

When I came to, Rodhi's back was to me, arms stretched behind him like some runner perpetually crossing the finish line. There was movement, distant sounds that could've been the calls of birds. The sky was a stretch of blasted blacktop; houses and trees sprouted downward from it, into the cloudy blue ground. The skaters pushed off blacktop sky, defied reverse gravity as they attempted ollies. They stopped when they saw Rodhi, my limp body being dragged behind him. The last thing I caught of upside-down Meadow Lane was the stop sign, just in time for the shooter to put another hole through it, missing Rodhi's head by a couple inches. There wasn't the crack of an actual firearm, just the whiz and pank of a pellet shot on metal.

I breathed in a world where apartment complexes and trees and a pond hung like insignificant chandeliers. Breathed out pain.

Rodhi led us into the woods, over burs that stuck to pant legs and under branches that made swipes for heads. After he found a secluded spot, he flipped me over onto my stomach and pulled my pants down.

"What the hell?"

The pain answered before Rodhi did. It came from my

right butt cheek: a thousand wasps stinging the same spot, over and over again. When it was over, Rodhi came around with the bloody pellet—a consummate surgeon.

I hiked up my pants, sat up, immediately regretted that decision. Took a knee instead.

"You shouldn't sit for a while, I don't think."

"Yeah, thanks Rodhi."

Just the cicadas humming. Rodhi looked away.

"No seriously, thanks. Thank you."

He didn't say anything. I felt like I could kiss him, allowed myself to think that for a moment before letting it go. We walked out of the woods in silence. When we got to Bay Colony, we both went our separate ways.

23. Now I'm Fourteen

If our internal splintering as a family was great, externally we were doing just fine. We could head to the store and actually go the whole way without an argument. Drew and Dad hadn't hit each other in weeks, and my quitting football largely flew under the radar. There were only a few more months left in eighth grade, M & D were getting me prepared for Confirmation that was coming up soon, and it was my birthday. March 11, 2004. Officially fourteen. The party itself wasn't anything special, no inappropriate laser tag moments this time around. I insisted it be a deliberately small thing. Just Rodhi and my family, pizza and a cake.

The party actually went pretty well. Aside from my dad asking Rodhi all about Hinduism and Rodhi thankfully not taking offense and instead giving him a crash course on his religion, my family remained on good behavior throughout, and for a while I saw a glimpse of what we could be should we decide that dysfunction wasn't quite our thing.

But good luck with that in the long run. I was just happy to have a twenty-four hour ceasefire. Sure, Dad was on his tenth beer and getting pretty raucous, and sure, Mom hadn't gotten me anything and Drew kind of wanted to be somewhere else, but at least they weren't fighting. I was truly happy about that.

There was actually a moment there, as I opened up Christmas-wrapping-paper-wrapped birthday presents and scarfed down cake and ice cream, that I swore I saw the future. Saw Drew shipped off to Afghanistan, my mom dying, all the rest. It wasn't a scary vision, or even a sad one, as weird as that sounds. Just a reminder, the universe reaching back and telling me to appreciate this. See this. Feel this. Because it will be gone. It will be.

24. The Puppy

Drew decided he wanted to get a puppy. He decided this after school one day, about a week after I had my first beer. He'd handed the beer to me and pressured me into drinking it before getting into what was really on his mind. He'd gotten the name of his biological father from mom, or at least a partial name. Joe. So I drank with him and pretended to enjoy the taste as he opened up to me in a way he honestly never had before. When he opened another can for me, I drank that one too. By the end of it, my throat burned and I was nauseous, but I didn't care.

Drew found the puppy online, an Entlebucher Mountain Dog up in Northwest Indiana that someone was willing to give away for free. He hadn't asked for permission, and given the circumstances, I didn't press him on it. I just hopped into his rusty old Camaro and rode with him to get the dog.

We passed by downtown Chicago on our way. Buildings I'd usually only see in pictures were right there, standing so tall that I had to crane my neck and stick my head out the window just to see the tops of them.

The Camaro's engine blared. Cars swished past. Nothing else.

"Have you ever met him? Joe, I mean."

Drew drove in silence for a while. Decided he couldn't get away with pretending he hadn't heard me:

"No, and I'm not going to."

Humming road and awkward throat clearing. I figured I might as well see this through to the end.

"But aren't you curious? Don't you want to know what he's like? Why he just left?"

A searing look.

"There are certain things you leave alone."

"What? No. This is something I'd really want to know. Like really bad. Don't you?"

"Fucking cut it out, would you?"

My cheeks were hot. Quiet for a while.

"Anyway, it wouldn't be fair to Mom and Dad."

"What do you mean 'wouldn't be fair'? This guy made you. And anyway, you... You said all that stuff about Dad before, so..."

"So just 'cause I say something in a fight one time means I mean it forever? Get your head outta your ass."

"Well, I don't know. It seemed like you meant it."

Drew had nothing to say to that. Nothing but:

"We're here."

He parked the Camaro on the street outside their house. Left me to catch up as he made his way to the door.

Guilt swirled around behind my eyes, my teeth, but I put it away and made myself smile as the door opened and this scrappy puppy bounded for us, tiny claws clattering against the hardwood, cartoon-running. When he got to us, he licked our hands, nibbled our pant legs, tried to lick our faces. He was no bigger than your average house cat.

The previous owners were nice enough. A young couple. The woman came in with a baby, careful to hold it a distance from the dog. We made introductions. They weren't worried about Reb seriously hurting the baby or anything, but they said he could get rough in play, and they didn't want to take any chances.

In five minutes, we were on our way, a tiny collar around Reb's neck, and an equally tiny leash attached to that.

The dog got Drew and I talking again, and as we passed back through Chicago on our way back home, I reminded Drew of the little finger man running game we used to play on long car rides home, how we'd make him run alongside our car and jump over obstacles, sometimes even scaling the Sears Tower. I caught a smile on his face, a hint of recognition in his eyes in the rear-view mirror. And that was enough for me.

25. Swan and the Pond, Take Two

The weeks that followed passed in a haze of denial and silence. Mona didn't want the dog in the house, but she also didn't want to talk about the reason why Drew got the dog in the first place. So the dog stayed.

There was a shift in the language my mother started to use toward me. It was a subtle change. Gradual. First it was picking on my clothes, wondering why I didn't wear this shirt or change into these pants. Then it was my hobbies. Turning me down when I asked to be signed up for chess club, because I needed to get outside more. Then the food I ate, and how much of it I was eating. How I was gaining weight.

It got so every time I went into the kitchen for a snack, I'd brace for an insult or a criticism—a perfect Pavlovian reaction. Being ignored I could take. Being picked on by LC— no problem. Even being *stabbed* by LC was doable. But I hadn't calibrated verbal abuse from my own mother into my defense strategy. And so I'd get silent, a fog of confused anger and sadness hanging in the air, smoke I couldn't study or grasp or identify. The silence would fuel her.

Dad never said anything, and she was always careful to

say things when Drew wasn't around. It was meant to be just between us.

I started spending a lot more time outside. Explored every inch of Bay Colony, made covert excursions into the defunct fisherman's lagoon to catch glimpses of smoke rising, and I'd make a game out of guessing whether it was coming from a fire or some kids getting high. Theirs was smoke I could understand, that I could trace with my eyes— see where it originated and where it dissipated. It wasn't a calm, but it was the closest thing I'd get to one then.

The night was balmy, sky cloudless, stars fighting against the light pollution. I made my way down to the pond in the center of Bay Colony. Watched the moon ripple lightly in the water: a tired sickle breathing in the light waves.

I walked down to the rocks alone and hoped I'd stay that way for a while.

There was a pained sound, coming through PVC pipe lined with broken glass. Something I'd heard before. Everything seemed slanted, uneven—like a VHS tape that's caught in the VCR too many times. I sprinted for the spot where I found the first swan and saw two figures in shadow. One was human, its back to me as it kicked and hit and grabbed at the second figure: a swan with neck craning and wings flapping.

For some reason, my body didn't freeze up like it usually did. My legs moved, and I followed them. Body got low in preparation for the tackle, just like that coach taught me years back. I hit hard, heavy contact on my shoulder. The figure's legs fell out from under him, and he was on the ground. He flipped around to face me, his eyes terrified. It was Mario.

I watched from outside of myself as my fist went up, saw it come back down and connect with LC's nose. Waldo's fists landed again and again—first LC's nose, then both eyes, then his mouth. He scrambled and scurried to get loose, but Waldo grabbed him and pinned him to the ground. LC cried out like an animal caught in a trap. Waldo roared at him to shut up, spittle flying from his lips and landing on LC's face.

Waldo let up, and there was a thought:

Is there a way out of this?

"Me" was gone, and LC was more battered than the swan was. Both eyes black and puffy, nose bleeding, lips split. Waldo got up from what he'd done and walked back to his complex, shoulder aching, hands shaking, tears stinging his eyes. The swan had stopped crying out by then, but LC hadn't. He could be heard the whole walk back.

26. Laying Low

I made my way from school to home and back again, day after day, always looking over my shoulder. It wasn't a reciprocal beating I was worried about. It was the thought of my school finding out. Of me being somehow expelled with only weeks to go till I was done with eighth grade.

Passing teachers in the hall, I could've sworn a few of them gave me weird looks. LC was absent the entire week after, which made my paranoia even worse. And the really weird thing was that none of the other kids seemed to know why. Consensus seemed to be split down the middle: Half assumed he'd gotten some kind of life-threatening illness (or maybe even hoped for it), and the other half figured he was ditching to get high or something.

I waited till Friday of that week to relax, no sign of LC whatsoever and not so much as a call down to the principal's office.

You can imagine my surprise to find a 9mm bullet standing perfectly upright on the welcome mat leading into our apartment.

I pocketed it before Drew or M & D could get the chance to see it and slipped inside, my heart pounding a syncopated beat in my ears.

27. Shadow Day

The next few days, I was Winston Smith in Miniluv, waiting for a bullet to enter my brain. Every corner I approached, every street I turned down presented itself as the Harbinger of My Death.

I didn't tell Drew or my parents. The way I saw it, it was my problem, and I was going to have to find a way out of it. I mostly stayed inside, dealt with Mona's verbal bullets instead of the possibility of real ones outside. I let that familiar old mental static take over whenever she got into one of her rants, ignored most of what I heard until she told me I'd be shadowing at Our Lady of Piety in a couple of days.

Our Lady of Piety High School for Boys is an all-boys private Catholic school in neighboring Niles, a place I never thought I'd be even visiting once in my life. As far as I was concerned, I was going to the same public high school Drew went to.

Apart from the whole CCD thing, we were C and E parishioners—Christmas and Easter. The thought of going to a school devoted to the sort of thing I put up with once a week made me feel sick. But this was nonnegotiable, so when the day arrived, I dressed in the school's strict dress code of khakis, polo shirt, and belt, and I sat in silence the whole ride over.

The grounds sprawled over many acres, the lawn kept to an unnatural hue and the kind of thing you could tell was cut every day. The school was brick and mortar, with scant windows, emblazoned with its name and featuring a Pietà copy directly beside the main doors so that anyone coming into the school would have to pass by the lifeless corpse of Jesus and pained face of Mary first. Say what you want about Catholics, but they know how to make a first impression.

Mom drove off in a hurry, leaving me to fend for myself and figure out where I was even supposed to go. The receptionist inside directed me to the homeroom of a senior named Chad, who I was meant to shadow for the day. All classes began with a sign-of-the-cross and a Hail Mary, with bowed heads and closed eyes and mumbled words. I peeked a few times during prayer and observed the room. Crucifixes on walls. Polo shirts on students. The odd phallus carved into a seat. The musty stink of teenage boys with no teenage girls to impress. The occasional teacher lifting hands up to the sky during prayer, standing on tiptoes.

Lunch was Chad and his three other friends at the table talking over the previous weekend, when they'd all gotten "drunk as a skunk," "totally baked," and "fucking plastered." As their conversation switched over to girls and the static in my head came back, I comforted myself with the thought that I would find a way out of going to school here. That it'd all just been a test, or a misunderstanding, and I'd be able to go to public school with Rodhi instead.

28. Waldo Iz Ded

It'd be convenient for me to say that I lost myself in my schoolwork, but I really didn't. My usual As and Bs plummeted in altitude. It didn't help that Rodhi only shared one class with me, a class we happened to also share with LC and his crew. The crew, with their muttered insults and half-whispered plots that conveniently left the words "shoot" and "gun" audible.

I found myself trapped in a strange world where excitement at summer's arrival was killed by what I knew would happen. Because I *did* know. Even before the words "WALDO IZ DED" were found scrawled across my locker and gawkers assembled (teachers and faculty among them), even before calls were made home and my parents laughed off the incident as kids just being stupid, I knew what would happen to me.

*

My dog Reb was my only method of centering. There were videogames, of course, but I'd beaten most of them. Drew was especially absent those days, getting drunk with friends, staggering in when I was already asleep in the top bunk. With his bouts of drunken crying, the strong scent of urine wafting up along with his beer breath.

I'd feign sleep every time, knowing I should probably talk to him, at least say something when he'd whisper my name, then say it, then half-yell it to try and wake me, no response. I couldn't do anything. Or wouldn't. Maybe both. Because in those moments, every time I peeked with lids half open and saw him nearly fall over himself drunk, heard him reminisce over the girl he nearly scored with that night, I saw only chin and brow. Just another dumb OLPHS type. So I'd wait it out, night after night, past the guilt that was hammering around in my chest, past the sleep sounds I manufactured to make it seem more convincing, till his cries of "Waldo" finally stopped, till his regular cries stopped too. It was only then, in the post-drunk silence, that we could both get to sleep.

29. But Wait, There's More

It was the last week of school—the last hurdle till freedom. Eerily quiet. Ominous. I kept waiting for the other shoe to drop, a habit I didn't notice I'd picked up somewhere along the way. Even so, though, sometimes intuition is wrong.

LC and his crew were nowhere to be found.

They weren't in any of the classes I shared with them, weren't even hiding in the camera-less corner of the school blacktop they'd claimed for their drinking sessions.

At lunchtime, a few of the teachers crowded around TVs the same way they had years ago, when fire was consuming the upper floors of WTC 1.

Before the day was up, our class was huddled into the cafeteria, and we all once again studied for clues the tense stares of grownups totally at a loss for what to do, what to say.

Our principal took the floor. He explained that our classmate Fernando de la Paz had been severely injured in what appeared to be an accidental shooting.

Details were still scarce, but so far they knew that the gun was Fernando's father's, and that William "Chaz" Billington was believed to have accidentally discharged the weapon. That Fernando was in critical condition, and they'd have more information for us when it became available. They told us that counselors were on the school grounds and were prepared to talk to anyone who might need their help.

I sat perfectly still, as if to move was to be found out for something I didn't do. In my mind, there was that moment with the fog of the field, a cool moon above and a knife being inserted into my side. There were all the slurs Mario had called me, all the pain and the frustration and the fear that he'd put me through over the years. I thought again of what PGN would do, what I thought he would do. And so I waited like that, quiet but buzzing internally, until the day ended. I made my mind empty of thought, and when I finally did get home, I picked up my bike and started scoping out.

30. Scoping Out

My bike was a hand-me-down of a hand-me-down, more rust and dirt than metal and rubber, spray-painted in spots, covered in half scraped-off decals in others. I got it from Drew, and he got it from a friend way back. I used to put Pokémon cards on the spokes with Rodhi to simulate motorcycle sounds, and how we'd laugh and try our hand at making up BMX tricks. When that image returned to my mind, I had to put it away. What I was about to do had no room for that.

He was out by the western edge of Bay Colony, where the only thing separating the subdivision from highway was a crappy chain-link that'd been bypassed with wire cutters a long time ago.

But this is about me, and about LC, so these were the events as they happened:

I saw him, and he didn't see me.

His back to me.

Peeing on the fence.

My tires buried gravel.

He knew nothing.

I righted handlebars' angle.

Gravel kicked up in a spray.

He turned to look, pissed on his shoes.
I pedaled.
He just stood there.
Front tire struck hard, pants undone.
He fell against fence, pinned.
I dropped my bike, kicked him in the face.
He cried out, grabbed below.
I kicked him again, below the sternum.
Wind gone.
I started to cry.
My fist hit his face, knuckle skidded off his cheek.
Sobs.
He looked at me as I cried. Terrified.
I cut my hand on a front tooth.
The smell of urine wafted on the breeze.
He started crying too.
I kicked him in the stomach.
He curled into a ball.
He begged me to stop.
I grabbed his shirt collar, ripped it, hauled him up.
I yelled, but not words.
He closed his eyes tight, refused to open them.
I tossed him to the ground.
His head next to my foot. I looked at it.
I raised my foot, shadow over his eyes.
A bird's chirp over the drone of cars, our crying.
My breath as it came out through PVC pipe lined with broken glass.
I set my foot back down, beside his head.
Kicked him in the groin, listened to him cry.
I got back on my bike and rode off as the bird chirped and chirped and chirped.

31. The Magniterrible One

There were no more muttered insults. No more murder plots to be conveniently eavesdropped. No crew to stand by as a knife entered me. LC didn't show up for the rest of the school year. He couldn't be seen at his usual Bay Colony hangouts, either. Word on Mr. de la Paz was grim. Even if he did survive the whole ordeal, Mr. Billington's foreseeable future wasn't bright. Basically, the threat was gone, finally gone, and yet I couldn't seem to make myself happy about that fact. I couldn't seem to feel much of anything.

I started watching fight videos online. The more brutal the better. Kimbo Slice before his stint in the UFC. Backyard brawls that left guys with a loss of blood and consciousness. I was especially keen on knockout videos where you could see the light of life slip away from someone's eyes, watch their body revert to a primal backup state where nerves and muscles refused to work properly. I carved out a little time for myself before bed each night, when everyone else was asleep and it was just Reb and I still up. He'd sit behind my chair, tail wagging and tongue out, occasionally push his nose against me for pets. But I didn't want to see him. I wanted to see hurt. I wanted to see pain.

This went on for a few weeks, until it wasn't enough.

Until shadowboxing and stabbing boxes wouldn't do it either. So I went scoping out again.

At first, I couldn't find him. At first, he had me beat. He knew where I'd look for him and avoided those spots completely. A part of my brain tried to make me take this as a reason to stop. To let it go. Maybe talk to someone about the things I was feeling. But then I remembered the fear. The fog in my head. The hurt. And so I'd get back on my bike and scope out.

First time I saw him outside again, it was unseasonably chilly, rain threatening. He was down by the creek, by himself, in a place secluded enough that most wouldn't see him. But I did. He snuck a couple beers from the twelve pack he'd stashed there, drank and tossed cans in front of him. I made a game of watching where each one would land.

I waited till he seemed good and comfortable before going over. I let him see me coming. I wanted him to feel the fear, the dread as he realized he had nowhere to go.

Words left my mouth, words I'd never spoken before. Words like pussy, and bitch, and fag.

And there it was. That word we didn't know the meaning of when we were younger. The one he used to call me because the big kids said it, and even though he didn't know what it meant, he did know that it hurt. I hated myself after saying it. My throat burned. I didn't know who I was anymore. But I figured there was no going back now.

I hit him and pushed him down into the mud until he broke down. I stopped once he started crying. That was enough. I left him to the muddy creek, to his discarded cans. I got out of the woods and went back home, and the mud I trailed along the way seemed like so many pieces of myself being permanently shed.

32. Mass With PGN

I passed the entrance exam. Regardless of how I felt about OLPHS, something in me couldn't intentionally fail a test. The cherry on top was that I actually placed into AP English and History.

To celebrate, we gathered as a family unit (minus Drew but plus PGN) and went to Mass. Being C and E parishioners, something about going to church on a non-holiday seemed wrong. It wasn't the same without the Christmas ornamentation, or else the liturgy on death and resurrection and salvation. Salvation. The image of Mario and I in the creek was still just as fresh in my mind, and when PGN congratulated me for getting into OLPHS, I had to create a smile on my face even as something deep inside felt permanently broken. Barren. The church, too, was pretty barren, a subject that Father pounced on in his sermon. He argued that the best and only place to receive the Grace of the Lord was within the four walls of the church. That attending Mass regularly was as vital to spiritual health as flossing was to that of dental health. PGN nodded along.

I scheduled my attention in time with the two parts of Mass that my presence would absolutely be required during: Eucharist and the Sign of Peace.

Eucharist is when the rising hunger of Sunday morning stomachs is quelled with the body and blood of Christ: wafers and wine. The Sign of Peace is that part where the priest reflects on the legacy of Christ. That eternal enigma of something like peace coming out of so much suffering. He would speak on this peace, and we were to shake the hands of our neighbors and offer what we had of it to them.

"...peace I leave you, my peace I give you..."

As Father gave us our cue, I couldn't help but stare at the crucified Jesus at center. The Messiah was hewn from oak; slumped, with a surprising level of exhaustion and suffering emoting through wood's grain.

Peace I leave you, my peace I give you.

A bassy rumble came from my immediate right with each hymn sung, Grandpa providing the baritone. Before long, we were in the Eucharist breadline, Father doing an admirable job of seeming fresh each time he uttered "the body of Christ" and offered a wafer as the recipient gave a thankful "amen." I couldn't help but imagine Father eventually getting tired of the whole thing, pulling a wafer back from the tongue of a parishioner and saying, "You know what? No. Fuck this, I'm done. Grab your own wafers." He'd leave the bowl on the altar and walk out.

I was stuck on this mental image as I was offered the Body. I knew it was wrong, but I burst into laughter that only got worse the more I tried to stop it. I tried to consume the Body to make it better, but when that failed, I accidentally spit out bits of it onto the church's floor.

In a moment, PGN had me by the shoulder of the nice shirt that M & D had told me to wear. He was pulling me out of the church, and I was moving to keep up with him. Mom and Dad were right behind us all the way out.

Out in the hall, I made myself focus on the faint organ notes as they carried, between and underneath the doors.

Mona told Grandpa to let me go. Her words were dipping their toes in the water, cautiously checking temperature and tide. But he still dug his hand into my shoulder, and I tracked the scuff marks on the floor that we'd left in our exit. Marks that wouldn't just go away over time.

Everything changed after she yelled at him. His grip on my shoulder slackened, if only just a bit.

"Mona Pauline Collins."

That was all he needed to say. Her eyes went wide and glassy. Seeing her like that got my heart pounding. But she recovered:

"Let him go, Dad."

A silence so painful it made my chest hurt. Why did I have to do the things that I was doing? Why couldn't I just be good?

"Am I hearing you correctly? Are you trying to tell your father what to do?"

"I'm... No, I'm sorry..."

Again, the eyes. Looking away. But she fought it again.

"I'm... Yes. Yes, I am telling you."

"Telling me what?"

"To... I'm telling you to let him go."

I could hear PGN's thudding heartbeat against my temple as he held me tight to his side. He released my shoulder and reached for his belt, an instinctive move. He was yelling, but not words.

Something stopped him, belt half-undone. The same something made him grab at his chest. He took a knee, and suddenly there he was in one of those black-and-white leatherhead football photos he kept on display. It was as if he were only waiting to hear what his coach had to say at halftime. Mona was crying. She screamed for help, and cell phones were out, and an ambulance was called as Grandpa went down, all the way, onto the ground.

Interlude:
Phil

Today is December 1, 1950. My birthday. I am now twenty-four years old. There's been difficulty getting mail in, what with the cold. Thirty below some nights, or so they say. Haven't heard from Genevieve in weeks. No more, "Dearest Phil," "My Love Phil," "Sweetest Phil." Nothing but the blinding cold here in this godforsaken place, this Chosin Reservoir. They call us The Chosin Few. Ha.

Most days are spent rotating between who stands in front of the tailpipe, our vehicles kept running most of the time just to keep them from breaking down. One day, they gave us hot cereal over at regimental headquarters. The hot milk was frozen solid within thirty feet of walking away from HQ. I mostly just eat Tootsie Rolls now. They're the only thing that'll melt in your mouth, that won't freeze solid.

The Chinese have been attacking for days now. Nights, rather. They wait till we're sleeping, play recordings of babies crying, women screaming. Lie in wait till one of our men goes to investigate, gives up our position. They gun the poor bastard down, come for us. I've heard that the chinks get hopped up on morphine before they attack. Lets them take shot after shot before going down. Fucking animals. I got in a few firefights, tracers the only thing illuminating all that dark. No way of knowing if I got any confirmed kills, but I like to think I did. Hardest part about it was keeping your hands steady in the cold, heat sapped from your fingers in seconds.

I lie awake at night, my breath disappearing into the wind, icicles clotting my beard, my nose. In my breast pocket, frozen solid, is the letter where Genevieve first admitted she loved me. Whether it was out of fear she'd never see me again or something else, I'm not sure. But I know I need to see her again. Fucking terrified I won't. They say the Chinese like to come in three waves. First one carries rifles. Second follows up with grenades. And the third. The third just scavenges from the dead. These chinks fight like it's their homeland. You'd never know the difference.

I want to have children. Grandchildren. I don't want to die alone in this frozen hell, eyes glazed over with ice. I want to see my mom. Even my drunk of a dad. All that petty bullshit between he and I doesn't seem so important anymore. If I could just touch Genevieve's hand. Last I heard from her, she'd been having more spells. No sleep for days. Screaming at her parents. No one knows what it is. They have her on pills, but they don't seem to be working. If I could just be there with her, she'd be okay.

I don't know how many more times I can survive these attacks. Seems I haven't slept in days, each day melting into the next. Melting. If only all of this could melt. The cold's worse than the Chinese, and it never stops coming. I take naps during the day whenever my superiors aren't around. It seems like we're all just waiting to die. They've surrounded us. We're outnumbered. I don't know if I'll make it out of this, but I'll sure as hell try.

It's nearly dusk now, Korean sky the color of Pepto-

Bismol, stretching out everywhere around us. There's an eerie hush, the snow collecting all of the sounds and hiding them from us. I'm so hungry. Probably malnourished. But that's okay. Just as long as I can operate my trigger finger.

I'm rested now. Ready. I don't know how I know tonight will be it, but I just do. So I stand guard and watch as the sun disappears from the sky.

No recordings of babies crying, of women screaming. Nothing but less-than-silence, the lack of sound itself absorbed into the snow. I ready my M1 Garand. Exhale. Tap the letter in my breast pocket to make sure it's still there.

And then their battle cries. And then their uniforms, tan against white, coming in from the shadows. Shots pocking snow all around me, sending drifts of it into the air. Crouching and taking aim. Firing. Watching a man fall to his knees, then his face. Features erased just as his life is. Drawing a bead on another. Dropping another. I will not go down today. Not today.

A man falls beside me, red already spilling onto white. I look at him, and within seconds his blood on the snow crusts over with ice. I go to him, but another shot tears off his jaw. He falls on his back, lifeless eyes stuck to pink sky that's quickly fading to black.

I fire three shots. Create three dead bodies. The air is so cold I can almost taste blood. My legs shake so badly I think I might fall, but somehow I don't. Somehow I take cover behind a vehicle just as bullets ricochet off of it. All around me there are men, good men, squirming and flailing in the snow. One among them pushes his boots against the ground to stand back up. I run to him. Pick him up, sling his arm over my shoulder. He calls to me: "Phil. Phil. Phil." We make our way, the two of us, into the dark, to where I've heard there's a medical truck.

We finally reach it. I stop to load the man in. He looks up

at me: "Phil." Goes limp in my arms.

I load him in. Turn to go. The corpsman tells me not so fast. I'm to get in too. I look down: a neat hole in my side, blood frozen, saving my life. I get in.

When I come to, the doc's saying, "Phil. Phil. Phil." At the foot of my bed's a metal medical file. My initials and some numbers: "PGN-090190." I look at the doc.

"Don't call me Phil.

"Call me PGN."

33. Lutheran General

I remember praying that he wouldn't die because of me, because of something I caused. That Catholic orisonic muscle still worked, no matter how much I'd let it atrophy over the years. Mona and Roger tried to pry me away as we waited for the ambulance, but I saw PGN's face slide into gray, watched the consciousness (or life, for all I knew then) slip out of his eyes.

No radio on the car ride over, nothing to score the trip but the underwater sound of sirens receding and coming back again whenever Roger would catch up, Mona alternating between sobs and the noise I'd only ever heard come from her whenever she told us she was freshening up.

We pulled up to Lutheran General's ER entrance alongside PGN's ambulance. Mona was out of the car before it fully stopped. As I got out of the car, a powerful dizzy spell hit me, and I steadied myself against a pillar to keep from passing out.

I wanted to go in the room with him, but I wasn't allowed any farther than the waiting area. Mona and Roger were let in, and went, leaving me alone down there. Minutes passed like that, maybe an hour or more, time refusing to cooperate with someone who had fucked up so badly. And worse than it all was the look Drew would give me when he found out I killed him. That I'd taken away the only father figure he'd ever had.

After a long time had passed, Mona came down by herself, holding the stairs' railing, then the room's wall, her face the same off-white as the wall, her legs made of jelly, her eyes unable to focus on anything for more than a second or two. She sat down beside me. Let all the air out of her lungs. I hugged her. Or rather, I latched both arms around her as she stiffened up, and it was in that moment that I realized how thin she'd become.

She waited silently until I pulled away. Immediately got back up and left the waiting room without a word.

*

The whole waiting room took on a haze—a fume-induced vision where the place was filled to capacity, then emptied out, then filled again, the waves of the infirm swelling and crashing on the hospital's shore. It took me a second to process what the nurse said when she came over to tell me I could see my grandpa now, and was I ready?

I was ready, and so she led me to his room.

There were tubes and wires. Mona cried a little girl's cry. Roger seemed like he didn't have a clue what he should do with his hands, or his legs, or his face, or anything else. PGN was gray and barely conscious on his stiff hospital bed.

I looked at him and started sobbing. Cried and then realized what I was doing, turned away from PGN and acted like I was very interested in one of the room's corners.

PGN scooted himself up a couple inches in bed, coughed a little.

"Ah, quit your damn crying. I'm the one in the bed."

I stared out the room's window, imagining myself as one

of the birds out there, lighting on a concrete structure before taking off to some other destination, unknown and unknowable.

PGN took me out of it:

"The hell are you doing, daydreaming? Why don't you try listening for once, you might learn something."

I called his bluff, tried on something like defiance and forced myself to look into his eyes.

"I don't know what your malfunction is, but you need to sort it out, and fast. Get your shit together. Because Lord knows I'm not always gonna be here, and neither are your mom and dad."

He waited for my response, but I had none. He went on:

"You're headed down the wrong path. Got no discipline. No faith. No sense of duty. If I were you, I'd be scared. Real scared. But you're tough, and you're angry. I just don't understand. I'm some crazy old geezer who doesn't know what you're going through. And that's fine. That's okay. But you'll remember what I'm saying here right now. When you're older and ready for it, you'll remember."

No one said anything.

"I just hope by then it isn't too late."

34. Double Feature

Drew took the whole ordeal surprisingly well. He responded in typical Drew fashion, careful not to show any emotion. I was a little bitch for crying, but laughing in the priest's face was pretty funny, and did I actually spit out the Host? And yes I did, but it was only because I was laughing, and I didn't know why I was laughing, and I didn't mean to. And that's pretty fucked up. I might just be going to Hell for that one. And I might've already been going there for other reasons, but I didn't say that one out loud.

Freshman incoming at OLPHS was looming in the distance, a pendulous cloud threatening heavy rain. Drew surprised me by suggesting we celebrate with a brotherly day of arcade games and action movies. I accepted, figuring I'd beat him at *Tekken,* or, failing that, at least put up a good fight at *Dance Dance Revolution.*

The walk to nearby Golf Mill Mall took triple the time it normally would've, Drew stopping along the way to quiz me on car models and Bears players. His quizzes were the only ones I ever failed.

He'd point at McMansions we'd pass and insist he'd live there one day, or maybe there, once he made enough money to get us out of Bay Colony for good.

There was a weird edge to his words, as if everything he said was inexplicably important somehow, like each cutting jibe was going to be time-capsuled and preserved for the future.

"You aren't gonna bitch out once you get to OLPHS, are you?"

and:

"How was school and shit? You get all As like a fucking nerd?"

and:

"You're good with Reb, right? Won't just let him piss all over our room?"

I was about to remind him that he'd be there to look after Reb too, but something in his intense stare stopped me from saying it. The look was as un-Drew as you could get, and it made me uncomfortable.

*

The arcade is one of those places that survive because they don't change, whose only business comes in to reminisce and play the same beat-up old cabinets they tore up as a teen, with every gnarled joystick a badge of honor, another "Dude, you remember that?" and "Holy shit, they still *have* this?"

You knew it was going down when Drew stepped in the arcade. He pulled out a fiver. Then another. Tenspot too. By the end of his token exchange, we both had to tighten our belts by a couple notches to fight the sag in our pockets. It was *that* real.

I got my ass beat at *Tekken* to start off with, then battled my way back in a couple hotly contested rounds of *Mortal Kombat 3*. After that, we teamed up, locked and loaded for the token-guzzler that was *Time Crisis*. And what outdated arcade would be complete without a few tilt-detecting pinball machines, de-netted Pop-A-Shot basketball, and an air hockey machine with a suspiciously inaccurate scoring mechanism?

After the tokens ran out, we went over to the food court and stuffed our faces with Taco Bell, then headed over to the movie theater that a few years prior had been added onto one of the ends of the mall.

I'm pretty sure the floors were sticky the day the place opened, and there existed a layer of accumulated popcorn butter/pop residue at hand-level on nearly all the walls. You could only see the original paint job by looking at the places where hands couldn't reach.

It wasn't even funny how many cans of pop we snuck into the place, pockets stuffed to bursting with the cans, bags of gummy worms, boxes of Dots, and some Junior Mints for good measure. Drew and I maintained almost creepy eye contact with all the theater employees we passed, the idea being that if they were distracted by our awkward staring, they wouldn't think to look at our pockets. Drew got us tickets for a PG movie that was playing on the same side of the theater as our intended target: a double feature showing of *Kill Bill: Volume One* and *Two*.

As the story unfolded and The Bride embarked on her epic quest for vengeance toward those who wronged her, I felt a stinging sort of love for my brother. Waves of gratitude flowed like the blood of the newly christened amputees to B's blade as The 5.6.7.8's played and played and played. I kept a lookout for something looming on the horizon, some new shitstorm to blot this out. But it didn't come. Drew didn't start anything after the showing, and neither did Roger or Mona once we got back. As Ice Cube would say, today was a good day.

35. Summer's Swan Song

So there I was at fourteen, Confirmation only a week away, and a week beyond that I'd become an OLPHS Don, a Gentleman of Mary. Until then, though, I was just Waldo, a kid from Bay Colony trying to enjoy his last few days of summer freedom. Trying to remember what I used to be like before all of what happened happened.

I decided the best way to spend the time would be with Rodhi. The sun was shining, birds were out, wind nothing but a breeze, and we had two bikes that were screaming to be ridden, preferably with no hands. I buzzed his door and was put through to his mother, Maya. Apparently, Rodhi was already out and looking for me. He'd left an hour ago and should've been by my place already. I thanked her and headed out on my bike. Went back to my complex to see if Rodhi was there. No sign of him. I checked the woods next to Bay Colony. Nothing. Reluctantly pedaled over to Meadow Lane, dangerously close to where we got shot at that one time. Still no sign of him. Finally, I pried the storm drain cover off of my old hideaway. Rodhi was the only other person I ever showed the place to, the only one I trusted with what was inside. But all I found were my old, yellowed notebooks filled with silly stories and the jars of bugs that served as tiny lamps in all that dark.

I was about to give up entirely, head home and try again the next day, when I decided to ride over to the pond at the center of Bay Colony. That old cicada soundtrack was back again, low ominous thunder tones of droning chatter, insect monotony that scared by staying exactly the same and continuing on that way forever.

But there was something else, too. It rose and fell in time with a beat I couldn't hear but could sense beneath the sounds. With each pedal rotation toward the top of the hill, the notes became clearer, more pronounced.

At the hill's apex, I discovered the instrument behind it, or at least figured out how to classify it. It was coming out of PVC pipe lined with broken glass.

I tried to rush over like before, motions precise and measured. But when I saw Rodhi lying there by the edge of the pond, broken and bleeding, one of his arms twisted the wrong way and his mouth hanging open as he choked, my body shut down the way an ant's would after struggling with a glue trap.

The bike fell next to me and ripped up hunks of earth beneath its sideways pegs as it slid back down the hill. My legs tingled. Stomach turned over and hardened into a solid mass, and there was that familiar old hum in my head.

Rodhi's expression didn't change when he saw me. His eyes here hazy and hollow even as he registered that it was me, at a point beyond pain and fear. There was an acceptance in those eyes, and that made everything worse. Instead of looking at his eyes, I surveyed the damage. My brain could only supply me with visual facts, nothing beyond that.

His cheeks were puffy and distended, one of them knuckle-cut, both of them already turning a noxious shade of green.

His mouth was a pulpy mess of flesh, both lips torn open and bleeding freely down his face and onto his shirt.

Nose broken. Septum crushed.

Lump on the side of his head the size of a golf ball, a vein on the lump visibly pulsing.

Right arm broken. Shoulder pulled from the socket like one of the busted action figures Rodhi and I used to play with when we were real little.

Pants.

Pants.

Pants down. And.

And.

In that moment, I was in a place completely outside of myself, divorced from my body but still somehow making sound. I heard myself cry and scream for help. Wail until someone must've heard. Anyone. Someone just please help. Please do something.

36. Back Again

The sound that came from Maya's mouth as she looked at her mangled son in the back of that ambulance is something I never want to hear again.

I don't remember how I ended up at the hospital (Lutheran General again), whether I rode with Maya, or my family later, or took the bus, or whatever. All I know is that I arrived in a great circulatory system of a hospital room. The place had arterial pumps and wires everywhere, Rodhi serving as the barely living heart at room's center.

First there was intubation, and almost resuscitation, and a blur of MDs and scans and tests and it was all happening too fast.

Rodhi's eyelids trembled, the eyes behind them dipping in and out of view like actors going out of frame in an old silent film. Maya stayed beside him for as long as the MDs would allow; her tears collected in the palm of his unresponsive hand. She blotted them by holding his hand against her eyes, her nose, her mouth. Tear-wet fingers distorted her Bindi, but she didn't notice, or else didn't care if she did.

I tried to say I was sorry, but it only came out as an innocuous croak, barely distinguishable from a throat

95

clearing. So I shut up. The other side of Rodhi's bed was my only option. I took my place beside my scourged friend, playing the thief nailed up beside him. I didn't know what I'd stolen from him and Maya then, and I don't think even a decade or more could give me the answer I'm looking for.

And there were the restless birds again, outside the window. Their wings carried them on the breeze as they took off from their perch on the hospital's parking garage, sights set on a power line not too far away. Even the birds in this town can't seem to fly too far.

The MDs actually let me stay through most of it, through fluid exchanges and scans, specialists' opinions and machine tinkerings. That was, until they had to check the damage below the waist. Then I had to leave.

I wandered aimlessly through the halls, the hallway throbbing and pulsing from both directions. It tore me this way and that until I found the men's bathroom. Until I thudded into one of the stalls and slammed the door behind me. Until I pulled down my pants and looked for signs of damage that weren't there.

I waddled out of the stall, pants near my ankles, looking desperately into the pulsing, squirming mirror. I tried to find something that wasn't there—something I didn't even know the name of.

I stood there like that for who-knows-how-long, my brain a collection of ants and other opportunistic scavengers gnawing away.

Interlude:
Maya

Madhan called last night and told me he needed to see me, called late at night so that I had to pull the phone's cord as far as it would go away from Mama and Baba's room, so they wouldn't hear us talk. They thought I'd stopped talking to him after they told me to, but they were wrong.

I haven't gotten any sleep since I hung up the phone. I got back home from night school, slipped in quiet so Mama and Baba wouldn't hear, hid my books, and Madhan called right after, as if he knew. Maybe he did. I don't know. That boy seems to know so much.

The night moves into morning, and I spend it by sitting on the grass, in a field near my home, watching the way the purple of the sky turns to pink, the stars disappearing into nothing. This place I've been to with Madhan so many times before, lying on the grass and looking up at the sky, far enough from New Delhi's center that it's quiet, close enough that the city's lights erase some of the starlight.

Madhan said he'd be here by sunrise, like the times before, when we'd shield our eyes from the light and watch the city come to life, the stray dogs rising up from the ground like steam to wind their way through the city and find another meal. But Madhan isn't here. I told myself I wouldn't cry, but my eyes are clouding, letting the light take over everything. I'm standing up, the dew on the grass clinging to my feet, and I'm putting my sandals back on, trying to figure out which way to go.

I get to the bus stop, this bus that will take me to Madhan, that will get me the answers he suddenly doesn't want to give. I sit on the bench and wait, but after a minute I'm back up, pacing, waiting for the bus as the sun rises into my eyes and blinds me. Finally, I'm not even pacing, just standing, and this old dog comes up to me with his tail between his legs, big eyes looking at me, begging for food.

I put my hands out to show him I have nothing, but he persists. He sniffs both hands to make sure that I'm not hiding something, then walks behind me and sits next to the bench. I take it as a sign and take a seat, reach out and pet his head, scratch his nose, his gray whiskers moving as he smiles at me. I can see the dog's ribcage, and he limps on one of his hind legs, but this old dog doesn't seem to mind. He just sits there next to me with his tail wagging, brushing the dirt from the ground like a child who doesn't know how to use a broom. I pet him so we can both forget for a while.

When the bus is in sight, I want to leave this stop and this old dog and go back to the field, back home. Somewhere else. But I don't. I get on the bus, and I pay my fare, and I take a seat, and I wait for the stop that will take me to Madhan.

The beggar children try to stop me everywhere I go once I get off the bus. They cup their hands into little ponds that are waiting to be filled. When they reach out their hands, I hold them briefly and apologize. I have nothing to give.

I get to Madhan's door and knock. It takes a few minutes, but he finally comes to the door and asks who's there. When I tell him it's me, he waits a while before opening up, peeks through the crack between the door and the frame to make sure it's actually me. He opens it up the rest of the way and says nothing, only looks at me.

He puts on some tea and offers me a seat. We don't talk until the tea is done, and he pours my tea with shaking hands. He starts by saying:

"You know how I feel about you."

When he says this, my stomach drops. He sips his tea so he won't have to say anything more, and I do the same. Finally, he says:

"I have to do it."

It's his parents, he says. They'll never forgive him, never let this go. They hadn't approved of me, and they never would. Anyway, it'd be better for me. This way, we wouldn't strain things with our parents. He could marry who they wanted him to marry, and I could marry Suddho. And when I tell him I don't want to marry Suddho, I want to marry him, how Madhan takes my hands in his and kisses them both, first the left, then the right, then the left again. How he tells me we can still see each other, how he can visit me in America if Suddho is still to take me there. And when I ask him why we can't run away together like we'd planned, how he looks away so I can't see the tears clinging to his eyes. How he kisses me, deeply, and holds me to him.

We spend what feels like hours there, ignoring our tea, holding each other, barely separating, wanting this moment to never end. And when we finally separate, how he tells me he'll call, he'll see me. How I cry because I know this isn't true. We both know it isn't.

And how he takes me to the door, unwilling, and opens it to the bright sunlight shining in. How we kiss and we kiss and we kiss, and he moves me past the door, looks into my eyes and says nothing. How he closes the door. How I knock, and cry, and call his name over and over again. Madhan.

Madhan. Madhan.

37. Resting

It wasn't too long after he'd been admitted to Lutheran General that Rodhi started Resting. Of course, the MDs had other words for Resting, but there he was looking worse for wear but still Rodhi, still the kid who carried me to safety and pulled a pellet out of my ass. So no, I didn't hear coma. I heard Resting.

The days that followed were hollowed out. You could see right through to the other side. I strapped my bike to the front of the Pace bus bright and early every morning and locked it up once I'd been dropped off in front of the hospital. I spent every free minute I had by Rodhi's side. It got so I was there even more than Maya, so I'd fill her in on what had happened while she was gone, which nurse was on duty, any twitches or anomalies that might signal the end of Rodhi's Resting.

Mona and Roger didn't say anything about my being gone, but Drew took to joking about how I was quote unquote going to the park an awful lot these days, how the park must be grassy and smoking on a hot day like this, how I should make sure I didn't get too baked out on the grass. Wink wink.

I let him think what he wanted over the truth, because the truth would be final. It would be definitive. I pulled my lips up into what I hoped was a smile and pedaled off to the bus stop.

I remembered hearing something vague about people in a coma being able to hear through the endless black that was their consciousness, that that was The Way to Get Through for loved ones still on the other side. So I started telling jokes and stories.

I brought my GBA and a copy of *Warioware, Inc.* Plowed through a few of the game's thoroughly Japanese microgames, narrating for Rodhi every speeding hotdog car Wario had to jump over, every Wario-snot-rocketed booger pinball I had to keep from falling behind the flippers.

When the games and stories got old, I'd just start talking to him:

"Yeah, so I've got that whole Confirmation thing in a couple of days. Drew says I get like an extra saint name and everything. Only he won't tell me his, so who knows if he's telling the truth or not."

...

"It's gonna be weird when we're in high school, huh? I'll ask your mom if she can pick up your class list. Would've been cool if we went to the same school, but I guess OLPHS won't be that bad, right?"

...

"It's so stupid how posers try to act all cool by drinking and smoking. Like who cares about that crap? It's all a bunch of bullshit."

...

"She didn't even say anything. She saw the cans under his bed. Only she doesn't know I know she saw them, 'cause I was in the other room watching the whole thing. I didn't say anything. But then she like always has to start in on me, right? Say I'm eating too much and—"

...

"You don't think I'm getting fat though, right? She was just being stupid, that's why she said it. We're all kind of stupid sometimes."

...

Etc.

When I got sick of that, I went back into my storm drain hideaway and fetched my musty old stories, pages curled from moisture, ghost-pale from darkness.

A deep, lizard part of my brain knew that he couldn't really hear me, that I was speaking into an assemblage of beeps and blips and wishful thinking was doing the rest. But I still clammed up when I started reading those old stories, heart still palpitated knowing that this was the first time they'd be read aloud.

I got to the end of the stack of pasty pages that took years to write within a couple hours, all of the characters and scenarios bleeding together (and making me want to pull my hair out). I called the head nurse, asked for a pen and a pad of paper, and pulled up a chair next to Rodhi.

I wanted to write an especially crazy one for him, one with alien worlds and post-apocalyptic dystopiae abounding. But when I sat there and let the words flow, there was no Walgar with his really awesome sword. No alien abductions or grizzled Lone Wanderer to right wrongs in the waste of the world. All that came out was a story about a chubby kid from the torn-up part of town navigating the treacherous labyrinth that was pubescence, his wit his sword, his nerdiness his shield.

I filled up the first sheet in minutes, then the second, then the third. You could almost see smoke rising in little wisps above the paper. I called in Nurse Esperanza (I knew all the nurses by name at that point) and procured a second pad. Let my hand take a break and read what I had to Rodhi in the meantime. I'd pause and repeat the parts that didn't sound right, revise the sections that refused to come out the way I'd first imagined them.

Other voices came to me as I wrote. Other points of view, other ways of seeing the world. I saw other stories populate my brain, then my page. I don't know if it helped or hurt more to get out of my own headspace, but that's what I did.

The stories were soothing balm for a while, but they couldn't cover up the nagging Truth scratching away at me— I wouldn't be getting confirmed in a week's time, and I wouldn't be going to OLPHS a week after that, either. Because in a few days' time, I'd either be in jail for what I was going to do to LC, or in the morgue for what he'd do to me.

38. No Scope

The pond was calm and clear, a glassy blue, one giant mirror. LC wasn't there, of course. He wouldn't make it that easy.

I scanned the usual spots:

Muddy creek beer alcove: nothing.

Expressway-flanking fence: nope.

End of the drag race track known as Good Avenue: nada.

I circled the subdivision, checked all nine courts. No sign of him.

I turned back to the Scalverettis' complex—the one closest to the pond. I stopped in front of their door and waited. Held my arms out like an oak-hewn Jesus out beneath the gray and faintly sprinkling sky, awaiting the wood I'd be nailed to. I actually imagined dying for a second there—feeling the cold black wash over and pull me into the undertow. Just as long as I could take LC with me. As long as I could—

Hit.

Black.

Reset.

Panting.

Dull fire.

Look up.

LC. Game. A baseball game.

Hit.

Black.

Reset.

Swing for the fences.

Good eye, good eye.

Where's Waldo?

Hit.

Black.

Reset.

Legs dead weight. Can't stand.

Looming. Yelling.

Hands up. Protect the face. Protect the—

Hit.

Black.

Reset.

"...off him..."

"...the fuck..."

"...here right now..."

Lid.

Sky.

Lid.

Sky.

Ragged.

Lid.

"I'm sorry!"

Lid.

"Dad, I'm sorry!"

Wail.

Lid.

Bat. Shoes.

Lid.

Collar. Scruff. Beet red.

"...fucking kill him..."

"Daddy, please!"
Hit. Cry. Hit.
LC. Ground. Chooch.
Hit. Cry. Hit.
"...fuck's wrong with you?"
Split lip. Beg. Grab.
"Daddy."
"Don't daddy me. You're—"
Hit.
"...going—"
Hit.
"...to—"
Hit.
"...the fucking—"
Hit.
"...academy."
Hit. Wail.
Bat. Hand. LC's eyes.
"Daddy, no."
Arm up.
"Daddy."
Whip.
Tip. Grip. Tip. Grip. Tip. Grip. Splash.
Breathe.
"...you okay? Jesus."
"Dad, I'm s—"
Hit. Wail.
"...you get up?"
Lift. Slump.
"C'mon, kid."
Moan.
"...inside right now and pack up. Right now."
Scurry. Scatter.
"...sorry, kid. Really sorry."

Shoes. Door. Clatter.

Black.

Deep.

Reset.

Sun on the water. Night coming. The moon across from it, waiting.

No one in sight. Vacant courts and quiet streets.

Reach up, toward the pulse in my temple. Blood when I pull away.

Heel digs into dirt, slides into goose shit masquerading as mud.

Hands come down on same, fingers squelch in it as I push through the pain.

Heat radiates through ribs, right shoulder, left pinky. Lips clog breathing.

Plop back on goose shit, topple back and supine, snow angel and eyes on the sky.

Head is double its normal size, maybe triple. Tailbone now has a fault line. It is...

No. No more is. Only *was.*

The sky took on the pepto pink of a Chicagoland dusk. Dark clouds spread across in thin wisps—gangly fingers stretching and snatching up, fighting some cumulo gang war up there.

Then the rain returned. Icy drops, droplet size set to random. Gutters already clogging with soaked leaves. Blood at shirt collar diffusing, turning a faint pink as if to match the sky's hue. I tried to get up and failed. Tried again. Failed again.

Then Rodhi came.

His cheeks were no longer puffy; eyes un-black and un-blue; lips not ragged strips of flesh but whole again. He stood in the rain in front of me, the only thing clear in all that fog. He smiled the way he did when he pulled the pellet out of my ass.

He crouched down, eyes on mine the whole time. Reached out with his unblemished hands and put them in mine. The warmth was as strong as the first bat-crack against my skull. The warmth got me to my feet. Rodhi led me away from the pond and toward my complex, helping me up when I'd fall and waiting by my side when I needed to gather my strength.

It was near the end, when my complex was in sight, that I noticed how the raindrops refused to fall on Rodhi.

He led me to my patio door, the one with the faulty lock. Waited as I wobbled, fell, rose, and wobbled again. He knew I could do it on my own. I propped myself up against the door and looked back to see Rodhi one last time, but he was gone.

Interlude: Mario

The seat belt burns my skin as I buckle myself in. Dad gives me a look in the rearview mirror as he pulls out of our parking space. As he pulls away from the pond, where I can almost see Waldo sprawled out on the ground, head cracked open by my bat. It's gonna take some time, Dad says. That's all he'll say to me. He'd threatened me with the Academy for years. He had friends, old military buddies, on the inside. Was just waiting for an excuse, and I gave it to him. A single backpack sits next to me, packed with the only things I'll be allowed to bring with me. Everything else gets left behind.

Dad barely let me get any time with Macchiato before leaving, the dog cowering in the corner of my room after I slammed the door shut and packed my shit. I pulled him into my closet and cried onto him in the dark, Dad yelling shit behind my bedroom door, pounding on it, yelling at me to hurry up. Even in the dark, I could see that Macchiato's ear was turned inside out. I fixed it for him and opened up the closet door.

And there's something else.

Nights spent camping out in my closet, before we even

got the dog, that's how little I was, and the way Dad would stagger down the halls like a drunken ghost, sometimes crashing family pictures to the ground as he reached out to steady himself on a wall. And I'd push myself farther into the corner, and wait, and try not to breathe, and close my eyes, as if he wouldn't be able to see if I couldn't. There was a stuffed animal my mom gave me, a little swan, and I'd hold onto that in the dark, clutch it to my heart so tight that it was like the swan had come to life. And then the steps came close to my door. Closer. Heavier. Right outside.

And then I'm there.

The doorknob turns. Door swings open. I let out all my air like a punctured tire. I'm clutching my swan so tight that my fingers hurt. The door slams behind him. Loud enough for Mom to hear, but she won't do anything. What can she do? Dad opens drawers and shuffles through my things. A couple seconds later, I can hear him lifting up my mattress, slamming it back down.

I should be able to hear footsteps before he opens the closet door, but I don't. He opens the door so forcefully that a shirt falls on my head. I hope that it'll hide me from him, but I know it won't. He grabs the shirt and pulls it, some of my hair in his hand as he does. I want to yell, but I don't. I know better. I squeeze myself into the corner till I can hardly breathe, clutch my swan so tight that I'm sure my knuckles would be white if I could see them. And then Dad turns on the closet light, blinding me.

He slaps me across the face, sending my cheek to the wall. Abrasion of drywall against skin, then tears being squeezed out of my eyes. I chew on the insides of my cheeks so hard that it's a wonder they don't open up and give me a permanent smile. He's towering over me now, not even his usual wife beater on, just hairy chest and sweat, dried puke that was stubborn even after a good scrub, then drinking after puking to make up for the lost buzz. He crouches down, into my closet, and gets so close that I can smell him. His beer breath makes my eyes water.

He grabs the swan from my hands, asks me what he told me about carrying around that faggot doll. I tell him I don't know, but I do. He slaps me so hard that I can feel my head start to bruise after it makes contact with the wall. Tomorrow morning, he'll ice it for an hour so the bruise won't show. He's done it before, and he'll do it again. He reaches at his waistband and pulls out his trusty old knife. Flicks it open as if he's done it a thousand times, 'cause he has. He brings it to the swan's neck and hacks at it while I cry and scream. Stuffing touches the floor as the knife pulls through, jagged cloth hanging from the decapitated stuffed animal, the placid eyes staring at me, questioning why I did nothing.

Dad goes to put his knife away but stops when he sees where I'm looking. There's a jagged, mangled scar that goes nearly from Dad's navel to his back. He asks if I want to know where he got the scar as if this is the first time he's asking me. As if I don't have one of my own, going from my navel to my side, half-completed. As if he hasn't cut into me time and time again, held a lighter to my skin to stop the bleeding afterward. Held the knife at my throat and threatened to open it if I ever told a soul.

He pulls my shirt up. Touches blade to skin. I don't fight or squirm. I don't know why I don't, I just don't. Tears well up in Dad's eyes, and he mouths words I can't hear as he slowly slides the knife inside of me.

And that's it. That's where the memory goes black.

39. Slipping

I didn't want to leave the top bunk. Didn't want to pull the blankets away from my face. Didn't want to hear the phone as it rang with no one around but me to answer it. Because I knew it was Maya. I knew. But I answered anyway.

He slipped away was all she could say, as if all along he'd been hanging by the fingertips from a cliff, waiting for someone to haul him back up to safety. He'd been hanging, and we didn't help him back up.

Silence was our way of consoling each other. I remember counting the heartbeats as they hammered in my eardrums, as they reverberated loud enough for Maya to catch through the receiver, I was sure. But if she heard anything, she never let on. She just breathed in slow and quiet.

And then her voice, barely a whisper, cut through all the quiet:

"You are good boy, Waldo. You are good boy."

The words flipped a switch. I cried so hard my head instantly ached, so intensely the cries would only come out in silent gasps for air. Tears squeezed out and ran down the old corded, gathered in upside-down rivulets that traced the cord's curlicue contour before dripping onto my lap.

My tears must've been an invitation, because she let go

too. She let herself fall from that cliff despite what she might be falling into. I knew if I were there beside her she'd hug me close like Mona never did and I'd let her. Let her clutch me in place of Rodhi and she'd let me hug her in place of Mona. It'd be a fair trade. But she was on the other line. The best we could do was cry and listen.

I don't know how long we sat on the phone like that, but the hurt I let out was enough to hide the pain in my head, ribs, face, and hands, where LC's bat's sweet spot connected again and again. But as the conversation turned to the topic of *antyesti* (Hindu funeral rites), that familiar old pain returned.

He would want me to come and see. I was good boy, and her *pyara* would want me there for final *sanskara*. I stayed by his side all of the time and read all of my stories, and her *pyara* would want me there. And would I come in three days' time? And I would. Of course I would, Mrs. Boshi. Of course I would.

It'd be easy to accuse me of knowing ahead of time that Rodhi's funeral would coincide with my Confirmation, and that I'd accepted the invitation accordingly, but that wouldn't be true. Even all these years later, after all the beefs I've had with the Catholic establishment, I'll still stick to that. Because it's true. I didn't know, and I didn't care. Rodhi saved me, and I had to be there beside him as the wind took him away.

40. Compound Interest

It's amazing the things people let slip when they forget you're around.

I stayed holed up in my room for the next three days, one of Drew's old hand-me-down hoodies on to cover the bruises and a blanket over that to cover up the spots the hoodie missed. I used the feeble excuse of being under the weather (at the tail end of summer). Maybe it was my persistence in not leaving the room, or maybe my voice had a raw, hurt quality they'd all decided they'd rather not fuck with, but no one pushed me on it. Not even Drew. Reb was the only one I'd let near me.

But the slips.

Drew was gone. I assumed he was getting drunk and/or high with his friends, but I'd later find out he had a meeting with his recruiter. Mona and Roger were in the living room, and Mona was doing her conspiratorial whisper, the one she used when she wanted to pretend like she was being secretive but was in fact trying to let everyone hear.

"Well, what do we tell him?"

"Just tell him what's happened."

"But we don't know if that's why yet."

"Mona, that's why. You know that's why. Don't be

stupid."

"Don't call me stupid."

"I—"

"Well I'm not going to Lutheran General alone."

"Fine, take him. But what about OLPHS?"

"We're *not* telling him about that."

"Yeah, fine."

"What do you mean 'fine?' "

"I mean fine."

"It only makes sense."

"Yeah, sure."

"Drew *should* have to help out after all the—"

"I said fine."

"And I already checked what he'll get for base pay. Should cover most of Waldo's tuition."

"Fine, Mona."

"What would Drew use it for anyway? It's not like he wants to go to college. This is the right thing."

...

"Right?"

"Yeah. Right. Okay."

"Right."

"If you're gonna tell him about your dad, just do it now."

"Don't tell me what to do, Roger."

"I..."

Roger trailed off as Mona walked over to my room. She gently opened my door.

"Hey, Wally. How you doing?"

She only used "Wally" when she was up to something.

"Not goo—"

"That's good. Look, Grandpa's in the hospital again."

...

"So are you gonna come with and see him?"

"Wait, what? What happened?"

"He got an infection. They don't know what exactly yet, but it's bad."

"How'd he get the infection?"

...

"He got it in the hospital, right? After he had the heart attack? Just say it."

"Well, they don't know at this point. He—"

"That's why. I know that's why. You know that's why. Don't be stupid."

I let one eye peek from the fortress of solitude that was the hoodie and blanket combo. Braced for the explosion. Dimly imagined the aftermath: jagged hulks of buildings, shadows burnt into walls. The works.

She opened her mouth to say something. To yell something. Took a deep breath.

She closed her mouth. Turned around. Walked out of my room and slammed the door shut behind her.

41. Return to Sender

The swelling wasn't as noticeable three days later. My eyes were still a little puffy and turning a nauseous green, but that's what the makeup was for. I pilfered it from Mona's collection, waited till everyone else was done getting ready to sneak into the bathroom and conceal the damage. I had to be quick to make it there on time. The antyesti would be performed at 10—same time as my Confirmation.

Hanging on the door handle was my jacket for church. Sharp, severe, a too-large gray that matched the hemmed and re-hemmed slacks I had to wear, the whole ensemble handed down from Drew's Confirmation. A crisply stale dress shirt, pressed and ironed, the faintest of yellow stains around the collar. A black-and-white-striped tie that hadn't been in fashion when it was purchased, which who knows when it was purchased.

The makeup claimed each splotchy bruise as its own and eliminated the competing colors. The yellows and purples and blues all faded with each application, till a dull and poreless approximation of Caucasian skin prevailed. I looked like I should be on the news. I put on the too-big jacket, cringed at its itchiness that was somehow worse than the dress shirt. Cringed again when I had to lift up the shirt's collar and look briefly like one of the popped-collar fools at OLPHS. I lowered the already-tied tie over my neck and collar, cinched it tight, and adjusted till it was centered. Brought the collar down and tightened the tie some more, till my face's dull fleshy tone turned a shade of red.

I looked in the mirror and assessed. Seeing my slightly puffy eyes without the discoloration explanation made me look misshapen. Off. I felt like I was looking at an uncanny valley version of myself. Even so, there was no concrete evidence that I'd received a brutal beating just a few days before. The person in the mirror looked fine.

My heart rose to my throat as I gripped the door handle and planned my escape route. I would open the bathroom door and walk briskly—walk, not run—to the patio door. I'd close it quietly so they wouldn't know. They'd know eventually, of course, but by then I'd be at the temple. I'd walk just as briskly down Potter Road to get to the temple I'd only ever seen passing by, the one that had its windows broken after 9/11.

I gripped the handle. Turned it. Walked briskly toward the patio door. I should've been alerted by the perfume, but I wasn't thinking clearly.

"Waldo, come here."

I looked out the patio door. She called me again. I stopped, looked at her. She held an old disposable in her hands.

"Let's get some pictures before we leave."

She came over and cinched my tie some more, smoothed my hair, and was about to wipe at a blemish on my face before I pulled away and made up some excuse about being too old for that Mom, come on.

I tried to smile, or at least pull my lips back and show some teeth. I felt my eyes crinkling. Flash. Adjust pose. Smile wider. Flash. Black. Reset. Just one more, come on. Lips jagged flesh, acceptance in the eyes. Flash. Black. Reset. Hold it, hold it, that's a good one. Don't look down. Don't see what LC did to him. Flash. Black. Reset.

We headed outside together as a family unit, all of us approximating fancy dress clothes as best as a lower-middle class family from the torn-up part of town could manage. The sun was too bright, shining right in my eyes. I saw Rodhi a couple paces up, in clothes of white, telling me it's just a little farther, that he'll see me there.

"Waldo, where are you going?"

I stopped. Turned around. The rest of the family was about thirty yards back, looking at me funny.

"Waldo, let's go."

I saw the heat in her eyes, a tiny sample of what I'd see over a decade later with all the wires and tubes attached to her and the beeps and blips of bulky machines, eyes looking death into me—her death.

"Waldo, this isn't funny. Get in the car right now."

I had urges, temptations to tell her to go fuck herself, that I didn't want this, that my friend was dead, that I knew why PGN was back there, that I caused all of this shit and it was my fault, but that didn't mean I had to go through with this. That I could make my own choices and live my own life.

Yes, I thought all of those things. But I didn't say anything. Not a word. What I did, what I actually did was walk back to Mona. What I actually did was climb into the back seat next to Drew and buckle myself in, seat belt molten against my hand. I stared straight ahead as we drove down Potter and past the temple, didn't say a word as we drove to the church. I just sat in the back seat and tried hard not to cry. I started reciting Hail Mary and Our Father and all the rest, anything to shut up the screaming in my brain.

Lead us not into temptation, but deliver us from evil. Amen.

You lead, and *you* deliver, will you? Because I can't do it for myself. I just can't.

42. Confirm or Deny

When we got there, Mona paraded me in front of the church and took some more disposables. She had me stand in front of the phallic obelisk at the main entrance, a gilded crucifix atop it, glinting in the sunlight. Marched me over to the stained glass windows, Mary Magdalene cleaning the feet of Christ. I could already hear the organ spilling its music, timbre low and foreboding.

And there was Father. And oh wouldn't you like a photo with him? And where are your friends, the ones from CCD? Why don't we snap a couple with them too while we're at it? And oh you should just see yourself, Waldo. Your face looks different. Like it's glowing or something. PGN would be so proud to, well... let's go inside.

The oak-hewn Messiah still cried out in wooden silence. Peace I leave you, my peace I give you.

The organ's notes pulsed in my sternum as I marched down the aisle of pews, itchy collar drawing beads of sweat from my forehead, threatening my news reporter makeup job. I started to wipe but thought twice. The sweat was too close to the muted purple and yellow.

Candles danced behind the altar. A mousy young lady stood in front of them, ostensibly singing along to the accompanying music but more allowing the organ to drown her out. The bishop and his entourage were set to arrive any minute, but until then Father retained his stranglehold on the congregation, setting a couple of the giggling soon-to-be-confirmed straight with admonishing glances, smiles to passing parents as needed.

Mona took out the old disposable and got a couple good shots of me standing in the foreground as Jesus remained forever frozen in pain in the background. She chose a kid at random, one of my "friends," and took a couple shots of us. Got Father to come over after calling his name enough times where he couldn't fake that he hadn't heard anymore. His sweaty hand rested on the place between my shoulder blades, fingers digging in, searching as Mona checked the flash, and the batteries, and had us hold the pose as she wound the film, finally got a shot she deemed acceptable.

Father trailed his fingers down my back as we left our poses and retook our positions. Everything shifted. The organ's notes became dissonant. The mousy singer's voice went all over the place. Mary Magdalene's off-yellow pellucid face let in a patch of sunlight that blinded me more than Mona's disposable's flash did. Harmless adolescent chatter might as well have been a crowd of people for how it sounded to me.

The entourage arrived right as I seriously considered wiping my forehead. The hush announced their arrival—all chatter ceased. The mousy singer let her tentative voice fade out completely. Even the organist calmed down.

The entourage's line was organized by rank, in ascending order. First came the altar boys and girls in their white robes with gold trim. Then the less senior of the church's clergy, in robes befitting the occasion as opposed to their usual plain black vestments. And there at the back of the line was the bishop with his amaranth zucchetto (think a yarmulke with a stem at the top), waving and smiling with hands whose rings could've easily paid my OLPHS tuition.

The procession circled the congregation as if to lock us into a holy force field. All but one went round the perimeter. He stood there, perfectly unselfconscious and pleased with himself, an easy smile on his face and his white robes so blindingly bright that I couldn't see any sort of texture on them, just a featureless white. Rodhi stood, and stared, and smiled, waiting patiently for me to take the hint.

I looked over at Mona and was suddenly made aware of the singing going on around me, the half-mumbled words occasionally shifting toward something resembling a tune.

I looked past Mona, at Drew. He was past fake singing— he just stood there and waited for it to be over. Roger stood beside him, letting his mouth go through the motions.

I looked to my left. Open pew. It led straight out into the aisle. If I was going to do it, it had to be now.

I started walking before my logical brain could catch up. Heard Mona call my name.

First the whisper so as not to draw notice from other parishioners.

I kept walking at the same speed.

The inevitable outside-voice version.

I sped up a little. Eyes on me.

Then the grand finale, the I-don't-care-if-the-whole-world-hears scream.

The organ cut out, the mousy singer quit for good, and I was out the door and sprinting faster than I would with Dumas on my tail during summer suicides.

The door slammed open again. Mona's banshee screams carried as she tried to bring me back. Drew yelled my name briefly then laughed at my supreme insubordination.

The sweat ran rivulets down my made-up face as I huffed and puffed in itchy clothes that weren't mine. Clothes I didn't want.

I loosened the tie till my circulation returned, till I could think again. Yanked it up, over my head. Tossed it aside. I ripped the jacket off and let it fall at my feet. Left my white dress shirt on, the too-wide collar flapping in the breeze as I scuffed my dress shoes on gravel and sprinted down Potter toward the temple.

43. On the Wind

I had spurts of lucidity as I sprinted along the gravel roadside masquerading as sidewalk. Then came the temple's golden spires, concentric circles stacked atop one another in geometrical precision. Pillars and arches and fractals. The temple's beauty set against the humdrum backdrop of Potter felt simultaneously wrong and right. Only in Des Plaines would that make sense.

The next light was a quarter mile up. Too much time. I played my hand at Frogger and sprinted across the street with barely a look in either direction. Felt calm as the cars passed mere inches from me, as horns spilled doppler sounds. I moved my body where it needed to go, in my wake a buildup of brake-slammed cars. No accidents, somehow, but plenty of pissed off drivers. I left them behind and ran on to the towering double doors that served as the temple's entrance.

All worries of proper attire disappeared as soon as I opened the doors. Rodhi's entire family was there, all of them wearing variations of white. Some were in *saris*, others in Western garb, but none were in anything approaching black. I stopped at the entrance and forced myself to hitch for breath in silence, to be unobtrusive and mature and respectful.

I'd be lying if I said they didn't all have the same what-the-fuck-is-he-doing-here look on their faces, and not just because of the cheap makeup running down my face, the deep U on my shirt's front and beneath both arms. I was the only white person in the place. I caught my breath in silence, avoiding eye contact as best I could.

Maya approached, her eyes mournful but still not shedding tears. She said nothing, just stood there and smiled a sad smile. She waited until I took off my shoes and set them beside the rest, then led me toward the family. The effect on the rest of them was immediate—all judgment they might have held floated away on the wind, like smoke.

The temple's interior hit me all at once. There were pillars, ornate statuary, and a polished stone floor that shone brilliantly. Representations of gods and goddesses, steps leading up to...

The casket was simple. Seeing it there at first, I was almost ashamed that Rodhi should be placed in something like that. But I know he would've been fine with it. Was fine with it. He never asked for much, never needed much.

We went as a unit without speaking, our steps soundless. Incense wafted from every corner, a comforting smoke. Smoke I could understand. With each step toward that humble casket, I fought back tears that wanted only to be let out. But if Rodhi's family wouldn't cry, then I wouldn't either.

It looked like him, and that's all I needed. There was none of the artificial bloat of the beating, or else the effects of embalming. It was Rodhi lying there, maybe still Resting. Maybe still alive. A few of Rodhi's family members sat on a cloth on the ground, preparing offerings of *pindas* (balls of rice and flour), flower petals beside them. When they finished, these offerings were distributed, and the flower petals were scattered on top of Rodhi's body. Maya applied *chandan* (sandalwood paste) to Rodhi's forehead as the rest of the family recited hymns and mantras in *Malayalam*. I couldn't understand the words, but I understood the feeling. I did the best I could with what I had available:

"Peace I leave you, my peace I give you."

The rest of the family didn't question my words, didn't even look as I said them again and again. They let my words carry along with theirs. Our words, whatever they are, are the last things we have.

My feeble attempt is what did it, I guess. Maya's hands trembled as she applied the last of the fragrant paste, eyes downcast. She cried soundlessly. I put a tentative hand on her shoulder. She looked at me. Let it happen. Let me cry along with her. I wasn't as strong as her. Wasn't as soundless.

We stayed as long as we could, but eventually we had to go. And soon, very soon, Rodhi would be taken away on the wind.

Peace I leave you, my peace I give you.

PART II

44. Tasteful Representations

The rest of the day was windless and serene, not so much suggesting a storm was coming as recuperating after enduring one. I let the recursive architecture fall away and accepted Maya's offer of a ride back, her condition that I stop back at her and Rodhi's old apartment for some naan and aloo palak and lassi if she had some, which was like saying she'd give me water as long as she had it on tap.

The drive was quiet—nothing more than whooshes of wind and blurs of color.

Maya pulled into her Bay Colony parking spot and sat a while with noonlight pouring in and highlighting the flush that was spreading high on her cheekbones, her profile like a face you'd see on an obscure coin.

Tasteful representations of many in the Hindu pantheon adorned most of the apartment's walls, a night and day situation from the typical Catholic fare. I took my shoes off at the door, was led in and told to sit. And did I want something, maybe that lassi? And I'd just have whatever she was having. And I didn't want to cause any trouble—any more trouble. And I was assured that I was never any trouble—*could* never be any trouble, and that I'd have my lassi now.

I took baby sips of the sweet drink, a habit from when I'd share with Rodhi at lunchtime and inevitably need the lassi to cut against the heat of whatever I was sampling that day.

I couldn't quite look Maya in the face, even in profile, so I kept my eyes on the wall. Maya leaned in to point at one of the works, a haunting telling of Vishnu in oils. As she did, her breasts brushed lightly against my shoulder.

"This is by Suddho. My husband."

Her breath hitched on the last word, as faintly and lightly as her body had brushed against mine. I gulped down some lassi.

"Before he..."

Her eyes glistened in profile. She pointed to a figure in the painting, a young boy lying on grass beside a baby elephant doing the same, both of them beneath the shade of a tree. It looked playful, vivacious. A bit unlike the rest of the painting, but that wasn't necessarily a bad thing.

"Rodhi made this part."

Again our bodies made brief contact as she leaned over to point, her finger gesturing to the figures in the painting. We sat there, muted, our legs touching just barely on the couch, both of us looking at the painting.

Maya reached for my free hand, the one that wasn't holding the lassi. She took it in her own and held it gently, let her warmth flow into the bitter chill of my hand. I kept looking at the painting even as she adjusted her hand and brought her thumb gently to my palm, as she caressed my lines, movements subtle, graceful.

I glanced at her face in profile beside me. It was so close, impossibly close, light giving it a glow, almost haloed. She turned to face me, lips somehow inches from mine—full. Her eyes were lost in half-forgotten memories.

She leaned into me and pressed her lips against mine. She held herself, us, gentle, quiet, frozen and waiting. Weighing. Her lips broke for a moment, retreated. Swept in again. It felt like the world was coming in faster than I could process. My inexperienced lips mimed and tried, because I thought that's what she wanted. Her hand rested on my lap, beside the half-finished glass of lassi now trembling terribly in my other hand.

Again and again her lips found mine—persistent. They broke together, met again, parted together. Black. Reset.

Her hand at my buckle, unfastening. I didn't know what to do. Zipper down. Pants unhitched, hauled down as tongues touched. My penis poked at boxers' edge, was then pulled free of the waistband. The warmth of her hand as she searched and found. Kisses so deep they hurt. Kissing through me.

She made a sound halfway between sob and moan, stopped kissing. She got on her knees, between mine, hot breath against me before her lips and tongue made contact. Black. Reset.

That sob/moan muffled by the rhythmic motion. She wouldn't look me in the eyes. That sob/moan came from both of us, built, mingled in the air. I found myself in another place. And then she released me. She pulled away and let the come shoot lazily past, onto my pants and the couch.

The sobs/moans were gone, and ragged breath replaced them. Tired. Chests heaving. She looked at my penis, eyes clearing as come still seeped from it. She looked up and past it, into my eyes. The flush came back, high in her cheeks. She got to her feet, didn't say a word to me. Didn't look back. She ran to her room and closed the door behind her.

It was quiet outside. The cicadas droned from far off. Greenery teasingly peeked through the slits of patio blinds. The sky a deep blue, little cirrus whirls dancing on it. The sounds grew quiet, faded away. My penis softened, toppled over.

I got up without wiping myself off, hitched up my boxers and pants, and went to Maya's room. I knocked but didn't enter. Asked if she was all right. Knocked and asked. Asked and knocked.

"Maya? Maya? Maya?"

45. Black. Reset.

She never did answer me. Never did come to the door.

Outside, there were cirri etched into the piercing blue by some immeasurable cosmic hand, clouds pendulous but not threatening anything other than a bittersweet eye-ache.

I went out to the warzone that was Meadow Lane. That pellet gun shooter and his friend were a distant memory by then, their families packing up and leaving some years prior, creating a power vacuum that still hadn't been filled. I pried up that familiar old manhole cover and barely squeezed through an entrance I'd once been able to clear while wearing shoulder pads. There was no bug light to guide my path—the insect lamps were out and sprawled on their backs at the bottoms of dusty jars. Kids can be cruel.

The words came easily that day, that night. Hundreds of them, sprouting, populating pages in the weak light coming in through the gap I left between cover and hole. I closed one eye as the sun set and kept it closed for hours. Waited till all daylight died, nothing more than streetlights to illuminate, and opened the dead eye. I had nearly perfect night vision to last a couple hours till the other eye was shut long enough.

Nothing but scribble sounds and droplets plunking into distant, standing pools as one page filled after another. I wrote until my hands clawed and stiffened around the pen. Wrote until my back throbbed. Wrote until adductor muscles shut down and turned off all thumb activity for the night.

And there was Rodhi, dressed in his funeral white and standing at the far end of the labyrinthine concrete cavern. He materialized out of the dark and stayed a while.

He disappeared into the distant tunnel wall, plunks to mark his departure. Fickle moonlight came in through the gap between manhole and cover, bounced off of chicken-scratched paper.

Cloud cover swept in, so I set my notebook down and sprawled out on the cold concrete. I adjusted position, rolled and squirmed. I cried the shame I felt out softly, quietly, until sleep came. Black. Reset.

46. Advance in Retreat

I woke up stiff-necked in subterranean morning, the sound of birds chirping transmuted into something like an underwater struggle. Out there in the distance, where Rodhi disappeared the night before, the wall was slatted with a notch of light. Between that wall and where I stood were hundreds of notches of light, one for each portal into the Overworld.

I left my notebooks in my room, dead bugs to stand guard as I followed the notches of light stretching down the concrete hallway, head turning in Michael-Keaton-Batman fashion left and right thanks to the stiffness. My destination was Away, and I'd get there in record time by following Des Plaines' catacombs.

I heard cars rushing overhead, felt sprinkles of ancient dust fall into my hair whenever an unauthorized semi would pass by and threaten to buckle the roadway.

It occurred to me that if the universe was infinite, then there was an infinite array of stars, planets, and possibilities. There was in existence some place where a nearly identical Waldo explored nearly identical subterranean tunnels. Maybe that Waldo was descended from reptiles instead of apes and the tunnel he traversed was made of diamond or something, but the gist was the same. Another place where Waldo went through with the Confirmation and met up with a still-alive Rodhi afterward to joke and laugh, a couple of jesters.

A place where Maya was still Mrs. Boshi.

I walked for hours like that, the distant sound of passing cars punctuating adolescent philosophical jumble, sore feet marching through stagnant puddles, stomach complaining, brain buzzing and chest heaving and bat wounds still burning, almost as fresh as right after it happened.

I came to a stop at one of the light-notched holes above me. I took the rungs slowly and pushed the cover at the top. Nothing.

I went back into the endless concrete hallway, hundreds of notches spilling light as far as the eye could see, both forward and back. I chose forward then, but I'm not sure what I'd pick now.

I ran as if I was being dogged by Dumas, a suicide sprint underneath my crumbling town, looking for a splash of light that'd give away another manhole cover with bolts pre-pried. I couldn't look back as my feet beat an echoey track in the tunnel that went on and on.

It wasn't until all energy left me and I fell over and sprawled out on chilly concrete and breathed in gasps that I accepted there was no way out. That I wouldn't ever reach the end by running away. I'd have to go back to get out.

47. In Which Foot and Mouth Meet

It was after midnight, dead outside. I got in through the trusty old faulty patio door. The apartment was barren, scrubbed of sound. Reb was asleep in our room and so thankfully not able to alert M & D as I sat down at the kitchen table and looked at the moonlight spilling in, diffusing across oak that wasn't Messiah-shaped but maybe Messiah-carved, it was that old—one of the pieces of junk Roger hauled me into the car for during Picking sessions we'd have when I was younger, sessions where he'd covertly pour PBR into an old McDonald's cup and shush me conspiratorially, insist to a five- or six-year-old me that Daddy's drink was our little secret as we passed through Park Ridge and Morton Grove and Wilmette and went Picking. After his sixth or seventh McDonald's cup refill, the car would drift lazily toward the curb yet miraculously avoid cars as their horns blared and my tiny laughs would jolt up to meet his bigger ones, and he'd look at me and not the road and shush some more, and I'd yell for him to watch out, there's a car, Daddy, and then more laughter.

"The fuck you been?"

I smelled him before I saw him, beer stink wafting out of the darkness. Drew wobble-fell over the living room's coffee table, jolted back up again.

"Shut the fuck up."

"I didn't say anything."

"Yeah, but you were thinking it."

"Sorry, thought police."

"You are in deep beyond your *wildest* dreams when Mom wakes up."

"Maybe. Maybe not."

"What do you mean, 'maybe not'?"

"I mean maybe I won't be around to get in deep. Maybe I'll be gone before then."

Beer breath wafted past Drew's smile.

"Oh yeah, smartass? Where you headed?"

"I dunno. Got any ideas?"

"Plenty. Fort Benning for starters."

Quiet, then a hic-burp from Drew. An oops-did-I-say-that look.

"Just kidding. Shut the fuck up. Why'd you leave?"

"I had... there was something I had to do."

"Right that instant? Couldn't wait?"

"Oh shut up, it's not like you give a shit. You wanted it over with so you could come back here and drink some more anyway."

DEFCON level plummeted rapidly to 1. He opened his mouth. His eyes started to water. I couldn't tell if it was on account of the alcohol or something else.

"Okay, Wally. Okay."

And that was it. He turned and staggered off in the general direction of our bedroom, wobbly feet making him take a couple extra pit stops on the way over. He shut the door as quietly as possible so as not to narc me out. He even shushed Reb when he gave his excited puppy whine. Fucker had me good.

48. Footmouth, Take Two

"I want you out."

I opened my eyes, early morning sunlight cutting in. Mona sat at the head of the table, bottom lip invisible. There was drool at the corner of my mouth, which I wiped instinctively.

"Get the hell out of this house. Right now."

"What?"

"You heard me. I said get out."

My drowsiness was splashed away with a bucket of water.

"I'm fourteen, you can't kick me out. And this isn't even a house, anyway."

"If you're not out in five minutes, I'm calling the police."

"And they'll agree with me."

She slammed the table with her fist, nearly put a crack in it. It scared the shit out of me.

"I'm not fucking kidding, Waldo. I want you out. I've had enough of your shit."

"Really?"

"Yes, really."

"So you've had enough of me not going through with something I didn't want, but it's okay for Drew to get drunk and high whenever he wants? That's fine, right?"

A "what the fuck?" from our bedroom. Footsteps from same. Mona:

"Stay out of it, Drew."

Footsteps stopped.

"For your information, your brother is... going to be helping the family."

"Right, and he's too much of a little bitch to tell me himself. Everybody can know but Waldo, right?"

"You better shut your fucking mouth."

"Or what, Drew? You gonna guzzle a couple more beers and whine about how you've never met your daddy?"

The words burned my lips as they came out. My throat closed to pinhole size. I braced for the charge, for chairs to be splintered on walls and table to be smashed through.

It never came. The only thing that came was the silence, at first. The quiet cries, ones a civilian might mistake for labored breath after a workout if they didn't know Drew. But I knew Drew.

"You get the fuck out of this house right now."

"Mom, I'm sorry."

"Get out!"

"Mom, please."

"Fuck you. I hate you."

An image. Roger reels in a big splasher. Clubs it on the head once it gets to shore. His knife works past bones and internal organs, slices a clean line right down the middle. Neatly eviscerated.

...

I left.

49. Something Like Confession

Dawn light screamed in my eyes as I ran to the abandoned fisherman's lagoon to retrieve my bike I kept locked against the fence, through the jailbreak hole cut into same, late summer reeds on the inside wilting, their cigar heads dipping toward a barren lake they'd never reach. No marijuana smell yet—it was too early for that. Just goose shit and boggy moss wafting in.

I got to the spot at the fence's far side, to the lock neatly snipped and left on the grass. Abracadabra. My bike disappeared.

I punched the fence. More a test than a punch. Light. I punched again. Harder this time. Nearly disconnected it from the top post. Punched again. Blood at split knuckles.

"Fuck!"

I kicked it. Harder and harder, till the fence mesh groaned. I put all my strength into the last kick, and the fence gave way. It ripped clean of the top post and toppled forward. The force of the kick kept me following the fence's fall. I fell on top of the rusty thing and slid down the steep embankment leading to the muddy creek adjoining the woods. Reached the bottom and squelched through mud. The cicadas whipped up into a frenzy.

I got up.

Took a deep breath.

Squeegeed mud from my shirt, pants.

Checked my pocket for change, found a buck fifty.

Squished through the creek's mud and variegated overgrowth.

Left the Lost Woods and merged onto Potter, waited at the corner bus stop.

Acted like being covered in mud was absolutely normal when the bus got there.

My appearance didn't help my case when I got to Lutheran General, but the receptionist recognized me from my Rodhi days and reluctantly let me sign in.

The first thing that struck me was how *tired* he looked. He had dark eyebags, pendulous. His pale skin sagged and melted away at the jowls, threatened to do the same at the cheeks. His bushy white caterpillar eyebrows were bigger now, or at least they seemed that way at first glance. It was only after a double take that I realized PGN had lost some weight. His eyebrows weren't getting bigger—he was getting smaller. He had several pillows behind his back to prop him up enough to watch C-SPAN.

So how he looked was scary. But what he said first was even scarier:

"Hiya, Waldo. How are you?"

He tried to smile, but his body had other ideas. He settled for a pained grimace.

"I'm, uh, good."

"Glad to hear it."

C-SPAN drone for a painful while.

"Actually, no. That's not true. I'm not good at all."

The look on PGN's face: more amused than concerned.

"Mona's... I mean, my mom's not letting me back in the apartment."

"What'd you do?"

"What'd I... I don't know. I mean, I know, but I don't know if I want to tell you."

A tired smile. Eyes lighting on the window, then back at me.

"I appreciate your honesty. But the M1 Garand's at home, so now's your chance to tell."

More waiting. Stalling.

"Confession, huh?"

"Yeah. Something like that."

"Are you sure you want to hear it? 'Cause once I start, it might not stop."

PGN looked down at his frail self, back up at me.

"If you haven't noticed, I'm a fairly captive audience."

"Yeah. Okay. I guess I'll start with the worst one first. I didn't get confirmed."

"I know."

"You know?"

"Your mother nearly screamed my ear off over the telephone about it. Told me over the cellular right after it happened. I could still hear the organ playing in the background."

"And you're not..."

"Not what?"

"Not gonna like shoot me, or disown me, or something?"

"If I'd do that, then I should've stoned your mother for having Drew out of wedlock too."

"But aren't you mad?"

He studied the clouds for a while, the birds that dipped in and out of them.

"You know what I am, Waldo? I'm tired. I'm tired and blocked up 'cause I haven't taken a shit in over a week, and my pecker burns where they put the catheter in, and these blasted nurses won't leave me alone with their tests and their questions and their phony smiles. I'm too tired to be mad. So get on with your confession."

I told him everything. And I mean everything. There were more than a few awkward moments of silence, and by the end I was actually sweating from the anxiety of the whole thing, but I said it all: my beefs with LC, Rodhi's antyesti, Maya. Everything. His military stiffness kept through the whole telling, which didn't help my anxiety. His face was unreadable.

"Is that it?"

"Uh, yeah. That's it."

"Why'd you tell me all of that? You didn't have to tell *all* of it."

"I don't know. I'm sorry."

"Don't apologize for honesty. Never apologize for that."

"Sorr— uh, okay."

"Jesus, Waldo. What the hell am I gonna do with you?"

"I dunno."

"I know you don't know. And I don't either."

I stole glances at the big man made small, siphoned off possible tears through strategic blinking.

"Did I do it right?"

"Did you do what right?"

"Everything."

"Waldo, no one does everything right. Most of us are lucky if we do maybe ten percent of it right. That's what life is, kid. An accumulation of shit you've done wrong with a sprinkle of good choices on top. Best we can hope for is a familiar face at the end of it all. That and not being blocked up with shit and having a tube shoved up your pecker, so I guess I'm at strike two at the moment."

Big, hearty laughs that took the place of tears. By the end

of it, when the sun was past its zenith and I knew I had to leave soon, I considered holing up under Grandpa's bed or behind one of the machines they had hooked up to him. I suggested as much, but he waved me aside and asked for the phone. Sorry, the *tele*phone.

"You're not calling Mona, are you?"

A look.

"Sorry. My mom. You're not calling her, are you?"

A muffled ring. Muffled hello.

"Let the boy home."

Mona didn't have what you'd call a discreet telephone voice, let's just say that.

"I said let him home. You listen to your father, Mona."

A couple seconds more of her voice. Then a click.

"Get on home."

"Grandpa, can I come back—"

"Some other time. You should be home now."

I made a show of untying and retying my laces as I plucked up the courage for:

"Love you, Grandpa."

I said it after both shoes were tied, right before walking out the door. I hazarded a glance back. He looked at me again, amused.

"Yeah."

50. First Day

There were meals (frozen, fast food), there were quiet trips to the bathroom, there was guilty silence, there were sleepless nights on the living room couch. After a few days of that, there was a bus pass and some cash for lunch on the table, a note that said I was going to school.

All I could see as I put on the uncomfortable polo/khaki/belt combo was smeared makeup on stiff hand-me-downs, sweat running, the smell of incense and sandalwood. Maya's eyes fighting emotion. Her sitting next to me on the couch, our bodies lightly touching. How she wouldn't look at me as she did what she did to me.

We hadn't talked since then. Hadn't seen each other. Some desperate part of me wanted to buzz her door, tell her I wanted it back how it was before, that we could forget about what happened, just spend time together again. The other part wanted to take it further. Wanted to be taught and shown and led. Desperate thoughts fueled desperate searches on desperate nights alone with headphones in and mouse on the X button, but for a very different reason from the old fight and gore videos. There were endless queries with endless permutations, each more desperate than the last.

Countless variations on the same theme, penes and harsh closeups and exaggerated groans at videos' and acts' completion merging together into one moment, one more hit as the come dribbled weakly out of me and I went limp as soon as it ended, cleaned myself off, carefully erased the history, wanted to erase my head, closed out the browser until the cycle would repeat itself the next night.

It was only right that I missed my bus on the first day of school. And so I huffed and puffed, the sweat gathering under pits and neck, burning in my eyes. My only consolation was not having makeup to add to the burn.

I ran for a half hour, till the next bus's driver was considerate enough to pull up beside me. He picked me up no more than two blocks away from the school, but it was better than nothing.

I felt eyes on me, eyes that scanned my sweat-stained uniform, eyes that looked away before I could reciprocate. Scornful looks on faces. Eyes caught mid-roll. Obviously I was some snob from Park Ridge or Wilmette and was only taking the bus because of some pretentious parental lesson on "grit and responsibility" before being given my Beemer or Lexus as compensation for my public transit trauma.

Here I was catching my breath and wiping sweat from my face, and what the fuck did they all know about me, sitting there in their piss-stained seats, seeing only some white kid in prep clothes? Did they know my brother was about to go to war to pay for my school? Did they know that the little money my family did make was lost to bills and debt collectors? Did they know that I recently took the beating of my life and sat by my best friend's side as he slipped away? No, they didn't. So they could keep their stupid eyes off me and keep the judgments to themselves.

In front of the Pietà knockoff, there was a mass exodus of Bentley-, Mercedes-, and Jaguar-exiting freshies, all of them congregating in front of Jesus to loiter and adjust backpacks from one shoulder to the other, because only losers use both backpack straps as a general rule in American schools. I still had time before school would start, so I gathered with the other freshies. There was chatter about football camp, about leaving St. Mary's or St. Margaret's or St. Francis'. Talk of girls and stealthy inebriation, talk of weed and coke and creatine. I'd become an outsider before school had even started. I sort of stood off to one side by myself, acting like I found nothing more interesting than a representation of a mutilated dead man being cradled in the arms of his mother.

*

First period. Ethics and Morality. Our teacher looked barely older than the students, and his duckbill hairdo didn't help much in that department. Next to me, an artist drew a certain part of the male anatomy on the chair in front of him. It seemed to be a running theme. Chatter stopped by that teacher thing where the teacher stands perfectly silent until everyone shuts up. He let the silence carry a little long, though. Uncomfortably long.

"In the name of the father, and of the son, and of the holy spirit."

Signs of the cross all around. Clasped hands. Closed eyes. Inevitable peeking.

"Lord, bless this exciting new beginning as we welcome in a fresh class of young men to learn your way. Please open up the hearts and minds of these young men. In Jesus' name we pray this. Amen."

Everybody:

"Amen."

The teacher seemed on the verge of starting the first

lesson but then led us again into prayer:

"Our father who art in heaven, hallowed be thy name. Thy kingdom come, thy will be done, on earth as it is in heaven. Give us this day our daily bread, and forgive us our trespasses as we forgive those who trespass against us, and lead us not into temptation, but deliver us from evil. Amen."

It's amazing how reflexive that was to type, even all these years later.

"Lead us not into temptation."

He paused for effect. Wrote his name on the board: Mr. Felter. Turned back to the class.

"Lead us not... into temptation. What does that mean to all of you?"

...

"Now, as young men in our society there will be certain... *pressures*, certain urges and feelings that you'll deal with as you... develop."

Uncomfortable glances. Painful silence.

"People have been arguing for centuries about why these urges exist. Some will say they're natural, that humans as a species are a product of their urges. That these urges should even be... prioritized. Maybe people don't say that directly, but they imply it with the kind of... *content* you'll see on TV on a regular basis.

"These urges are not natural. They're an outdated part of our brain, just like wisdom teeth, tonsils, and the appendix are outdated parts of our body. Maybe at one point in time men had to kill their food, but we've become civilized. We've developed a better system. And just like how we have supermarkets with all the food we could ever want now, we need to develop a better system for our *other* urges too.

"But maybe 'develop' isn't the right word. That makes it seem like a better system doesn't already exist. But it does. That system's right here."

He picked up a KJV from his desk and held it up to the class.

"In the teachings of Christ. In prayer. In the act of confession."

Silence. Felter's eyes were on me.

"Yes. Mr...?"

"Collins." A croak. "Waldo Collins."

"Mr. Collins. Did you have something to add?"

Many more eyes on me.

"Uh, no. Why?"

"Well, you were trying to say something with nonverbal communication there, so I thought I'd give you a chance to tell the rest of the class what was on your mind."

"Nonverbal communication?"

"You rolled your eyes, Collins. Don't play dumb."

"But I didn't."

"You're sitting there telling me you didn't roll your eyes after I mentioned confession?"

"Yes. As far as I know."

"As far as you know?"

"I don't know, maybe I could've rolled them unintentionally."

"Do you often mock your own faith unintentionally?"

"I try not to do anything unintentionally."

"And now you're smarting off to a teacher. Not the best way to start your education here, Mr. Collins."

He went over to his desk. Made a show of opening one of the drawers. Pulled out a pink slip and a pen. Filled it out in silence.

"There won't be anything unintentional about JUG, Mr. Collins."

He walked over and handed the slip to me.

"You can spend the rest of class in the Dean's Office."

51. JUG

Justice Under God, before you ask. Yes, that's a real thing. Tried and true punishment of the Catholic educational establishment since the use of corporal punishment was outlawed and a whole generation of ruler-smacking nuns were rendered obsolete.

They didn't waste any time laying the disciplinary smackdown: My JUG was served immediately after last period. From the remainder of that first period to the last, there hung in the air an unspoken knowledge of my judgment. Other freshies fell into two camps re: how to acknowledge me—either not at all, or as one might look at a death row inmate.

There weren't many of us, and the ones who were there were all upperclassmen, all accustomed to the process, and commonly referred to (I'd find this out later) as the Juggernauts.

*

Dean Boyle stood on the immaculate lawn, arms folded behind his back, golf visor on to shield his eyes from the sun.

There were twenty-six acres to the grounds in all—

delicate shrubbery, planters, some very un-Illinois-like hills thrown into the mix. Boyle couldn't help but smile.

"Gentlemen."

He let his arm pass slowly over the grounds as if he was giving away a prize car on a game show.

"Weed."

And with that, we were off. The Juggernauts got to work pretty quickly while Boyle was watching, careful to save their un-gloved hands by grabbing at the root, stuffing the weeds in their pockets. I tried to keep up with their pace while Boyle's eyes were on us. We were rewarded for our efforts a few minutes later, when he finally left us to it and headed back inside.

As soon as he was out of view, the Juggernauts gathered in semicircle around one in their group. The Head Juggernaut, I guess. He reached in his pocket and retrieved a rolled up sandwich bag.

"Gentlemen."

He held up his arm, baggy in hand.

"Weed."

They all laughed. HJ pulled out a one-hitter and started packing it. One of the other Juggernauts lent him their lighter.

HJ lit up, inhaled deeply, didn't cough, passed it along. He turned to me.

"So what'd you do, freshie?"

I watched the one-hitter get passed around. I was fifth in line. Then fourth. I turned back to HJ, told my voice not to shake.

"Got in a fight."

"Really?"

"Yeah, really."

Third in line.

"They suspend you for that shit. I call BS."

"Maybe they would've suspended me if they saw me doing it. I hit the kid when the teacher wasn't looking. He just heard us yelling after."

"No shit?"

"For real."

Second in line.

"What'd he do?"

"He was trying to talk shit. Realized that was a bad idea."

Impressed nods. Expectant stares. I looked down. The one-hitter was placed in my hands. I appraised it like it was an heirloom on *Antiques Roadshow*. Watched the faint glow pulse and fade from early fall wind. Watched. Waited.

I raised it to my lips and took the Hit to End All Hits. Held it for a second, then inhaled. If I didn't know any better, I'd say the Juggernauts almost looked worried. I finally let the smoke flare out of my nostrils dragon-like and willed myself not to cough. I did anyway, though, at the end there. There was laughter, but it wasn't judgmental.

"Good shit, freshie. Good shit."

Good shit. Sure.

52. Good Shit

The Juggernauts weren't stingy. They let the one-hitter ring around the rosie more than a few times, and I smoked at least half of it. I smoked it the way I was eating in those days—too quickly for my body/consequences to catch up. The Juggernauts laughed as I coughed up a lung, and it was like that usual burning buzzing in my head had transmuted to something else. Something I couldn't understand. A few minutes passed. I raised my hand.

"Put your hand down."

"No, seriously, guys. Seriously."

"Kid's a lightweight. Look at him."

"Get off the grass. Boyle's gonna yell at us if he sees us on the grass."

"Kid, chill. Chill."

"I'm chill. I'm ice cold. I'm fucking frozen."

"Kid's at critical fucking mass. Get him a doctor."

"Guys. Guys. Guys. Guys. Guys."

"Holy fuck, kid's tripping."

"No I'm not I'm fine."

"You're not fine."

"Fuck off."

"Get up, you fucking moron. Stop laughing."

"I'm all alone go away. I'm all alone go away."

"Fuck's sake, pull your pants back up. Jesus."

"I can see Rodhi. Can you see him? I can see him. Ha."

"Who's Roadie?"

"He's behind you. Never mind. It'll be all right, right? It'll be all right."

"Breathe. Breathe."

"I'm breathing all the time, see? I... can... breathe... faster... than... you."

"Amazing."

"What kind of fucking poser am I, huh? Fucking poser."

"All right, shut up. Boyle's coming. Get the fuck up. Not kidding."

"You get the fuck up."

"If you don't get up in like two seconds, you're gonna be in shit like you've never seen."

"Fine, I'm up. Oh look, a weed. Get it? Start picking."

"Good point."

"Still hard at work I take it, gentlemen?"

"Very much so, sir. I hope you don't mind if I call you sir."

"Not at all, Mr. Collins."

"Good to hear, sir. Very hard at work, sir. Picking every last weed, sir."

"That's enough, Mr. Collins."

"Sir yes sir."

"What was that?"

"Nothing, sir. I was being silly, sir. Forgive me. Sir."

"All right, cut the sir business."

"Yes s—"

"Ixnay."

"What's going on here?"

"Just some good, wholesome weed grazing, sir. Picking. Weed picking. Ha."

"Shut it, fresh."

"Mr. Collins, care to explain your behavior?"

"Not particularly."

"Not particularly. That's rich. How would you like to come back tomorrow and try explaining then instead?"

"Whatever floats your vessel, Deanwise. I'm game."

"You might actually set a new record. I can't remember ever suspending someone on their first day before."

"Oh goodie. Do I get a prize?"

"I'm sure you'll find out when you get home. Come with me. We're going to make a call."

53. Wracked

Sunlight pooled in the melted blacktop—an oily rainbow sheen. If you slid back and forth, it was like looking at a holographic card. There were coins with faces of dead people in my pockets. Enough for the bus, but I was getting a ride.

An image. Dr. Seuss read on PGN's lap: *Hop on Pop*. A hand-me-down '90s shirt, sections split up by bombastic primary colors. Zigzag zebra pants. Shoes that light up when stomped. Lights in the shoes in need of batteries, I used them that much. Primary color lights to match the shirt. Face planted in the Neck Brace of Mystery. PGN giving an obligatory hug, and me requesting another volume, but it was time to go. Next time, kiddo.

I was woken from the reverie by Mona's death stare, car idling. I got in. Was driven off.

I was a fuck up. And Mona couldn't believe how stupid I was. Did I know how stupid I was? Oh yes, I could assure her I knew. I was going to get a slap across the face if I mouthed off some more. And what did I have to say for myself? But I wasn't too keen on earning that slap across the face. And shut up, smartass. Always think you're so smart. But when did I ever say that? And if I said one more word I'd be out on the street. And maybe that'd be preferable. But I didn't say that

161

part. Just thought it.

My spine was stuck to the seat as I watched sunspots come and go out the window, as THC sent tingles to areas of my body I didn't know could tingle. I scanned the skies for UFOs so I could tell Roger... or Dad... over a PBR for him and a coke for me. We'd catch a couple largemouth weeds and snap some disposables outside the bait shop, me with my bowl cut and eyes asquint against summer sun. Ha.

Apparently the "ha" was audible, because what the hell did I find so damn funny? A: A lot of things, I guess, Mom. A lot of things. But I didn't say that either. I could be such a little bitch sometimes. Drew would've loved that, right? Key word being "would've."

He was gone when I got home. No sign of him. Drawers cleaned out. Toiletries emptied from their resting spot in the bathroom. Even his sheets were stripped from the bottom bunk. He wouldn't need his sheets in the war, would he?

Tingles turned into shivers, elbows forced inward. Reb put his tail between his legs. I guess I would too. And Mona. The look on her face as she stood in my doorway:

"You did this."

She slammed the door. Another one added to the litany.

54. Nowhere to Go

I didn't move for days. I mean, my body ambulated. I ate meals, vacated waste. But some essential part of me was divorced (duh-*vorced*) from the rest.

The family battles still continued, just with one less combatant. I'd shush Reb and turn on the PlayStation 2, pump up the volume and put in *Katamari Damacy*. There was the King of all Cosmos, goading his puny son to roll up all he could see into a giant ball. Small things first. Pencils, cassette tapes, milk cartons. Then dogs. Trees. Small cars. Houses. Saki Kabata sang her bubbly sweetness in clipped lines about lonely rolling stars in the background, the synthpop barely letting on that something's up, that it's just you out here, rolling endlessly. That the whole world is yours to collect in a neat little ball, but then what? The King of all Cosmos will inevitably shoot you with his laser eyes, or at best scoff at your mediocre katamari rolling abilities.

It's funny the things you don't appreciate about someone till they're gone. For Drew, it was hygiene related: heaps of dirty boxers, pants, shirts as mountains, valleys of chip crumbs that Reb hadn't gotten to yet, broken AOL trial discs and Eminem/Dre/Snoop albums under that. Games if we were particularly unlucky.

The way Drew would talk in his sleep—an incoherent mumble. The overwhelming smell of cologne, Drew making up his own definition of "apply liberally" before clubbing. How I'd make a show of plugging my nose. The stale air when he went away.

I started digging through his things on the third day. Slid his rusty lockbox out from underneath his bottom bunk and played around with the three-digit combo. I had time.

After an hour or two of work, my efforts were rewarded with a cache of material: old receipts, movie tickets. Phone numbers hastily scrawled on scraps of paper with names' "i"s dotted with hearts. Old football collectibles. Sacagawea golden dollars.

Then condoms. I didn't know what they were, so I opened one up. I recoiled from the sliminess, set it aside on its wrapper without further unrolling. I kept digging. Found some dice. No pips, though—words and pictures. Lube. I kept digging. An old polaroid, frayed at the edges. An unnamed girl from Drew's class, posed topless, with the first two fingers of her right hand caught below the lacy fringe of her panties. Her eyes screamed seduction, hair wild and covering one of her eyes. Nipples forever hardened. Bottom lip stuck in mid-bite.

I grabbed the condom. Scanned the box's directions and worked my head around the logistics. I unzipped and tried it on. Wrong way. Wouldn't unroll. I flipped it around. Wet chill.

Stroke almost automatic. Almost unthinking. I kept digging. Another girl from another party, in bra and panties and on all fours on a bed, head turned back to face the camera. I kept digging through his trophies, and the pile only got bigger. One more, that was it. Just one more, then I'd be done. Okay, one more after that one.

Another polaroid, hidden deeper than the rest. Another

classmate.

This one male.

He was naked, flexing pectorals, one hand wrapped around himself. No. Stop. Not to that one. Not to that—

Too late.

I took a while to catch my breath, the last polaroid in my hand. I stuffed it back down in the lockbox. Returned the rest of the pile, too.

I sat there for a second, watching the window's light filter through the cloudy tip of the condom. I took in breath and let it out slow. My spermatozoa swam, collided, swam some more. Nowhere to go.

I snuck a coke can out of Drew's garbage and deposited the condom in it. Tossed it back in the trash.

I rooted around some more under the vacated bottom bunk, past old chip bags and what I hoped weren't more of what I'd just tossed out. I made contact with something different. Pulled it out. It was an old photo album.

First picture: tiny, oblivious Drew in corduroys and primary colors. Second picture: PGN giving a piggyback ride, neck brace as saddle. Third picture: Drew covertly snapped by the camera as he flicks through a View-Master. And on and on.

And there it was. The last picture. I looked and hoped it wouldn't be as big a surprise as the last "last" picture. But it isn't a surprise if you've seen it before. Because I'd seen this older man with his arm around Mona, with his assured smile and his Drew-given face. But there was something else there, too. He was all sharp lines and angles, like someone ordered him out of a catalog or something. But I couldn't see that. Wouldn't see that. So here's what I was going to do. I was going to shut the album and walk away like I saw nothing. I was going to go on keeping Joe as some amorphous paternal blob. I was going to scrub away the familiarity I thought stopped at Drew. Close it up. Put it away.

Quiet steps now, to the bathroom. I didn't want Mona to hear. I turned the door handle first to silence the hinge click. Ran the faucet and didn't look at myself in the mirror. Breathed quickly and watched the fluorescent bulb pulse and burn. Sterile, white, terrible. Fucking terrible. I lifted the seat. I wouldn't need it, but I turned the faucet on just in case. Ran a little water through my hands, hair, face. Breathed some more. Breathe. I wouldn't need it. Stop thinking. I knelt down in front of the porcelain, each grouted tile a vast plain for microscopic things. I let it go. Let it collect in little bile ripples, waves from the inside out. It lapped the curved shores of the bowl, fluorolight dipping in at odd angles and reflecting back into my eyes that were squeezing out of their sockets, stomach twisting like a shirt pulled prematurely from the dryer and hand-wrung, bullied for every last drop. It would flow over. I flushed it down for the next round. I kept my eyes on the tile and off the bowl. Just let what would happen happen. This was good. This was natural. I tried not to see the little chunks making laps around the porcelain, looking for a way out. Because there was no way out. There was nowhere to go.

Interlude:
Roger

55. Here Here Purpose, Bone Nooey

I laid low. Kept my polo tucked, belt secured, mouth shut. Took notes and moved silently from class to class. Scrounged up what remained of long ago birthday/Christmas money and made a habit of catching Saturday matinees at the theater in the Golf Mill Mall. Sat by myself in the back row, no illicit cans this time around. That was a Drew thing.

After about a month of this, I filled out an application. I hadn't been planning on it, and I definitely didn't have parental permission, but it felt like the right thing to do. A week later, they gave me a call. I mustered up some flimsy excuse for M & D of having to stay after for a school project.

The interview (group interview, as I immediately found out), was about as official as an interview at a movie theater could get. We were questioned in a meeting room that doubled as a location for birthday parties, balloons and streamers stuck in corners and taped to walls. Here's who the "we" was, according to the "HELLO my name is" nametags:

TOPHER—Maybe two years older than me. Short and a bit mousy, with oversized glasses to complete the picture.

169

WALLACE—Probably Topher's hypothetical age. Tall and lanky, with a mane that would make Jim Morrison proud.

TALLULAH—Also slightly older than me. Dirty blonde punctuated by green eyes that caused perspiration.

Our interviewer was Dave. Dave was thirsty, so he left us to mingle in his absence. Our dialogue:

WALLACE: All right, who's here for the free movies?

Two hands go up.

WALDO: Not a movie fan?

TALLULAH: They're fine. Mostly.

TOPHER: Mostly?

TALLULAH: Yeah, well. Maybe I'm just picky, but it seems like Hollywood's getting a bit lazy nowadays. Not taking enough risks on original ideas. I don't know.

WALLACE: I mean, I guess I could *kind* of see that, but—

WALDO: Yeah, that's true. What you said. Tallulah.

Awkward silence.

Dave comes in with slushie-filled courtesy cups for everyone. Scene.

And there were packets, training manuals, interview questions that Dave was putting check marks next to as we slurped quietly. Finally:

"So it's often said that the customer is always right. How would you, in five words or less, describe— No, wait. That's the next question. Here. Well."

Awkward shuffling of pages. More slurping. Dave put the pages down and looked us over.

"You know what? Screw it. You guys know how to operate a broom and dustpan?"

Nods all around.

"Know enough basic math to give change?"

More nods.

"Think you can deal with the occasional... No, let's be honest here. The *frequently* annoying customer?"

Slightly more tentative nods, but still nods.

"Works for me. Come back at 5:30 on Friday. You'll all train together."

Topher and Wallace went off to the Replay arcade together. Apparently, they wanted to see if Big Bertha (the large cloth woman-game you were supposed to throw plastic balls into the mouth of) was still in service, and to possibly shark some noobs at *Time Crisis*. Tallulah stood on the line where the theater met the rest of the mall and took a field sobriety test, her red-laced black Converse touching heel to toe, heel to toe. I asked her what she was doing and choked on my spit in the process. It came out as what are you do haw doing. She pretended not to notice but smiled anyway.

"Waiting for the parentals to pick me up."

"Cool."

"Yup."

...

"You?"

"Nothing, just... I don't know, hanging out."

"Why are you here?"

"Why am I here?"

"Yeah."

"Because I want a job?"

"No. *Here* here. What do you want, what's your purpose, what's your thing?"

"Here here? Purpose?"

"Oui. Here here purpose."

"I don't know. What's your here here purpose? What's anybody's?"

"Good eye, good eye."

"You're a strange bird."

"Strange bird like a fox."

"Or like a strange bird."

She kept her head down, in a trance as she walked the

line. Dirty blonde avalanche covered her eyes, but she'd push it back and take another two steps. When she got too close to me, she'd salute, about face, and repeat. I looked at her:

"So what's your thing?"

Left. Right. She cleared her face of hair. Left. Right.

"My thing?"

"Yeah. Your thing."

"I don't have a thing."

"BS. Everyone has a thing."

"Incorrect. You yourself claim to not possess a thing."

"No, I said I don't know what my thing is. Big difference."

"Touché."

"Right. So do you have a thing for French, or..."

"La femme mange une orange."

"Something about an orange?"

"Oui. Je suis un petit requin."

"I got the oui part."

"L'homme et le garçon sont d'accord avec l'éléphant et l'œuf."

"A home and a waiter's accordion elephant love."

Her laughter: a you-caught-me-off-guard thing. She paused mid-sobriety test and looked in my eyes. Dimples showed up, but then got scared, ran away.

A honk from outside the theater's doors. This was before cell phone proliferation, so a car's horn did the job just fine. She pushed her hair behind her ear. Lifted her eyes toward me.

"Bonne nuit, Waldo."

"Bone nooey, Tallulah."

56. Released

Golf Mill has a neighboring park where the dealers assemble after dark. Before dark it's all right, as long as you don't mind the possibility of rusty-chained swings collapsing under you, of every surface you touch having been peed on many times before, sometimes by animals but more often by humans. It's a woodchip park, but I took my shoes off anyway and set them on the ground. Socks, too—I stuffed them into my shoes' toes. The smell of late-season barbecue drifted in from farther down Milwaukee Ave; it looked like rain. The cicadas couldn't decide if they should go or stay, so half of them called out while the others hunkered down for the night. An unmarked cop car glided past, slowed, kept going, and disappeared. It'd be back come sundown, no doubt.

I told Mona I'd be back by now. Told her I wouldn't be late, that I was just working on a project. She'd lock me out if I was late. She had before, and she would again. I checked the clouds. Might hold till morning. Trying to predict the weather in Chicago is an effort in futility.

So. My thing. My here here purpose. I looked out at the setting sun and wondered if Drew was seeing it too, maybe giving me the go ahead with the whole Tallulah thing and insisting I not botch it.

173

When I was a kid, I used to walk to this park. I'd jump and slap at willow fronds that lined the street on the way over, take running starts to dip into ditches and have enough momentum to get to the other side, try not to splash hand-me-down sneakers in the questionable water along the way. Before that, it was Mona pushing me along in the stroller, guiding us both to those micro speed bumps on the side of the road, the ones that are spaced out a ways and meant to warn drivers that they're veering off course, that they need to right their path. And we'd come to this very park, and I was much too tiny to know that there was anything other than that moment, any experience other than slapping willow fronds or going "ah" to let the microbumps make a beat with my vocal cords, too young to know that there was anything like frantic, anxious, can't-catch-my-breath love, that the universe could grab you by your lapels and shake you around a little and take you over to a person and say look at this, that there exists a system in place to guarantee certain permutations are actuated, that there can be an order to it all if you want there to be.

The sun was licking at the willows; there were worms in my head. It was getting dark. A couple figures were coming into view, not walking so much as sauntering, so I'd call it a night. I almost needed a bindle, but I'd just have to make do without. Early dusk's purple smoglight cut through the fronds, and the fronds made that chittering rustle I remembered from all those years back, like a thousand tiny maracas being shaken. Late season leaves came free and helicoptered to the ground around my feet, but I couldn't stand there. I ran on down the road, letting the fronds whip my hands as I went. Here were the microbumps, but I didn't have any wheels to get the full effect. Just a tiny, geometrical mountain range under my feet as I ran on and on and on.

I remember laughing till there were tears in my eyes, and

not knowing what to do with them. Lights streamed in. I kicked up grass blades on someone else's lawn, flew over sidewalk rubble and gathered speed, on to the Colony.

The pond was posing for a picture that'd never be taken, late night lamplight as flashbulbs for nonexistent cameras. Fog flirted with tree trunks, car bumpers, my kneecaps. My complex was the spookiest of all, but I couldn't tell you why.

The door was barred when I got there. Forget the faulty lock—Mona had *shoved* a two by four between door and frame just to make sure my ass wasn't getting in. Yanking didn't help—it only woke a sleeping Reb, whose barking I didn't think would exactly help the situation.

I hoofed it over to Bay Colony's park, this one also woodchip and not nearly as expansive as Golf Mill's, but far more secluded.

I spent hours swinging, attempting pull-ups on the monkey bars, getting stuck in the baby slides. I watched the moon climb and chase after the faint white blurs that were the stars in the pepto sky. Laid on the woodchips and felt my chest rise and fall. It was one of those nights. At least it was until Maya showed up.

Her headlights blinded me, put spots in my eyes that made it hard to make her out when they turned off, still in her uniform from a long night of cleaning other peoples' messes. I'd sat up by then, watched as she went to turn toward her complex, stopped, did a double take, and stared at me. She took a tentative step, stopped, went the rest of the way. She stopped a few feet in front of me, lamp- and moonlight behind her haloing the hairs that'd slipped free of her ponytail.

"Why are you not inside?"

"Got kicked out."

"Your parents did this to you?"

Nod.

"Do you have a place to go to?"

Head shake.

A sigh. She turned her head first to the left, then to the right. The coast was clear, apparently:

"Would you like to come inside?"

I finally noticed the insect chatter. A low-flying O'Hare departure screamed overhead and left a faint contrail in the sky, white on pink. Maya blinked.

"Yes. Yes, I'd like to."

Her door's lock refused to cooperate at first, but it gave after some jiggling. Her elbow brushed against me as she pulled the key back out. She set her purse down on a stack of final notices on the kitchen table and soundlessly slipped off her scuffed work shoes. I was let in and did the same with my sneakers. I closed the door behind me and met her eyes. Remembered to breathe.

No lassi this time around, no artistic small talk. I was pinned against the door with her mouth on mine. Our hands came together, fell apart. She kissed me till I couldn't breathe, forced my shirt over my head and blanketed the final notices with it. I reached for the buttons on her blouse. In another apartment, someone was fighting with their spouse, both voices muffled and underwater. A car honked distantly, a brief solo over the harmony of car-doppler down 294. Maya was leading me by my belt to her bedroom, and I was letting her.

I was told to remove my pants, bitten on the shoulder while I did so. I reached behind Maya's back and fumbled a while at her bra strap. She reached and unhooked it in the time it took our lips to detach. I watched the straps fall down her slender shoulders, cups loosen, breasts fall out, moonlight spilling in from the lightly curtained window. Her hand was in my hair, dexterous fingers swimming through it, gently pulling my head closer, closer. Her nipples were full, complete. A stifled sigh as I rolled my tongue over them. We let it happen for as long as it needed to. Our pants mingled on the linoleum floor, boxers then panties. She went on her back for me.

Her fingernails traced parallel lines down my back, lines that'd never intersect, never touch like we were touching. The ten parallel lines dwindled to five as she reached down and guided me into her. I had to look her in the eyes as she did it. Her toes let go of the bed sheets and legs wrapped around me, bedpost hit wall again and again. Her teeth were on my shoulder, then tongue to make up for the teeth. Rhythm stopped. Disconnected. Desperate squeezing to stop the flow. Too late, oozing onto sheets and dribbling down leg. Her eyes telling me it's okay, don't worry, it's your first time. And there was the other first time in my head again, on the couch. Return the favor.

Moans of surprise from her, hand over mouth to hide them from the fighting spouses. I peeked up to see her breasts, billowing hills on uncertain ground, one hand half covering the view, up and over to stifle sounds. A rising tide before her whole body went limp. Silence.

We lay in bed for who-knows-how-long after that, her eyes on mine, her fingernails back at work. Now it was my flank instead of my back, sine waves instead of parallel lines. I tried to talk one time, but she shut my mouth with hers, so I didn't say a word after that.

She clutched me close to her breast and I let her. Cooed things I couldn't understand and kept our skin in constant contact. If I tried to pull away to look at her face, she clutched me tighter and reproached me.

As her chest rose and fell beneath my cheek, I thought of the potential hells we'd be sent to for what we'd done. Mine built by Alighieri. Fire and brimstone. Gehenna: a mistranslation. And where would Maya go? Was there a

Hindu hell? I'd yet to take World Religions, so her possible fate was unknown to me. Maybe she was in the clear and only I'd have to suffer for our sins. Maybe that's how it all works.

Something changed on her face. Her lips fell into something like fear. Brows met. She looked at me as if I'd just teleported naked next to her in bed. Before I could ask what was wrong, she was on top of me, kissing it all away. Not letting our lips part for more than a second. She grabbed me again and put me back inside of her. Her thumbs touched, palms against my stomach. She wasn't looking at me so much as through me. Seeing something else on the other side. She made me release her, gathered rhythm and released again. She pulled away and lay on her belly. Released. On her side. Released. She made me stand up with her. Released. But I couldn't, not again. I don't know why. She tried to make me, but I told her it wouldn't work. I might as well have cursed her from the look she gave me when I said that. She pushed me back onto the bed and sat on me, forced me against the bedpost and tried some more. Used her hand. Her mouth. Nothing.

"It won't work, Maya. It's done. Over."

She slapped me across the face. Nothing in the room but our breath—heavy. Freight trains way out, whistling down the tracks. Fire in my ear as she slapped me again. She hauled back for a third time but stopped when she saw me flinch.

Her sobs were quiet at first, but they came in after a while. They got so loud I didn't think I could take it. She was crying from her gut. It was a cry that was beyond her and I. I couldn't comfort her, but I tried.

Once she gathered herself, she shut the light off and lay back in bed next to me. My night vision came slowly. She wasn't looking at the ceiling so much as keeping it from falling with her eyes. Breathing in real shallow, then deep, sometimes muttering quietly to herself but mostly listening to the sound of us. Our sound harmonized, merged with the post-industrial soundscape outside and collapsed in on itself in the dark. Hours must've passed in that bed with those sounds before I got to sleep.

*

I woke to the smell of *uttapam* wafting in from the kitchen, my plate prepared and plate preparer nowhere to be seen. She came in once I'd nearly finished, sat down across from me at the table and let her eyes play at the blinds, at the parched and yellowed "greenery" behind and outside of them. Our eyes met a few times, and I pulled away each time. Maya kept looking at me like she had no idea why I should be so uncomfortable. She passed me a napkin. I needed it.

I followed her out to her car without a word, and she drove me over to OLPHS in silence. I tried to turn on the radio one time, but she brushed my hand away before I could. So I put my hand on her lap instead. She didn't brush it away that time.

She parked far enough away from the front doors that no one could see us. Let the sound of us gather before she leaned over and kissed me. She leaned over farther and opened my door. I didn't look back the whole walk up to the main entrance, couldn't look Jesus or Mary in the face as I brushed past them either. I just walked right in.

Interlude:
Drew

I'm on fire watch. It's Fort Benning. Hot, humid, clouds of fly sex every five feet as you walk. The barracks are quiet, everyone asleep, and I'm thinking of what to say. Mom tells me PGN is sick. She doesn't want to say too much, but I can tell it's bad. They keep moving his room in the hospital. It's hard to get a hold of him.

I'm the only one on fire watch tonight. I've been waiting weeks for this, to be able to do what needs to be done. High fences box us in, open fields beyond them, no roads in sight. I remember staying long after Red Devil practice was over, still in my football pads, after everyone had left, and standing out in the middle of the field, surrounded by grass.

The phones aren't supposed to be operational after sundown, but there are ways around that. I've got our phone number memorized. Memories of me dialing with Waldo, turning it into a song to help him remember. He couldn't have been older than two. Two, and tiny, and the way I'd prop him up under the armpits for one of Mom's polaroids.

Who knows what my drill sergeant might say, or do, if he caught me doing what I'm about to do. He already put a guy's head through drywall for defying orders. Made the same guy clean up the mess after a recruit attempted suicide with an M16, his face and jaw fragments sticking to the ceiling, unsalvageable, and by the time they did surgery on the poor fucker he was barely recognizable.

I go outside, look over the barracks, take in the fact that this will be the last time I see them. And there's PGN at my age, in Korea, the details fuzzy now, him never quite wanting to relate them. The recruiter told me I'd be deployed to Korea's DMZ, that I'd never see combat. He lied. I'll be shipping off to Afghanistan.

I make my way over to the comms room and shut the door behind me. I dial our number. Take my time on the last digit. Eventually press it. Ringing. And ringing. And ringing. Someone picks up. Waits a while. Breathes. Doesn't say hello, but hell. Voice croaks on the last syllable. It's Waldo. Even hearing it, knowing it's him, it sounds like Roger, like a higher-pitched version of him. Maybe I don't answer the phone like Roger because he's not my dad. I wonder if I answer the phone like Joe, wherever he is, whoever he is. All I have to go on is an old polaroid, his arm around Mom like he owns her, a punchable smile, body all sharp lines and angles. I found his number once, snooping through Mom's room. Never called. Now I'd never get the chance to. I'll never be home again.

There's a bruise on my shoulder from where the butt of the drill sergeant's drilling rifle made contact, his idea of correcting the way I did jumping jacks. It's like that one time Roger cut Mom's eye open and we hurried to put ice on it, blood still flowing, speckling the bottom of the bathroom sink. Roger, drunk, punching himself in his own eye, asking if that was enough. Did he need to keep fucking going, or was that enough? His eye already blackening, blood trickling down the corner of it, like a statue of the Virgin Mary weeping blood. We didn't bother with Roger, just tried to get Mom's bleeding under control. And when we couldn't, me punching Roger out so he couldn't take the keys, us piling into the car. Waiting outside the hospital as they looked at Mom, Waldo and I jousting with tree branches and wheelchairs, bruises on shoulders no different than mine now.

Waldo doesn't say anything else. What can he say? What can I say? I can see him now, sitting alone, Mom and Roger asleep. Maybe writing another one of those stupid stories. I don't know. What I do know is that I can't keep going. What I do know is that I need to hang up. So I do.

When I'm ready, I enter the arms room. I grab an M16 and take a seat. A seat, like strapping into a ride at Six Flags with Waldo, the kid nearly pissing himself on the Batman ride, Seal's "Kiss from a Rose" playing in the background, the sealed-off floppy rubber Batsuit melting in the summer heat when we get back. Running back to the front of the line, waiting in nacho-stink till the front car opens back up. Here I am now, sitting with the M16 in my lap, reclining. Like all those days with Roger reclining in his chair, waiting till I'd get home to start his shit. Mom disappearing to the bathroom, running the faucet, probably trying not to let us hear her cry, eyes like black holes when she'd come back out. But more than all of that, it's spinning Waldo by the arms in an empty field in Dee Park, and when I put him back down, him telling me the sky looks like Pepto-Bismol, and me saying he should use that in one of his stories. That it was pretty good, kid. Pretty good.

I put the M16 under my chin, barrel touching my neck. I don't want to fuck this up. My finger touches the trigger. Nearly squeezes it. And there's Waldo and Mom and Roger and PGN. Their faces at my funeral.

I put the M16 down. I close my eyes. I breathe.

57. Unspooling

Keeping my head down at school got a little easier once I had the theater. It wasn't a cakewalk, let's be honest, but it was easier. Times I'd usually spend in my fortress of solitude, looking forward to masturbating before bed, testing out ninja skills around the house to avoid being called a fat fuck, were now spent at the local movie theater, where the worst I had to deal with was exploded corn debris and annoying customers. Topher, Tallulah, and Wallace worked the same shift I did—always weekends, always late nights bleeding into early mornings. Ours was one of those rare immediate connections, made night after night as we'd open up theaters as end credits played and people filed out to go back home. Hanging out with them at that theater was the closest I ever felt to being at home somewhere.

Topher, Tallulah, and Wallace all went to the same school (Central South High School). T, T, and W were all sophomores. T, T, and W, as it turned out, were also creatives. Tallulah loved to paint and draw, although good luck getting her to show you any of it. Topher inked and wrote comics religiously, occasionally played the odd adolescent hitman/zombie slayer in one of Wallace's short films.

183

It got very quiet the first time we talked about our work, our roundtable not a table at all but a series of theater seats. Topher sat next to me, broom and dustpan spread out on the seats beside him as if to reserve them. Wallace and Tallulah were in the row in front of us, Wallace standing in front of his seat while Tallulah folded her legs under and kneeled seiza on her seat, the seatback obscuring all but her face peeking up from the top. Her messy hair fought against the black derby we'd all been forced to wear. They passed their art-related stories in semi-circle at first, semi because I wasn't participating. And then there was silence, and Wallace cutting in with:

"So what do you do, dude?"

"What do I do?"

"Yeah."

"How do you know I do anything?"

Wallace gave me a look. I glanced at Topher and Tallulah. Matching looks. The accusation made me smile.

"I write stories sometimes, I guess."

Tallulah:

"You guess?"

"I guess not. I guess I just write them."

Topher:

"What kind of stories do you gravitate toward?"

"Well... I tend to like..." Molemen. Aliens. Doomsday scenarios. "I guess I go for more intellectual things, you know? Literary. Stuff with characters who feel real. That sort of thing."

Topher: Skeptical.

Wallace: Eyes glazed.

Tallulah: Mildly impressed.

Only the last reaction mattered in my eyes. She must've known I was thinking about her, because:

"Why don't you bring in some of your stories next

184

weekend?"

"Yeah, duder. Maybe we can shoot one of 'em, too."

"It could be... interesting."

And so the other members of the roundtable had given me their counsel. All eyes were on me. After an unbearable couple of seconds:

"Totally. Sounds like a plan."

*

I didn't even get my uniform off before the writing marathon began. Clip on bowtie still securely fastened, dress shirt half-untucked, only the derby off. I put it on Reb's head, and he gave a dog smile for a while before knocking it to the ground and sniffing it out. It was Sunday night. I had plenty of homework that'd slipped through the cracks over the weekend, but it could wait. The theater peeps wanted stories. And not just that—they wanted that fancy *literary* shit. I pulled out my notebook and pen and got to work. I caught myself writing about a mutagenic outbreak in an all-boys Catholic school. Crumple; toss. Zombie infestation in same. Crumple; toss. Okay, zombie outbreak again, but this time it's like the zombies don't even *matter*, man. It's all about the *people*. Crumple; toss.

It went on like that for hours. I started playing crumpled-paper-ball catch with Reb. Started singing old cartoon theme songs from childhood. Started translating old cartoon theme songs from childhood into French (I'd picked up a few library books on the subject after meeting Tallulah). I made my main character a lone wanderer, then a rugged explorer, then a fish. Shifted from one character's POV to another and then back again in the same paragraph. In the same sentence. I had a story about a character in a story coming to life, then one about a writer scrapping a character he made in a story that'd come to life. I wrote in the past tense, then present tense, then future. Wrote a story with sentences that all began "Waldo Collins says..." and another whose sentences all ended in question marks whether they were questions or not. I asked Reb if I was doing an okay job and he got up, went in a circle and pawed at grass blades that weren't there, laid back down again.

I got so desperate I actually un-crumpled a couple of the paper balls, smoothed them out, and tried to come up with excuses I'd offer for their frumpy appearance when asked.

After a while, I put down the pen, set the paper on Drew's old bunk, and sprawled out on the floor next to Reb. I shooed him away the first couple times he tried to lick my face, then he got the picture. Left me to it. I put my hands palm-down on the floor and felt the air in my chest move my body closer and farther, closer and farther. I felt an itch on my thigh, ignored it. Soreness in my back, but I didn't budge an inch. I just lay there. Just breathed and listened.

Maybe an hour passed, two, I don't know. What I do know is I sat up, gathered my supplies, and started on a fresh sheet. I didn't let the pen rest for longer than a second. Didn't know what it was going to be going into it. Had no idea. When characters appeared, I let them. I went on while Mona and Roger started up another of their fights. Conjured a character whose brother was off at war, whose mother hated him, whose best friend had died. I wrote about how his chest felt like it would burst from all that Hurt, the pain brushed in sepia tones, turning everything to shit. Standing outside his mother's door, calling her name, waiting for a response that'd never come. Saying it, singing it, screaming it. Pretending to have a broken arm, paralyzed legs, a fractured spine. Sitting on the floor where the dust eddies would blow in because of the apartment's funky central air, swirling a few around his fingers and writing messages in the dust.

Watching them blow away, still calling her name. Heading to the park to climb jungle gyms that haven't had a fresh coat of paint since the '90s. Peeling off flaking chips and letting them fall at his feet in neat piles. Letting the loneliness collect in sine waves, each oscillation a mountain. Playing woodchips with himself and speaking aloud to his brother and friend, letting them in on What was Going Down. Taking his rusty bike off the fence it'd been chained to and riding nowhere in particular, doing all the tricks he'd learned as a kid: Look ma, ho hands. I believe I can fly. Tea party. Butt steering. The works.

I wrote till I believed, because I wrote even when I didn't. I wanted to turn the thing into confetti more than a few times. I cursed my name, my age, my race, my gender, cursed my parents and all the other faraway ancestors. Here's a kid moving through the frames of his life, twenty-four a second, as the projector clacks on. Hurtling forward, unspooling from the reel, twisting around my ankles and leaving sprocketed impressions from the heat on my skin. Soothing balm nowhere in sight. Just picking up the film in great heaps, piles that were bigger than me. Taking on more than I could handle and the reel still spinning. PGN's voice booming from somewhere, the point upon which the rest of the universe pivoted and turned. Mona and Roger down there in the auditorium, not seeing or hearing my difficulties up in the projection booth, sitting on opposite sides of the theater though they were the only two people in there. Duh-*vorce* tchick-*tchicking.*

All beautiful, holy-shit, knock-you-on-your-ass creative expression comes from the deepest Hurt, the pit inside that you refuse to show to anybody else in the whole wide world. So I had to show mine.

58. The Birds, The Bees, and The Boys

So we're at the lunch table. We is me and a couple other freshmen I haven't yet gotten the names of. They're big and stocky, and they're sitting with me because I'm big and stocky. Their minds fit their bodies, but my mind doesn't fit my body.

But we're at the lunch table. I'm picking pickles off my burger and setting them down neatly on a napkin. There's a conversation:

"Sarah Metzler totally jerbed me off. She had to use both hands."

"I doubt that."

"The jerb or the two hands?"

"Both."

"Then there's Chloe. Blowie Chloe. I heard she took it too deep and puked all over Schneider's dick."

"Fucking gross."

"Fucking right, fucking gross. Dumbass Schneider wanted her to finish, too. He got pissed when she didn't."

The lunchroom faced a glassed-in outdoor courtyard. Delicately cut shrubbery, carefully tended pond. Benches crafted to resemble pews. I looked out at it as my brain went to static, as they swapped their stories.

Outside, a mama bird hung from a sun-limned branch, looking first this way then that as her young complained for food, beaks little Vs crisscrossing in the afternoon light. She doled out the meal in equal parts as other birds and critters cawed and called for mates and food, mostly mates. One of the groundskeepers had left out a push mower. A family of chipmunks was just then gathering under its dormant blades. I put my food down. Started to get up.

"What about you, Collins?"

Big one on my left, shoving meat in his mouth, chewing loudly, open-mouthed. Dude next to him tipping his head up.

"Huh?"

"What about you? Any jerbs? Beejays? You get fucked?"

I looked at the chipmunk family starting to nestle in. The groundskeeper was nearby, clearing rocks and sticks from his mowing path.

"No."

"Never been fucked?"

My hands got cold. Face heated up to compensate.

"No."

"Never gotten a beej?"

The groundskeeper headed back to the push mower.

"No."

"Shit, dude. Not even a jerb?"

I walked away, opened the door to the courtyard. The groundskeeper stared me down as I displaced the push mower, but he didn't say anything. The family of chipmunks scurried off as mama bird watched nervously from her branch and the other animals went on and on about how much they wanted to get laid.

59. Adaptation

It's 2 a.m. on a Saturday night. I've got ringlet burns on my fingers from cleaning the popper. Tallulah's sweeping up the last of the exploded corn debris. Wallace is storyboarding in the break room, and Topher's ostensibly sitting in a 3D movie on glasses duty but is instead sneaking a cigarette in the men's upstairs, blowing into the vent but still stinking it up. I know these things because I use the bathroom after him and have to hold my breath during, then I get badgered by Wallace to stand in for a sketch as the lead role in his *Pulp Fiction*-esque gangster short in between changing out of dress shirt and bow tie.

No one's out here but us. Tallulah celebrates this by cartwheeling from one side of the theater to the other after clocking out. She insists I do a barrel roll when I tell her I can't do a cartwheel. Barrel roll is her term for somersault.

When she's tired, she sits on a bench and catches her breath, blows the hair away from her eyes. Someone's torn the hand from a promotional cardboard cutout, some celebrity giving the thumbs-up. I give it to Tallulah, and she says she'll treasure it forever.

Tallulah gathers the group into a circle. We sit cross-legged on the stained carpet, the idea being we don't get up until we've got an idea for what to do now that we're off work. Brainstorm time. We could hijack Dave's boombox and have a dance party. Claim the empty mall as our kingdom. Steal some shopping carts from the parking lot and joust with dustpans.

Eventually, there's a lull. Tallulah gets a look. Gives the look to me.

"Wait a second. Weren't you supposed to be doing something?"

Wallace nods.

"Yeah. There was totally something."

Me:

"Are you guys sure? I don't—"

Topher:

"They're right."

"Sorry guys, I can't think of—"

"Wait, shut up!"

Tallulah jumps up in excitement, remembers her own rule, sits back down.

"You were supposed to bring your stories for show and tell, mister."

I look at her. My face starts to heat up. All I can do is give a shaky:

"Oh?"

"Yeah, oh. You knew. Know."

"Did I? Do I?"

"Enough stalling. Cough 'em up."

The folded pages bulge from my back pocket. I retrieve them to exaggerated whoops and cheers, pass the stories out with shaky hands.

When you're letting someone in on your work for the first time, every eye twitch is a judgment. If brows even come *close* to furrowing, you've messed up completely and should give up because you're awful at what you do. When they're smiling or on the cusp of laughter, you're leaning in and laughing too loud along with them. When they're quiet and somber, you're checking which part they're at to see if that reaction was intended or not. They have you dangling over a pit of endless black by a thread that could give at any moment.

After about ten minutes of this, they finished, their copies resting neatly on their laps, all of them silent, still looking down at the pages. Basically, I felt like I was about to have a heart attack. Wallace broke the silence:

"That was really fucking good."

The other two just nodded. I didn't say anything. Tallulah:

"I didn't expect that."

"What does that mean?"

"No, it's a good thing. Well, I guess it was bad that I didn't expect much to begin with. But then it became a good thing. It was a metamorphosis."

"Thank you?"

"Yes, thank you. And you're welcome. It felt... real. Like you meant it."

Tallulah nodded at her own comment. Wallace stared off into nothing. I glanced at Topher out of the corner of my eye, then turned to look at him. The rest of the group did too. Bassy rumblings came from auditoriums to our right and our left. Popcorn stood out against carpet. That too-bright light that comes from any artificial light at night. A lone nacho chip with coagulated cheese in Topher's dustpan, staring at me as I stared at him. Then:

"You made some... interesting choices."

Topher scratched at stubble, looking at nothing in particular. We all just nodded. I think I muttered thanks. Wallace:

"Dude, let's film it."

Tallulah tried to hide a grin but didn't do that good a job:

"Right now?"

"Hell yeah. I'm dead fucking serious. We can take the bus down to Park Ridge. It's totally abandoned outside now anyway. Shit, dude, this could win an Oscar. Wow."

"Nearly all of the scenes he wrote took place indoors, Wallace."

"Well then we *interpret* them, Toph. Take, like, creative *liberties* and shit."

Tallulah turned to me:

"Well? Shall we?"

Tallulah watched me. I tried to act like I wasn't admiring the way her eyes look when she's waiting for an answer. Finally:

"Yeah, that'd be awesome. Or whatever."

*

Wallace was out with his battered old JVC camera, the one he always brought to work even though the break room's lockers didn't lock. Topher was smoking one cig after another. Tallulah was pinching the full moon between her fingers, then my head, keeping one eye closed to enhance the perspective effect as I played someone who'd just been decapitated. Wallace had a red pen that was nearly out of ink, and he was using it to quickly transcribe my prose into screenplay format on the backs of my pages. He gave me the pen to take over so he could start setting up shots.

I scanned the format for clues. Third person narrator. Present tense. "Prose" made up of three elements: the scene's location, description, and dialogue. Nothing that can't be seen or heard. No paragraphs longer than five lines. Plenty of white space. Tallulah stood next to me in the waxing moonlight, muttering suggestions past hair that wouldn't cooperate. I watched the way the streetlamps haloed her as she took my pen and crossed out extraneous dialogue here, unnecessary exposition there.

Wallace and I traded off on director of photography duties, Wallace giving me a crash course on what a DP does, which is setting up lighting as well as the shots themselves. Wallace pulled out an old light meter he kept in his back pocket and held it in front of Tallulah's face so we could adjust the ISO. Next came Topher, the male lead.

The story we filmed resembled the story I wrote as much as a chimpanzee resembles a human. But this chimp was sweet, and it meant well, so it wasn't as bad as you'd think.

Wallace had to step in and stop me mid-take when I'd film Tallulah. I'd pull in too tight, he said. Topher was lost in the background. The mise en scène was jacked, whatever that meant. Tallulah would smile in that mysterious way I hadn't quite decoded yet. So I pulled out. Gave Topher some shots. Took long breaths when he took her hand as the script required.

We made our way to the train station to film our denouement—the love that got away. We spent a half hour discussing how we'd film the departure of our female lead, what clever angles we'd use to make it look like she'd climbed aboard the train to leave her love behind forever. Halfway through discussing this, the bells clanged and railroad crossing sticks descended. Wallace was on DP duty. He ran over beside the tracks and pulled a wide shot, impromptu steadicam as the train clanged and rolled into the station. Topher and Tallulah instinctively bolted into the shot, assumed character, and said their goodbyes. Then the kiss. The incoming train became very interesting to me during the kiss. And it arrived, and they detached, and the doors opened. The film gods were smiling on us that night—there weren't any gawkers, and the conductor didn't notice Wallace in the dark. Tallulah got on the train. Looked back at her love for the last time. Really showed the loss in her eyes. Wallace got the shot and called cut just before the door shut on her.

"All right, Lula, we got it."

A smile. That smile. And something else with it: a wave. The doors shut, and she watched us, laughing, as we sprinted down the platform after her, the train gathering speed and leaving us behind in its noisy, windy wake.

60. Our Night

We snagged the only two unlocked bikes in the station. Lucky for us, one of them had a peg on the rear tire. A peg, mind you, not two. So Wallace grabbed one bike, and I grabbed the other, pegged one. Topher hopped on and balanced on the lone peg, an unspoken agreement between us that he be the one to do it for two reasons:

1. He was the lightest and smallest of us.
2. Fucker got to kiss Tallulah.

He tried to put one foot on top of the other, but that didn't work, and soon enough he was falling off. So he ended up standing on his right and holding his left in the air, fingers digging into the muscles of my shoulders, hands shaking, sweating through my shirt.

Here's Wallace, camera out, pulling B roll, laughing his ass off, swerving to avoid tire-sized potholes. Here he is turning around while riding at the speed of the cars on busy River Road next to us so he can get some footage of us and our peg setup. He's almost falling off his bike laughing, tire wobbling, pitching toward the road a few times but righting itself each time. Topher's left leg out like he's standing on an invisible peg. Wallace:

"He's lighter than air, ladies and gentlemen! A fucking

magician!"

"That isn't very helpful!"

"Fuck's sake, Toph, lighten up. Topher Copperfield, ladies and gentlemen, the great Toph—"

Light pole.

Camera skidding alongside bike and body, my brakes squealing and Topher leaning toward his invisible peg, then standing on it, then hitting ground. My own bike wobbling in balance compensation, handlebars twisting arms. Heading toward the break wall that separates River Road from Des Plaines River. Swerving, running over battered JVC instead of Wallace's forearm. Smacking loudly into break wall and jumping off the bike. A barrel roll on gravelly sidewalk but otherwise unscathed as Wallace and Topher get back up and collect JVC and pack of cigs respectively. Wallace nearly pissing himself laughing as he points at my bike and howls like a banshee.

"Look at it go!"

The bike ghost riding itself down the sloped sidewalk of River Road, miraculously avoiding light poles and break wall. Some cars watching, others honking because they don't know what else to do. Us three running after the getaway bike, Tallulah's train just then pulling in. The bike rolling off the sidewalk and through several lanes of traffic, cars missed by inches, handlebars adjusting after a bump and angling to the left. The train laying on its horn as the getaway bike uses up the last of its potential energy, as it rolls onto the tracks and intersects the train's path, as the horn dopplers and wind nearly blows us over, as the bike becomes a collection of tiny, tiny parts glittering under moonlight, shredded tire rubber flapping like wings before landing on the train station's roof, the rest of the bike skittering out along and on the tracks, the train complaining as it lulls itself into the station.

It's clear fairly quickly that we won't have to wonder

which door is Tallulah's, the conductor chasing her out, burly guy stuck between responding to Lula's not paying, or the bike that just exploded, or the kids pointing and laughing at all of the above. Wallace has the JVC on, screen dangling by a couple wires but otherwise functional, the conductor's angry face zoomed in on and twirling as the screen does the same. Tallulah's leading us back, her work clothes in one hand, wearing her high tops and shorts and knee-high socks. Us over the bridge, still laughing as the train finally pulls away. The Des Plaines River beside and below us, glassy and still. A mirror into ourselves without a cloud reflected. Just pepto sky, stars like pixels in the distance and fading as the moon takes its place in the sky, monstrously huge, almost like the moon from *Majora's Mask* but not angry—a Majora moon that's at peace with itself.

We ran, and the night ran with us. Past Wallace's stolen bike, past a couple of the cars still stopped and onlooking. I could've sworn we passed a group of four on the way back, taking their time over the bridge. Walking as we ran. Faces identifiable but with some sort of uncanny valley going on— something not quite right. Their eyes scanning our exit, smiles visible. Our faces. Our smiles. Us from a time and place removed, walking together again. Everything changed but then nothing changed at all. I turn back, and they're gone. Just rolling pink sky and downtown Des Plaines.

We ran on for centuries, millennia, eons. Ran till Des Plaines relinquished its hold over the landscape and fell again to the plains it was named after, tufts of vegetation peeking through concrete before it cracked and fell away, rolled back into the ground. Till the light poles fell and break wall collapsed. Till the abandoned cars rusted from the inside out and window glass melted in translucent pools and rubber popped and disintegrated into reverse-motion flowering patterns. All was changing except for us. All was standing still except for us. And that was the night. That was our night.

61. Satan's Secretary

Felter gave us a research paper on the second Vatican council. It was originally going to be a two page paper, but then I wiped eraser dust off of my notebook and onto the floor, which obviously warranted an extra page being tacked on. You can imagine the reactions. I was Mr. Popular for sure.

So I'm down in the dining/computer room at midnight on a Tuesday, finishing up my bibliography, giving the thing a final read-through. Then a writing session, the urge striking a lot more often now that I had an audience. Next is internet porn—query after query, bleary eyes, and peeks over shoulder. There's a plastic crucifix above the doorway I expect intruders to come from. My eyes stop on Jesus' ragged plastic body. He's appalled at me, and I don't blame him. Next is masturbation in the bathroom, into tissue. The light taking on an intensity as it happens, that familiar wave of guilt coming in as I flush it all down. Then it's the phone ringing. The phone.

I'm standing there, waiting for the phone to do something other than ring. We can't afford a voicemail machine, you know the kind with mini tapes, so the phone's going to ring for as long as the person on the other line wants it to. I count twenty-five, twenty-six rings. Reb nudges the bedroom door open. He's by my side, tail wagging to the rhythm. There's a stirring from down the hall. From Mona and Roger's room. So I go over and I pick up the phone, breathe into it. The person on the other line doesn't breathe into it. I stand there, looking first at the innocent eyes of my dog, then at plastic Jesus, then at the moon through the window as it overtakes 294, sashed with clouds, partially obscured by fog. The person on the other end breathes once, then again. I try to say hello but choke on the second syllable, so it sounds like I'm either condemning the person or am Satan's secretary. I clear my throat, and the other person breathes some more. Before I can say something else, they've disconnected. I listen to the dial tone a while and scour for clues, but they don't come.

62. Our Parts

My nighttime walks home from the theater on the weekends took me past Lutheran General. There was a car dealership nearby, and its too-bright lights gave a brief interval of daylight before it'd all darken again in front of the hospital. Orderlies would congregate around the doors sometimes, cigs in hand. Sometimes it was an RN who needed a breather. One time, I saw a nurse napping in one of the wheelchairs meant for pregnant arrivals, the ones I used to wheel around in as a kid after particularly bad fights between M & D, when the bag of peas wasn't enough and the blood wouldn't stop. I'd wheel around with Drew and joust with branches he'd boost me up to from nearby trees. He'd make sure I had a good grip and then let go so my weight could snap it off. We'd have silver dollar bruises on our chests after. Whoever had the least won.

A couple of those nights, I walked to the automatic door and stepped on the mat that granted entry. I'd never get past feeling the AC drifting out of the main lobby, maybe a front desk person shooing me away. Then I'd head home. But this one night. This one night, I walked in. Bypassed the front desk. Went up to see him unannounced. I still reeked of butter and pop. Still with my bowtie on, crushed-up derby in hand. I spiraled up the concrete stairs in silence, the only sound the clack of my work shoes. I hid, peeked around each corner once I got to his floor. His room.

Here's PGN on *his* bed, sitting in *his* room, eyes drifting between *his* TV and *his* window. All of it *his*. *His* head not quite able to rise from *his* pillow and look at me as I walk in.

He's melting into the bed. There's no other way to say it. Arms hollow, brittle, like bird's wings. The skin once filled out with muscle now loose, slack, sliding away. Here's the face of a big man, sunken and withered. Cheeks concave and shadowed. Nose crooked because it's barely there, the cartilage being eaten away along with everything else. Cheekbones so prominent they might poke through the skin. Lips cracked and gray, endless black behind them. Hospital gown dipping into a valley at the chest, arms more like ornaments than real arms. Wrists no thicker than the branches Drew and I jousted with all those years ago. Hands giving way to knobby knuckles, knots on the branches maybe. Nothing like the big hands that used to carry me, hold me, pick me up from the dirt and send me on my way. Fingernails blue and translucent, glowing in the sliver of a moon, pointing towards me. Hands lifting up just enough to show there's life in there. And there are his eyes, those piercing blues that give off their own light, now graying. Giving up. The lips opening slowly, then coming together again. My own teeth chattering, then stopping. My mouth opens, sags, falls. I don't know what to do with it. Then a nice, steady tone, comforting, not at all a cause for alarm like in all the TV shows and movies. Carrying on in night's quiet. Those gray blues looking at me, maybe through me. I'm taking a step back, and another, and another, and the door's falling away. I'm in the hallway, feet moving fast. Down the staircase now, down the endless spiral, falling down, down, down. Just like that, and all I hear is the muffled tone of comfort from his room as the nurses go in and play their part. My part's over, and so is his.

63. Genuflect

What do you do with a human life? Do you collect it in a lockbox you've been hiding under your bed, with pictures and receipts and tickets to movies that no one remembers anymore, tickets that have lost their ink and are now blank? Do you write about it, cry about it, scream it into skies sliced open by 747s? Do you listen to the nighttime phone calls from your brother who never had any trouble speaking before, now his breath the only sign someone's there? Do you knock on your parents' door and tell them everything? Do you sit out in one of Dee Park's fields at night, when the sprinklers spurt, in a dead zone where no water will fall? Do you watch an orgy online and eat a whole fucking chocolate cake and jerk off till the skin where the head meets the shaft is peeling and bloody, so you need to keep your hand at the base and it all takes much longer? Do you take a breath, open a book, read a passage, flip a page, come back again? What do you do? What do you *do*?

So here's mine, I'll tell you. I'm sitting on a flea-ridden bed in a motel, in the town where I grew up and lost myself and maybe even found myself, waiting for the courage to go see her, see Mona, make that leap, waiting in rooms where kids point at aquariums and say Nemo, where the smell of needles and gauze sinks into your clothes, your hair, doesn't leave till you've washed up and even then it lingers.

The detritus of my adult life is gathering at my feet, waiting to be sorted into piles. Here go the dead ones, all of them. Here go the misplaced lovers, the bullies, the friends, the bullies who became friends. Here goes another year's me, each one a still in a time lapse shot that's over in a few seconds. Here go all the days spent in quiet contemplation when I'd been born and raised on banshee screams and bottles hurled at walls, when the brown stains would explode and coat the wheels of my old Fisher Price walker, make a line at the bottom to mark the height of the World's Tiniest Man. When Mona would tell a five-year-old me we're only kidding, that's all, smile all teeth and crinkled eyes. Here's a cookout at PGN's, plastic pool in the back gathering grass blades and shadows on the water's surface where I'd dip my face in and see how long I could hold my breath, Drew talking underwater, trying to fuck me up, then laughing. Hot dogs sizzling on the grill and PGN explaining refraction, turning those inexplicable wavy lines into something real, something smart and cool. Slamming my finger in the back door and crying as my nail turned purple and fell off, but it being my middle finger and so having an excuse to flick people off for a few weeks. PGN putting his arm on my shoulder as my finger swelled in the ice water, bringing me an ice cream to stop the tears, my favorite: strawberry shortcake.

Here's me dialing Lula, dialing Rodhi, dialing Toph and Wallace and even LC. Planting words between the rings, spots for me to say hello after all this time, to reach out from the past and grab onto a person who isn't there anymore. Looking back into that misty distance, risking salt pillar transformation but looking anyway, like when you were first told not to stare directly at the sun as a child and you did it just to spite all grownups, all authority everywhere. Now as then, there are spots in your eyes, cataracts burning from each person you've left behind or who left you behind, little floaters who might not impede your life but who will always be there, a silent reminder no matter where you go, what or who you see. Times like these you sprint down the sidewalk and through a sprinkler in all your clothes, let it soak you, let the stares come. You climb onto a bike that hasn't been ridden in years, perform tricks whose names didn't exist until you invented them. And they will feel our fluttering pain, our punctured happiness. They'll see it in our eyes when we're smiling, no matter the occasion. They'll hear it in the sigh after the laughter, the way we trail off at the ends of sentences. They'll feel it in hugs given halfheartedly even when we mean them with all our heart. You know the type just looking around you. In this room alone, I have access to 942 channels, free Wi-Fi, landline. If only they could get someone to answer.

When the pain hits, you can take shelter on Drew's bed with the dog on top of you, droopy ears hanging over your face, sobbing into the pillow to silence the cries but it's not helping, and your mother's coming in, and you can barely see her through your bulging eyes. And you can't talk, so you won't, and it's making Mona angry. Making your mother very angry, so you need to tell her. Need to see her collapse to the floor, on week-old clothes not yet picked up, arms spread out in prayer and fingers inches from the lockbox, nearly grazing it, with all the pictures your brother couldn't show to another soul, not even you. Especially not you.

You can almost see the person you've wanted to see all these years, the façade set down for just that blinding second. There's a TV show on in the other room, something with a laugh track, and they're losing it out there. Light's coming in from somewhere outside, somewhere far away, you'll never know where. The bathroom door is open. Mona's at it before you can get up, about to close the door, but you're there, stopping it with your foot, and her arm's up, and you're there beside her. Then the sting, bursting as the sound of the slap comes, a yell, a push, but you're still at the door. And her hand being swallowed, fingertips grazing uvula, gagging in front of you, other hand opening the toilet seat, fingertips jamming to force it out. And she's down in penitence, saying her prayers, genuflecting on tile, kneeling before her porcelain altar. It's all coming back up, and the sting still burns your face as you hold her hair back. Your father is at the door. Your father is watching. When it's over, he's in the living room and sitting on the couch, laughing along to the track. O'Hare's flight path is overhead and you notice it now, low-flying planes drowning out the track and the flushing, cars on 294 joining in. When it's over, you say nothing. When it's over, Mona says nothing. When it's over, Roger says nothing. You all go to your separate places and that's that.

64. As It Should Be

There are spaces only Drew can fill. He should be there at the funeral home in the early a.m. with extended family congregating around the coffee machine, little kids in store-bought black, trying to play, being gently admonished by their parents. Drew should be there with PGN's old pigskin from his leatherhead days, Mona allowing the tiny humans to play catch outside, go long and throw surprisingly straight spirals that eclipse early morning sun before colliding with arms, grass, the bumpers of hearses. Drew should be there at the altar of pictures, the ones that show PGN How He Was, How He Should Be Remembered, and not the wasted carcass in the casket with too much makeup on and a too-flashy suit. Drew should be here, but the Army says grandparents aren't close family, so he isn't.

Roger's wandering through the place, stopping here and there, drinking from a can he's gotten from who knows where, then another, then another. He is becoming a secret drunk. An alcoholic's drunk. He goes up to Mona, here, in the home, and tells her he didn't kill her father. His eyes wide and expressionless, telling her, almost pleading, assuring her that he couldn't have done it, it had to have been someone else, but not him. And she's crying to herself as he walks away to fetch another can, walks away and no one questions her tears because of the situation, so Roger gets away with it, leaves his empty on the windowsill behind heavy curtains, where there's a hidden pile.

So I'm up by the casket. I'm crying and becoming a vacuum of sound. I keep arms and legs inside the ride at all times. I do not chew gum. I do not wear loose articles. I do not have a heart condition, and I am not pregnant. The lap bar is locked securely, comfortably. When my time is up, I move down the track, approaching the end. This is a good ride, a fun one, just the right amount of loops on it, the anticipation milked till the last second before kinetic catharsis comes. When it's over, you can run back to the front of the line, wait in nacho-stink till the front car opens up and you can get on to do it all over again, stick your hands up this time, wear flip flops, expensive shades, scoff at your heart murmur, pray the faulty lap bar won't open on you, send you tipping head over heels in ragdoll fashion, seeing ground then sky then ground again, each moment you're airborne compressing itself into still longer moments, till a millisecond becomes a century and you're falling for all of time. All of these things are possible on this ride, this simulation where things contain other things which contain other things still. It's a good simulation. This is what we've been given. So you can either question it or you can sit in the front row at your grandpa's funeral and see him stagnant in that box, admire the way the clothing's black melds with the whites of walls. You can see snot bubbles in the noses of small children who are teething, smell the beer breath emanating from your father, watch your mother apply makeup for the third time beside you, her compact's reflection smudged with years of product, never cleaned, the same from your baseball days when you were told to choke up. And there's a versatile phrase, isn't it? You're doing it as you're thinking it. Isn't that fantastic? Here: You are okay. Really. You are fine and beautiful, and you will be okay. See how that felt? Wonderful. This is what you think. What you know. So see the moment and press record, let it happen how it will. Let your dad get drunk. Let your mom put on makeup. Let your grandpa be withered and dead, a shell of his former self. Let your brother stay right where he is. For this millisecond that's a century, this is all okay. This is as it should be.

65. Now I'm Something

Months melt away. Now I'm fifteen, sixteen. Now I'm something. The school year's over, and Felter's passed me. Drew's late night phone calls trail off after PGN's passing, the rings counting up to twenty, then ten, then not at all. Weekends at the theater include Friday, then Thursday, then Wednesday. My run-ins with Mona become a summoning of the Triple Fs—fuck-up, fatass, and failure. Magic words that make Waldo disappear: "I knew you'd be a fuck-up." Poof. Leaving for a bike ride. "No, go ahead and eat it. Not my problem you're a fatass." Presto. Time to shoot some hoops. "You want to become a failure like your father?" Abracadabra. Heading to the theater for a late shift.

If you can go back to your hometown, you will see yourself in the spaces you once inhabited, the phantoms of memory materializing like fog you'll see in empty fields at dawn, waiting for the bus that'll take you to kindergarten, then third grade, then public transit to high school. You'll hear voices you forgot existed and smile as the tears cloud your eyes. You'll go to the convenience store you stole shit from as a youth and gladly pay now. You'll try to dunk on that hoop you swear you were, like, five inches away from touching that one time, and without a patio chair to boost you.

At least this is my experience of that vast expanse of suburban decay and lower middle class desperation as I walk these streets, Reggaeton blasting out of beaters' windows—doom-dee-doom-DEE, doom-dee-doom-DEE, the drivers motionless, as if the beat isn't there at all and they're somewhere far from this place. The weather seesaws between Gobi hot and Siberia cold, often within the same week. I'm out on one of the few days of reason, temp steady, no threat of precipitation. I am twenty-four years old. I guess I should've told you that going in, but it wasn't important then. We're closer to the end now, so the present can slip in before it becomes more past, another shovelful to heap behind you, like dirt from a childhood tunnel to China that only got waist deep, drinking those Mondo drinks with the plastic spaceship tops instead of lemonade. I can show you the buildings scrubbed from Des Plaines' manuscript, the palimpsests in the form of fresh office buildings, fresh apartment buildings, fresh convenience stores. I can take you to Dee Park, where I choked up on the bat, where the Gujarati Thugs duked it out between games of cricket. I can show you the weeds that lay claim to the fields, even springing up in the basketball courts now, each rim chain- or net-less, just rusty hoops that no one would dunk on anymore, but where fights and deals still go down.

I'm walking these streets now, at twenty-four, the whole neighborhood changed and yet exactly the same. There's a funny thing about moving on. Like everything else, the destination seems so final. The happy ending. Roll credits. They all live happily ever after. That's bullshit. The end is that there is no end. Forgiveness is a garden that needs endless watering, pruning, and tilling. The work will never be over. The moment you think you've made it, you have to start all over again. Read these words. See these places. Exchange them for yours and fill in the blanks like ad lib games from childhood, but keep it appropriate this time. This isn't the story. The real story is yours, so tell it. And if you're going to bother telling it, make it burn through you. Let every person and place scorch you on the way back up like so much freshening up. Don't be afraid of the pain, the discomfort. Embrace it. Anything that's ever worth doing involves a degree of pain, discomfort, desperation. So own that.

Okay. There's a shovelful. Let's go back again.

*

The weekend. Saturday night. Wallace and Toph turned down extracurriculars after closing, offering vague excuses, looking at their feet. They hadn't been able to make it the night before either. I didn't push it. Just let it go. Lula had trekked home the night before, usually getting a ride from either Toph or Wallace after our hangout, whoever's turn it was to drive that time, and so not usually having to worry about a ride. She insisted she'd be fine walking back Friday. Like a dumbass, I said okay. See you tomorrow. But this time, Walgar—excuse me, Waldo—wouldn't make the same mistake. She insisted, and I made some lame joke about being a big, tough guy who could protect her. I got in a mess of explaining after she accused me of thinking she couldn't handle herself, which, let's be real—she could handle herself just fine. She took Taekwondo as a kid and augmented it with boxing as she got older. She'd match your play fighting with a hook at 60 percent that knocked the wind out of you. Tiny? Yes. Fierce? Also yes. After five minutes of self-deprecating jokes and getting her laughing again, she finally agreed, mostly so I'd stop bugging her.

Dave gave me the look on the way out. I rolled my eyes

and shook my head, but I could feel my pulse in my ears.

Outside, planes sliced orange creamsicle sky so high up you couldn't tell whether they were commercial or something else, my childhood brain jumping to UFOs, scanning for them like I would while fishing in the pond with my dad. We hadn't done that in years, hadn't talked in what seemed just as long. Even then, it was always something utilitarian: pass me a garbage bag; have you taken Reb out lately; did you track this in. Etc. With Mona, it wasn't even utilitarian anymore, just the Triple Fs. You'd think PGN passing would calm that shit down, but it only made it worse.

So here I am walking next to this girl I've known for nearly a year, this girl I've become close friends with, and I can't say a thing. I don't know what to do with my hands. Lula's hands are just fine, of course. Lula's hands are perfect. Fuck, I mean here's this girl who insists I call her Lula now, and I'm acting like we just met.

She drew first blood:

"What are you thinking about?"

"Me?"

"No, the guy next to you."

"I don't know. UFOs and fishing with my dad and weird stuff like that, I guess."

"You go fishing with your dad a lot?"

"No. Used to, though. When I was little."

A nod. Quiet, the occasional honk. Lula again:

"What's your dad like?"

"I don't know."

"You don't know your dad?"

"No, I know him. I mean, I know who he is, obviously, but—"

"But..."

"But, I don't know."

"No, you know. I've just hit one of your weak points,

that's all."

"Weak points?"

"Yeah. Like a boss in a game. King Hippo's belly in *Punch-Out*. Bowser's tail in *Super Mario 64*. Eyeballs in, like, every new Zelda game. Yours is your dad. Probably something else you're not telling, too. Nothing to be ashamed of."

Cars whooshing past.

"That simple, huh?"

"That simple. Everyone's got 'em."

"Really?"

"Mmhmm."

"And what would Lula's weak point be?"

"That I was adopted. That I've never met my bio parents. That I don't know if I want to, either."

Silence for a couple seconds. I broke it:

"It's so quiet out, huh? Kinda weird."

"You don't have to do that."

"Do what?"

"Change the subject 'cause you feel awkward, 'cause you think I'm uncomfortable. If I wasn't comfortable talking about it, I wouldn't talk about it."

"Oh."

"I don't know why people are like that. So afraid of awkwardness. Just talk about stuff that bothers you. Who gives a shit?"

"Some people might get offended."

"Yeah, well some people are giant babies."

His and hers matching laughter. Me:

"That was pretty good."

"I know. That's why I said it."

"You're a character."

"Why, because I say words out of my mouth hole?"

"I guess it's more about the kinds of words that come out of your mouth hole."

"I just say what's on my mind. It's not that crazy."

"I know, but a lot of people don't. A lot of people never deal with their shit. Giant fetuses and all that."

"Giant babies, but I like the sound of that too."

We crossed four lanes of traffic. Not at the light, of course. She just grabbed my hand and started running. We got to the other side, caught our breath, kept walking.

"So when'd you find out? That you were adopted."

"Third grade. Some douchey kids would say stuff at recess. I thought they were making it up, but I guess one of them overheard my mom talking to a teacher about it one time. I went home and asked my parents, and they froze up. Dad went back outside to fix the car. Scooted under with one of those rollie dealies. Mom turned on Pokémon and scooped me some mint chocolate chip. And that was that."

"So they never confirmed it?"

"Yeah. Well, yes and no. They didn't like verbally say, 'Yes, Tallulah, we're not your real parents. Sorry, kiddo.' But they didn't have to, I guess. Their reaction kind of said it for them, you know?"

"Yeah, I guess."

"You guess?"

"I don't know. I'd want to hear them say it. Hear it out loud."

"Yeah, no shit."

"You guys talk about it at all since then?"

"Negatory."

The convo trailed off a bit, but it wasn't uncomfortable. It seemed we could just be quiet with each other. We had to walk into the street a few times, the sidewalk closed for construction that never got finished. I tried to walk on the outside to shield Lula from traffic, but she insisted on taking it, would loop around me with a laugh whenever I tried. The cityscape gradually gave way to post-apocalyptia, the line separating unincorporated Des Plaines from the rest of the town marked by trash and potholes. I told Lula this was my hood. Like that, too, "hood," not "neighborhood." I shook my head at myself, but she smiled. And there was the defunct fisherman's lagoon flanking Bay Colony, the place I'd snuck into to smell the fumes of weed grazers before I'd done any grazing of my own. I told her as much.

"Well that's a fun coincidence."

"What is?"

Before I had my answer, she hopped the fence and ran off into the overgrowth. I gave pursuit as she wound her way through the trail so nimbly you knew she had to have come here before. We got to the clearing with two logs next to each other, one of them with "fuk" intaglioed into its wood grain. She lit her joint in the dark, cherry glowing burnt sienna.

That sickly sweet smell wafted off the joint's tip and hung in summer air a while. Spring's rains had collected into little pools by then, and Lula made a game of tossing pebbles into them as she took a deep drag and passed me the joint. I held the smoke in for way longer than I needed to and then let it out of both nostrils, dragon-style. Lula took a Lula-sized hit. When that joint was through, she had another ready, gave me the honor of lighting it up. She motioned for me to scoot closer to make passing easier, but I had high hopes that it was for other reasons. Lula would be an excellent poker player. We sat in the dark, headlights flickering through tree cover, looking like speeding lightning bugs in the distance.

She passed me the joint, and I inhaled deeply. It was at tweezer size. When she insisted I pass it back, I refused. I didn't want her fingers to get burned. She called me a "consummate gentleman" in a posh British accent. I thought the accent was sexy. I thought everything she did was sexy. She leaned forward, lips out to meet the tiny joint. Moonlight caressed her cheeks, chin, nose. She met the joint with her eyes closed. Her lips touched my thumb and forefinger as she dragged on it. She took another drag, lips grazing my fingers again. She took it in, held it, let it out, looked at me. Her smile said, "I know exactly what I'm doing, and I want you to know that I know."

When the joint burned out, I tossed it in the dirt. We sat there on our logs, looking at each other, waiting for the other to make a move, guns not at our hips but they might as well have been. My inner Walgar said, "fuck it," and I leaned in first, waited till the last second to close my eyes so I wouldn't end up kissing air. By some miracle of science, Lula was actually leaning in too. Her lips were soft. Warm. We kissed for seconds or centuries. When it ended, neither of us could contain our excited smiles, knowing what that feeling was, like the tingle you'd get from a Van de Graaff generator with your hair standing on end and tiny sparks dancing between surfaces and fingertips. When it ended, we pulled back and looked at each other. She reached out her hand. I took it, our fingers laced together, and we sat like that for a while. When it was time to go, we got up. I walked her the rest of the way home in happy silence. We kissed one more time under the false moon of her porch light, and she let herself in quietly. The last thing I saw was her face disappearing into the darkness of her home, still with that happy smile as she waved goodnight.

66. Like a Call

Everything else in my life that wasn't Tallulah Belyst became a hurdle, noticeable only in the interval that I'd either clear it or be taken down, even then scraping ground for a second before getting back up. My homework was fine. Felter was fine, and so was Boyle. Mona's insults were fine. Roger's silence and drunken stupors were fine. The hole that Drew left behind was fine. Reb shitting on the carpet when he was sad or lonely was fine. My grandpa being dead was fine, and so was Rodhi being dead. My porn addiction was fine. Jerking myself off to sleep was fine. Wishing my mom were dead and then hating myself for wishing that was fine as well. Not knowing who I was on a daily basis was fine. The mounting guilt of betraying Lula with what I did when she wasn't watching was fine. Not trusting Topher was fine. There were many things that were fine.

The one thing that wasn't so fine was seeing Lula at work the night after we kissed, me trying to look nonchalant as she walked in, bowtie in hand, red-laced black Converse on, allowed by Dave even though we were supposed to wear black dress shoes, going around the front desk to get to the clock-in computer, clearly seeing me as I made it look like I was sweeping the same stubborn spot of popcorn, clearly noticing me but refusing to even make eye contact. Then when she couldn't avoid it any longer, when she'd have to pass me on the way to the break room to put away her things, the platonic look she gave me, the smile hiding something, the too-formal "Hi, Waldo" before quickly brushing past, me letting out air like a punctured tire.

It was supposed to be Lula and I behind concession, Topher and Wallace ushing, but Lula inexplicably switched with Wallace, so I was behind the counter and doing my best not to lean (because if you've got time to do that, you certainly have time to do something else), trying not to make it obvious that I was watching when Lula and Topher would finish cleaning one of the theaters and head back to the main lobby, try to make it seem like I was just bending over to scoop up ice while I eavesdropped, decoded every laugh that Lula gave, every look shared between them. I watched how animated Topher was, his usual resting Topher state of cool apathy switched to something else around her. But maybe that was just Lula. It didn't matter who you were, she had a way of bringing out a side of people they didn't even know existed. So maybe it was that. Or maybe they'd kissed again, this time not in front of a JVC but in private. Maybe they'd done more. It was on these helpful topics that I was meditating when I realized my right pinky was grafted to the hot popper as I stood there preparing to scrub it out.

Luckily, there weren't any customers around to hear my booming F-bomb, lucky too that Dave was in the manager's office and out of earshot. But Lula heard it, and before my skin could blister, she was behind the counter, next to me, hands lightly holding the parts of my hand that hadn't made contact, leading me gently to the sink, turning on the cold water, bringing my hand under the water as I watched, as Topher and Wallace did the same. The water was excruciating, but the pain dulled when I realized that Lula's fingers were getting wet with mine.

It's safe to say I wasn't exactly expecting it when Lula reached in her pocket and pulled out the severed, thick leaf of an aloe vera plant, her tearing off the smallest of strips at the end so the cool fluid could flow out and onto my skin. I looked at her:

"Why do you have that?"

Lula with a blank stare.

"For times like these."

Obviously. With that, she tucked the leaf back into her pocket and headed out to the main lobby, grabbed her cleaning instruments and disappeared into a crowd that'd just let out of theater one.

*

We're out in the parking lot, buzz of the light poles as soundtrack, the occasional whoosh of a car speeding down Golf Road. Lula's shoes are off for comfort. Wallace's are off because he's trying to roof his shoe. We didn't have an exact measurement, but the theater must've been at least two hundred feet tall. Perched at the top, there'd be the inevitable pigeons, the occasional goose if you were lucky. Wallace decided it was his duty as an employee of this fine establishment to claim some of the birds' turf for his own. My shoes were still on, though Lula was goading me into taking them off, and I was ready to crack at any moment. Topher's shoes were on. Lula sat between us as we watched Wallace take a running start and get his shoe about halfway up the wall, its shadow long against the overhead lights as he waited under it with arms open like a circus clown ready to catch one of his own.

While Wallace planned his second attempt, Topher fished a cig from his pack and made a show of retrieving a

Zippo emblazoned with the logo of a band the rest of us had never heard of. He lit up, cherry burning as he inhaled deeply, holding it in for too long before exhaling loudly and looking away from the smoke. Lula asked if she could have one. Topher said sure. They leaned in towards each other and huddled against the wind. Topher lit it for her, and the cocoons of their hands—hers around her cig and his around his lighter—nearly intersected, fingers nearly grazed, but they didn't, only teased at it. Lula said thanks. Topher said sure. Wallace said nothing, because he was screaming and brandishing his sneaker at the goose holding its ground a few feet from him, but the bird wasn't having it. I told a joke, but I can't remember what it was. I told it for the reaction, which I got, Lula doubling over and putting her hand on my arm, careful even while laughing not to touch the bandaged hand. Topher chuckled for a second, then went quiet and took another drag. Wallace lobbed his shoe like a hand grenade, with mixed results. I'd catch Topher looking at me out of the corner of my eye while I talked to Lula, his eyes always darting away when I'd look at him, pretending he was studying his cigarette smoke as it dissipated into nothing.

And then Wallace screamed, ran over with a lot of "did you see that"s and "that was fucking awesome"s. We hadn't seen it, but it didn't take a genius to realize that Wallace was down a shoe, his big toe peeking through the hole in his sock.

"Un-fucking-believable. I don't even know how I did it, to be honest. I don't believe it. I refuse to."

Me:

"That's good? Is this a good thing?"

"I can't believe you guys missed it!"

Topher:

"Uh, Wallace..."

"Yeah?"

"Don't you think you might need your other shoe?"

"Who the fuck cares? I'll get another pair. Fuck, man, I should've filmed that."

We gradually migrated to Topher's ride—rather, his mom's ride, a minivan he'd been given permission to use for theater transportation. We sat inside for a while and listened to the band that Topher's Zippo advertised on a CD that Wallace found under his now shoeless foot, the tracks occasionally skipping, us yelling out "Remix!" as we jammed and lit up some exotic stuff that Wallace had acquired the weekend before.

I don't know what made Topher pull out of his parking spot and onto the tiny drag-racing strip that was the lot next to the theater, what got me to sit on top of the minivan's hood and howl at the moon. Maybe it was something in whatever we smoked. I don't know.

He started by revving the engine while in park, Lula in the passenger seat laughing. I pretended to thrust a sword in the air like I was a Roman general atop his war steed. Once I did that, Topher switched into drive and gunned it. Lula wasn't laughing anymore, and neither was I. My knuckles whitened as I clung to the wipers, the minivan's hood sloping down into speeding ground—gravel flickers and gray lines undulating like a blacktop polygraph test. The music in the van sounding underwater. Lula's voice a chorus of "no"s and "stop"s. Light brake taps, and here I am sliding down the hood. Here I am slipping off. Here—

Whip, crack, light piercing and sounds of falling, of screaming. Tumbling and ground overhead, engine like bombers like falling like...looking back you see the van's approach like time seeping through your fingers, it's coming, put your arm up, heat exploding from all of you, rust under the bumper, contact on forearm and heat running through, bloody knuckles like quarter games at lunchtime, fingers clenched over the bumper, wedged, keeping it from running you over, shoulder scraping pavement, shirt tearing to tatters, kneecap making cold contact and melting like a stick of butter held to a searing pan, other hand underneath, engine impossibly loud, and here is where you'll die, fear you've never felt before, here is where your life will end, fear like your head held underwater, bubbles at the top, face on blacktop, you've been grinding for centuries beneath this van, and here's the wheel beside your head, spinning endlessly, then brakes like a choir of fire alarms in your ears, a smell of burning coming from you, hollow warmth as the polygraph is shut off, tiny pores in gravel.

There's blood on the front bumper, streaked across blacktop, pooled at your feet. When you stand, firecrackers explode in your spine, and you look for the hat you dropped. There are faces. Some you know, some you don't. The light is too bright. You are to look down. You are to see the blood that's claimed your shirt and pants, cold now, already, torn everywhere, mouths on faces making big Os as they look at you, as your hand finds the left side of your face. More blood when you take the hand away, still more, dripping, like a horror film, and you wait a while for everything to come back, but you're sleepy if you sit. Better to stand and wait, here let me help you back up. And the firecrackers again, and the sirens, and the light, so beautiful and permanent. Questions coming from underwater, and you can go right into that ambulance. Here, let me help you.

You're waiting now, tiny animals screaming in your brain. You are to lie down. You ask the man who told you to lie down if you look bad, and he doesn't say anything. You ask again, and he says he's seen worse, but yeah. It's bad. You ask if Rodhi's coming, and he asks if you're in a band or something, or are you the roadie? You wiggle your toes after the man asks you to. You tilt your head forward, look out past your feet, to the opened ambulance doors, where there's a visitor. Where Mona stands there, howling, in darkness, making a noise you've heard before. You would plug your ears if you could, but the pain is too great. Better to lie still, hard even to tilt forward on the stretcher, hard even to look at her as she cries, but you have to, it's your duty for some reason, so you look until there's nothing or no one to look at, until the doors are closed and the engine's on and they're bringing you to that familiar old place—Lutheran General.

67. Exit

You're being rolled down what looks like a bowling alley. It's not like how it happens on the doctor shows. None of the personnel say vaguely medical things to you or anyone else. No one says much except the occasional watch it, careful, etc. The personnel seem almost bored. None of them look at you for that long. The pain has a taste—bitter, like battery acid left on your tongue. Corrosive. Even breathing sets off the firecrackers in your spine. Everything is too bright, and you're going to throw up. Your grandfather would tell you it's "get sick," not "throw up." Old habits die hard.

When the personnel do speak in medical jargon, they do it in a whisper, like parents doing a bad job of hiding a fight from their kid. Mona's in now, Roger too, and they're having one of those whisper fights over Roger's being drunk and so not able to drive them over. He's not a staggering drunk. He's a true alcoholic's drunk—not like what you'd see in movies or TV with slurred speech and fighting. A real alcoholic doesn't want you to know they're drunk. A real alcoholic is a consummate actor, as are most addicts. At least the ones who are any good at being addicts, anyway. The only thing that gives him away is, well, two things: that glassy look he'll get, and the vein at his temple. He'll try to hide them anyway, though. He'll wear sunglasses inside, splash his face with cold water. But the vein doesn't go away. The vein always gives him up.

The personnel let Mona look at you, not knowing her potential for making a scene. She'll wail so loud that personnel will let go of tubes, clipboards, pens, and gently grab at her arms, elbows, the small of her back, and lead her out of the room.

Your eyelids are two worlds colliding in space, crushing everything into powdery black oblivion. Each of your breaths is enough to fill a hot air balloon. You think your spine is going to break apart, like it's made of Legos. You tell the personnel this. They nod and return to what they were doing. There's a needle in your arm now, warming fluids passing through the needle and into you. You're told this after it's happened. There's vague murmuring of grafting, and you try to hear crafting instead, imagine you're a workbench being put back together, a weekend project that'll be fixed "in a jiffy." You remember that Lula saw all of this. You hear her screams and remember that she was crying. Crying so hard. Crying not because of that stereotypical crap about how women emote, but because you were suffering and she couldn't take it away. A forced spectator of a girl who was anything but. You wonder where this tough girl is, how she's doing. You hope she's okay wherever she is, that—and now you remember that she's high. That you were high—are high, and so are Topher and Wallace. That the police stayed after questioning was over, their red and blue lights still visible as the ambulance took you away.

You tear out tubes and needles and experience a pain you've never felt before, like ice shooting through your veins, beeping machines, the personnel used to this, forcing you back in bed. You look around for a mirror, a screen, any reflective surface. There aren't many options. You settle on the metal hand plate on the door of your room, where you look like an M.C. Escher piece, mostly just a Caucasian smudge with red smudges around your face, arms, legs, half of your face covered in blood, like Two Face. You wonder if Batman is coming. If he is, you hope it'll be George Clooney's Batman. You think you could take him.

Right before the morphine comes, you find yourself in a pain so great that it starts to feel comfortable, like a burned finger starting to feel cold after a while. You call out when the morphine finally comes, let the room breathe you in and out. You try to say Lula, but it comes out slurred. "Lula" becomes "you are," again and again. You are. You are. You are. No one looks at you when you say this. They're embarrassed. One of them opens the door, and Drew's there, in full military uniform, digital camo out of place here in this sterile white, these scrub-colored sheets, this gray night coming from a window like the one PGN would look through, the one with the birds outside. Here's your brother standing by your side, words useless and so not spoken, him setting his rifle at your feet, the thing as heavy as a safe, crushing your feet, but you're letting it so that Drew can be with you. An Apache helicopter hovers outside your window, several more lined up behind it, this window's so high up that you can see it all, and all of Des Plaines is a great desert now, sand on the ground outside the hospital, in your bed. Drew lifts you off the ground, the stump of your leg hanging over the sand, enemy fire coming from six o'clock, and he's getting you to safety. Your arms are around his neck like they'd be at Dee Park after teeball practice, fingers laced together behind his neck and him telling you to hold on tight, you're becoming the propeller to his helicopter as you both spin and spin, his face the only thing standing still against all that motion, the grass a green blur, baseball diamond a brown one, and you're laughing so hard that you can't breathe, legs weightless and centrifugal behind you, leaving ground, dipping low, toes grazing tall grass as Drew takes a step, pivots, legs lifting back up as he does, and you're a horse in a merry-go-round.

You have an appointment with the pain, so Drew has to go. When he does, you remember the little red button the personnel showed you, the one for relief, timed so you can't overdose, every half hour, and you press the button after the last second passes. Your chest is the size of the room you're in, then it's as small as your pinky. When the wave crests, it's "you are." When it crashes, it's "Lula."

The worlds of your eyelids collide, and it's a deep, dreamless sleep. And that's it. You're out.

When you open your eyes again, Lula's standing even though there's a chair next to her, early morning sunlight erasing her features, a tabula rasa you can fill in with memory. She's saying "you are," or rather asking it, and it takes you a while to remember. When you do, you bury your face in the pillow, on the scraped-up side, and she's grabbing the arm that wasn't dragged, pulling you up by it, propping you up in bed.

"Don't. You're hurting yourself, Waldo."

"I'm fine. I'm fine."

There are tears on her cheek, and she's not hiding them. Not insisting there must be onions nearby, her latest strategy when a sad story Waldo's told about his family life has really gotten to her.

I breathe, and suddenly I'm back inside of myself. I look at her:

"Where's Topher and Wallace?"

"Wallace is on his way. He's borrowing his mom's car. Topher's..."

"Yeah?"

"Topher's got a court date."

I nod.

"Have the painkillers kicked in at all?"

Lula's floating in the air, twirling in circles, weightless. She touches down and looks at me like nothing's wrong.

"Yeah. I mean, kinda."

When I inhale, the whole room gets pulled in at the center—an invisible belt pulled too tight. When I exhale, the belt is loosened and everything's okay again. Lula's staring, so I ask:

"What do I look like?"

Lula won't answer. She's blunt, but never hurtful. Her purse is on the table next to me. I reach into it with the hand that isn't wrapped in gauze, pull out a compact and look before she can take it away. The skin on the left side of my face has been ripped off like an overzealous kid with fried chicken, the tissue beneath a menagerie of color—the inevitable reds, cautionary yellows, some purples and blues, all circling the worst of the wound, a spot on my cheek where I was dragged nearly to the bone, a pond of blood at the center, the rest of the wound wide at the top and diminishing toward the bottom, an upside-down triangle, I'm looking at it from satellite view, and the blood's pooled in my ear, can't hear out of it, blood so thick you can't see the ear, how much is gone, if any, and I hand the compact back. Lula takes it but won't put it back in her purse yet.

"Don't worry about it. You'll heal."

...

"You'll heal."

Lula puts the compact away. Her hand comes back with a writing pad and a pen, the Uniball I told her was my favorite. I look at her while trying to hide the left side of my face. I'm not very successful.

"In case you want to write something."

"What am I gonna write about?"

231

"I don't know. This might make a good story, for starters."

"Maybe."

...

"So that was pretty fucking stupid, huh?"

Lula gives me a sad smile. I ask:

"Is Topher going to juvie?"

"No idea."

"Do you think he should?"

Lula tries to keep her face neutral, but her brows betray her.

"No. Of course not. Do you?"

"I was just asking. Just wondering."

"Do you?"

"I don't know."

...

"I don't, no."

"Good."

"Lula, do you..."

"What?"

"Nothing."

"Don't 'nothing' me. What?"

"Do you like him? Topher?"

"Of course."

My heart has been excised from my chest.

"I like him. I like Wallace. I like you."

"I mean do you *like him* like him?"

"Why are you being so weird?"

"I'm not being weird. You're being weird."

"I'm getting a territorial vibe. It's weird. It doesn't suit you."

"I'm not territorial, just curious. Just wondering."

"Oh yeah? What's your blood type? Social security? How many times a day do you shit?"

"That's not the same thing, and you know it."

"How is it not? My attractions or non-attractions are my business. Not yours."

"It's different because we... shared something."

"You mean kissed?"

"Yeah."

"Waldo, I kissed Topher before I kissed you. Does that mean I have to tell him everything about my life too?"

"That was for a movie. It doesn't count."

"So what does count?"

"You're just going in circles. Using semantics."

"And you're being all Nineteen Eighty-Four Big Brother-y. It's shitty. Look, you're a good friend, and I'm sorry you got hurt, but that doesn't, like, magically give you the right to act like you own me. Like I'm tied down to you because of some stupid kiss or something."

"So it was stupid?"

"You know what I mean."

"No, I don't think I do. What about it was stupid? Because to me it was pretty great. To me it meant something. But I guess I'm just being stupid."

"Yeah, maybe you are."

Quiet. The machines hum. A slight breeze comes in from the window at the other side of the room. It's colder than it should be. Colder by forty degrees at least.

Exit Lula and the part of my heart she keeps.

68. In Jeopardy

The personnel tell you that you have to sleep. They're amazed when the morphine doesn't do the trick, your eyes closed, willing sleep to come, but it won't. It goes on like that for hours, in the dark, then all through the next day, when Mona and Roger are supposed to come but have to work, only Roger's taken to putting on his starched shirts in the morning, cinching his tie, and taking a spin around Bay Colony, around and around he goes while Mona's working, this time at a gas station, the latest in a string of part-time jobs, her managers being "assholes" before she's let go. And there's Roger orbiting BC like a satellite, and you know this because you've seen it yourself while riding your bike around on a teacher's institute day. Tie still cinched, eyes blank, hands at 10 and 2, and he could be commuting for how his face looks, and it's on and on like that until 5, when he parks back in the spot and comes inside, loosens his tie, tells you all about his day, who said what to whom, the politics at play, when the next raise is likely to come, and meaning it, you can see it in his eyes, refuting it at this point would do nothing, and you get the urge to howl like a wild animal, strip down to nothing and yell, taste blood, and Roger stares at you with those too-wide eyes, the kind of liar who must hypnotize you into belief, the beer breath on him even after all those hours of circling, maybe fresh, you've found some in the glove compartment before, and he's telling you to stop looking at him, screaming it, and you do, but he hits you anyway, hits you once and winds up for another but then pulls away and gets back in the car to circle some more, that's his job, and he'll do it till the gas tank runs dry.

Wallace comes the next day. There's a catheter in you now, the burning down there hasn't subsided yet, and you can't shake the fear that you're pissing your pants when you go, even though the stream's safely redirected, can't get over the awkwardness of taking a piss while your friend stands in front of you, talks to you, looks you in the eye. He's got the JVC of course, naked without it, duct-taped in the spots that got damaged during the bicycle incident, the camera still somehow working, and you know this because Wallace is pulling a wide shot on you, sun coming in from the window at his back, good natural lighting, and he's using the rule of threes to get the best shot composition. You tell him to stop filming, will he please stop. Will he fucking stop. And jeez Waldo, he's just trying to, like, document history here. And you're not in the mood. Really not in the mood. He shuts the JVC off. Seconds lapse into minutes of silence. The tune for Final Jeopardy filters in from the room next door. Before Trebek can check in with the contestants, Wallace cuts in:

"I should've done something. Should've stopped him somehow. I'm sorry."

"Yeah, you should've."

"I said I'm sorry."

"Whatever."

"Look, dude, I'm not the one who did it. And anyway, it was an accident."

"Sure it was."

Wallace is looking at a stranger now.

"Seriously, dude? Really? You're gonna go there?"

"How the fuck do you not stop the car? How do you keep going by accident?"

"Dude, we were in orbit at that point. In the twilight zone. We should've been in a padded room, but he was behind the wheel. It's fucked up, but he didn't mean to."

"I'm glad you're so sure."

"Dude, what the fuck?"

"Don't even, Wallace. He's jealous of me and Lula. It's obvious."

"You and Lula?"

The way he says it and the smirk that accompanies it makes you want to hold his head underwater till the bubbles disappear. Wallace:

"Don't you think you're being just a little paranoid?"

"You know what? Fuck you, Wallace. If you're gonna be like that, fuck you."

Wallace looks more hurt than angry:

"It's like that?"

"It's like that."

Wallace stands there for a second, considering. He ejects the tape from his JVC and hands it to you, careful to put it in the hand that isn't injured. And then he walks out, just like that. You look at the tape, at its label. Hastily scrawled in sharpie, it says, "HERE'S WALDO." You set the tape on the table beside you as *Jeopardy!*'s audience claps and claps and claps.

69. One Bite at a Time

It's not you, it's me. I did those things.

I sat in bed in the days that followed, not knowing I was in the same room they put PGN in, waiting for my parents to come, but they never did, not even on the weekend, the pain finally subsiding, or at least the physical kind, and I had to sit up for scheduled parts of the day, prepare myself to stand up, to walk again. I was once again the prince in *Katamari Damacy*, endlessly rolling the garbage of my life up into one overwhelming ball, sickly sweet J-pop in the background, rolling up now my family, now my friends, their limbs wiggling in cartoon fashion just like in the game, and it's endless, just keeps growing, keeps rolling, out of control.

Days passed, only the personnel and my thoughts as company, thoughts as nourishing as cyanide, thoughts I'd return to in a year or two, when the hot water would be shut off and I'd have to microwave cups of water if I wanted to take some semblance of a real shower, trample over mounds of Mona's hoarded clothes and garbage to get out of the apartment for school, clear a space in all that junk for Reb to sleep on, a space where the bare carpet actually showed through, Mona strung out on ludes and who knows what else, Dad MIA, and the power went out next, bills unpaid, lying on a bed stripped of blankets in ninety-seven degree heat, the mattress bare but still not giving any relief from it, then trailing into wintertime when I'd have to wear pants to bed, then a sweater, then a winter coat, making a game of watching my midnight breath collect on my bedroom window, Reb under the blankets and burrowing as deep as he can into me for warmth, poor puppy, Mona taken to sleeping on the recliner in the living room now, a corrupted version of PGN, a sentry, standing (or sleeping) guard, coming awake right when I wanted to go to school, or work, or God forbid see my friends, barking out her usual shit, keeping the heat on the fire inside her till she'd get me to blow up and say something that'd add tinder, give it oxygen. Anything to keep it going.

So I called Lula. Straight to voicemail. Called Wallace. Same result. It hit me that the wobbly, hastily built construction of your life can come down in an instant, no matter how stable you thought the foundation was. So I cried. I allowed myself that for a little while.

Then PGN came into the room. The old man. PGN. How he was. How he is. Eyes lit up. Hands not knobby tendrils but back to their old thick selves. Everything.

"The hell's a matter with you?"

"What?"

"Trying to build a tributary to Lake Michigan?"

"No sir."

"Then quit it. What've you got to be so prissy about, anyhow? I'm the dead one, not you."

"I don't know. I fucked up. Messed up, sorry. I messed up."

"No, you fucked up."

"Yeah. I mean, how do you know?"

"I can see everything. One of the perks of being dead, I suppose."

"Wait, everything?"

"Don't be a pervert."

"Yes sir. Sorry, sir."

"Don't say sorry. At least not to me. Fix it."

"Yes sir. Sorr— Yes sir."

"Those kids are good for you. Especially that Tallulah."

"Are you real?"

...

"Are you?"

"What does it matter? I'm telling you something you need to hear, whether I'm real or not. You go around asking if every book you read is real? That's not the point."

"But I need to know. I need you, Grandpa."

"Don't."

He cleared his throat. Looked out the window. Turned back.

"Give me your hand."

He took my hand and held it up to my eyes.

"See those lines? Mona gave them to you. I gave them to Mona. No matter how much time passes, no matter where you are, where I am, I'm there. In those lines."

...

"And hopefully that'll stop you from jerking off so damn much too."

Both of us laughed through tears.

"You're meant for big things, kid. And I'm not just saying that. Something else I've seen. But it's up to you. When someone goes through the kind of shit you've gone through... the kind of shit you're *going* to go through... it either kills them or saves them."

"How could it save them?"

"You'll see. I hope. It's going to be hard for a while. Hell, it's going to be hard forever. But that's what being a good person is. You're not just either born a Mother Teresa or a

Hitler. Being good is a choice, like anything else. You have to consciously make that choice, again and again, to be the best 'you' you can be. It'll always be easier to be an asshole. To write other people off. Be cynical. Chase tail instead of stay true. What's harder is seeing how shitty things are and staying positive *despite* them. What's harder is to have others ruin your day in all their petty little ways and to stay kind anyway. Kind to them especially, 'cause they need it the most."

"So where do I start?"

"Remember that Silverstein book I gave you?"

"Yeah."

"Remember the one about the little girl who ate the whale?"

"Yeah."

"Well how'd she do it?"

"One bite at a time."

"One bite at a time."

70. Okay

They brought me a walker, the kind with tennis balls on the legs—Pacmen gobbling up the walker one bite at a time. Ha.

So:

Step right up, come one come all, to the stupendous, marvelous Walking Waldo! Watch with your very own eyes his steely resolve as nurses remove his catheter. Witness the daring of a young man learning how to walk again, legs as wobbly as a toddler's. Feel the pain that slips in as the morphine drip lags, as Waldo stumbles and falls on his bad arm, rips open partially healed skin and has to get wrapped up like a mummy all over again. Watch the nurses remove the walker from his room, and see Waldo escape to locate it. Walk with him as he paces late at night, past lights out, building his strength, hiding the walker before the nurses can catch him. Hear the triumphant groans of an adolescent navigating staircases again, white knuckles glued to the handrail all the way up, all the way down. Feel the freezing, spinal cold as Walking Waldo bends the wrong way, back giving out and leaving him splayed on tile floor to wait for the nurses to return. Get your tickets now, they're going fast, won't want to miss this one, what a sight, all of this, waiting for you, inside, underneath the Big Top.

I was discharged early the next week, with the mummy bandaging and a plastic back brace that made me look like I was related to RoboCop and Threepio. Mona was supposed to pick me up, but she never showed. After an hour of waiting, I caught the bus back home, same one I'd taken to visit Rodhi a few years back, those years feeling like eons. The pills they gave me for the pain shook in their bottle like a maraca after I got off the bus and walked back to Bay Colony, already used to the stares.

I walked into another of Mona and Roger's fights, this one so heated they didn't even notice me walk in and past them. All routine as I pet Reb, angled his licks away from my wounds, and got some things together for my journey. Journey where? Shit if I knew. I should've brought a bindle. Ha.

Even after all that time of knowing her, I only ever walked to Lula's place that one time, but I figured I could find my way again.

Summer sweat soaked my bandages on the way over. Not exactly suave-looking. I didn't have a cent on me, so I plucked flowers along the way and made my own bouquet—daisies, marigolds, tulips snatched from ample Park Ridge lawns when no one was looking, which was especially impressive considering I was covered head to toe in bandages. But I got the flowers, rehearsed my lines along the way, did mental rewrites, scrapped the whole thing and started from scratch a few times, eventually said fuck it, this isn't something that should be scripted, it needs to come from the heart, whatever that means, so I got to her house and screamed at my brain to come up with something. I started looking for pebbles to toss at her window, like all the old movies show you. Only problem being her lawn was fairly well maintained, so I ended up combing through pristine grass, first hunched over, then on hands and knees when my back started to act up. I was crawling around like a toddler.

"Waldo!"

At the window.

"The hell are you doing crawling around in my front yard?"

"Looking for rocks to throw at your window. Pebbles, sorry. Just pebbles. I didn't want to break your window. That's not why I'm here."

I stood up, sloppy bouquet in my hands.

"Then why are you here?"

"I'm here to... Look, can you like come outside or something? This is kind of personal."

"If you can say it in private, you can say it in public."

"Yeah, well... Okay. Okay, fine."

...

"Uh, you remember when we first met? And we were talking outside the theater, and you were giving yourself a drunk test and asking me stuff? About my purpose? My here here purpose?"

"Yeah, I remember."

"Well, I didn't know what my here here purpose was then. I'm still not sure now."

...

"I'm not making any sense. Look, I don't know what I'm here to do. All I know is when I'm around you, I feel like I do know. You make it seem like everything will be okay in the end. Like the world could end any second now and it'd be fine. You know?"

A hint of amusement on her lips, but she still wouldn't say anything.

"My heart's beating so fast right now, it's not even funny. I feel like I'm gonna throw up. Holy shit. Okay."

She laughed.

"Anyway, I feel like I'm supposed to be with you. Like *with you* with you. Not just friends."

Silence.

"Look, I brought you a—"

Half the bouquet fell out of my hands and scattered on the lawn. I bent over to pick it up. Bad idea. I locked up, went to stand but lost my balance, fell on my back like a turtle.

"Yep, that fucking hurt. I don't think I'm getting back up."

"Waldo, for fuck's sake. Hold on."

She bolted downstairs and out the door, ran across her lawn, grabbed my hands, and started to pick me up.

"No, wait."

"What is it?"

She held my hands as she waited for my answer. You better believe I paused for effect.

"I need an answer. Please?"

"Damn it, are you faking?"

"No. Trust me, this hurts like hell. But still, I want to know. Need to know."

"Need to know what?"

"If you'll go out with me. What, are you stalling?"

"No, I just wanted to hear you say it. *Needed* to."

She tried to maintain the deadpan but wasn't entirely successful.

"If I'm going to go out with you, you can't pull a John Cusack every time you want to see me."

"Understood. I'll call first."

"And no more of this jealous bullshit."

"Got it."

"I mean it."

"So do I."

She was still holding my hands.

"And don't be a jackass. If you're with me, you're with

me. Okay?"

"Of course."

"Okay."

"Okay?"

"Okay."

"I might start swearing when I get up to kiss you, but that's just—"

She kissed me before I could complete the thought. A small crowd had apparently gathered to watch that Belyst girl kiss some mummy boy on her front lawn, one of the onlookers loudly supplying the story to whoever they were on the phone with, a few others recording the whole thing. And how did Lula react to all of this? Well, naturally she hoisted me to my feet and together we ran, my arm over her shoulder, me limping like some wounded soldier as we escaped the battlefield of her neighborhood.

71. Telling Lies To Get At The Truth

When we got to the fisherman's lagoon, Lula helped me adjust the straps of my back brace till it fit okay. I pantomimed Threepio when she was done, and she laughed for me. We sat down, and she pulled a spliff from her Dia-de-los-Muertos-skull purse. We lit up. We took a few hits each and let the smoke take laps around us, kissed a couple times to confirm that it was still just as fun. It was.

Lula:

"What are you smiling about?"

"Me?"

"No, the other Waldo."

"I don't know... I've never been this happy before. I know that sounds stupid, but it's true. I don't trust it."

"Do you trust me?"

"Well, yeah. Of course."

"Good."

...

"So you mean it? About never being this happy before?"

"Yeah. Up until now, my life's been shitty with like a sprinkle of good on top. Maybe I'm being dramatic. I don't know. I'm kind of stuck in it, so I'm a little biased."

"Why's it been shitty?"

"Because... I don't know. Just because."

"You don't know, or you don't want to tell me?"

"The latter. Both. I don't know. Can't we just smoke? What kind is this anyway?"

"Nice try, subject changer."

...

"So you don't know your dad. Or you know him but don't really know him. What else?"

"Could we please not do this right now? It's kind of killing the mood, and—"

"Okay."

She stood up. Grabbed the spliff from my hand. Put her purse over her shoulder.

"Wait wait wait. Don't go."

Lula stopped and turned around.

"Are you going to lay out your baggage or not, baggage man?"

For a second there, I was ready to do it. If I could tell PGN, I could tell Lula. And there the old man stood, right behind her, without his trademark neck brace, hair not white but a dark brown I'd never seen before, never *could* see because any photo from that time period was black and white. So I'd have to fill in the details, imagine what my grandpa looked like at twenty-four, because that's what he is here, same age I am as I write this. PGN with all the questions and worries I have—not yet all-knowing, just a kid trying to find his way in the world.

Lula:

"I'm waiting."

PGN's gone. It's only Lula now, in the clearing. Only ever was Lula.

"Me too."

"What?"

"I love you."

...

"Fuck. I'm sorry. I don't know what I'm saying."

"It's fine. It's all right. Just talk. Tell me something."

What's there to tell? How about seeing Rodhi's mangled body, limbs bent the wrong way, pants down, mangled down there too. Or maybe lying naked on the frigid beach of Maya's bed, fucking and getting fucked, the two of us stumbling in the dark, reaching but not finding as cars doppler past down 294 and the moonlight cuts through pepto pink sky laced with violet, looking out this window as I thrust into her from behind, not blinking, not really feeling, just performing an action no different from brushing your teeth, her sex sounds insisting there's something more, something real, and when it's over so are we, hands losing grip on each other, drifting, falling through space, and all of this is telling lies to get at the truth. What else? Childhood memories of Roger stumbling in drunk to start a game of dogpile with Drew and Mona. Roger sifting through channels late at night, me beside him on the couch, him settling on porn, telling me to be silent, don't tell Mona about this, blanket over him as the motions start, only scratching, just got an itch, look at the TV. Watch. Or the screens I'd access later, still accessed then, before I quit, watching strangers fuck each other, women seen as nothing more than the holes they had. Or trying to remember something that's been erased, before my brain split, I can feel it. Or else Drew trying to force me into someone I wasn't, mold me, shape me into who he never was, who PGN never even was. But the image is there, and we have to chase it together, like a carrot at the end of a stick, all of us, all men, running in terror from our fear, not accepting the feelings we have, shutting them out, shunning them so they can come back stronger the next time. Here are the things I can tell her.

The things I will tell her. Right now.

"I..."

...

My pulse was giving me a headache. Light bent and twisted before it hit my eyes. The sun burned holes through leaves, singed my forehead. There was sweat everywhere.

"I can't. I'm sorry."

And her look. More disappointed than angry. Snuffing out the spliff beneath her Converse. Shouldering her purse. Walking away. Leaving.

Interlude:
Tallulah

At a little creek, beside the woods, a three minute walk from my old childhood Park Ridge home, there's an awkward stone bridge that someone made, the idea being that you could hop from one stone to the next to get to the other side, where the woods would give you enough cover to get high out of sight and smell of parentals. I didn't want to get high, but my tiny self did want to get across, if only so I could say I did. But every time, every damn time, I'd come up short about halfway across and fall into the creek, soaking my Converse. I'd have to turn back and head home in my soggy shoes, leaving wet footprints behind.

There was a gaggle of kids that would give me shit at recess, follow me home and shout taunts till I reached the house with the pitbull that was always in its yard, the pitbull that gave me slobbery kisses but growled at the kids anytime they got near. One day, I decided to pick up some rocks and whip them at the kids' heads. That got them off my back, until a couple days later when they told me I was adopted. This was before I found out that I actually was adopted. But anyway, that's what they said. Because you know. Escalation.

When I asked my parents about it, I got a bowl of mint chocolate chip and an episode of Pokémon. I don't know why I didn't ask them again. Why I didn't press it. But I didn't.

There's a thing you do when you've just found out something that huge about yourself and are trying to get to sleep that first night. Or at least there was a thing I did. I clenched my pillow with all ten fingers till my knuckles went red, then white, till my fingertips hurt and beyond even that. I smothered an invisible person and yelled into the pillow till I thought I might go hoarse. I punched the pillow, then the mattress, then the bed frame. I snuck into the kitchen, scooted a chair up to the fridge so I could reach the freezer, and iced my bloody knuckles. I didn't want the parentals to notice.

I remember sneaking into our partially finished basement, dirt floor in the farthest corner, the place where the light didn't quite reach, and plopping myself down, not caring if I got my pajamas dirty. Listening to the sound of the furnace dying out and coming back to life—a coughing, wheezing resurrection. I don't know why, but I started digging. It wasn't long before I found what I hadn't been looking for: an empty Jim Beam bottle. Jim Beam, what Dad had been drinking before he "quit." What he'd given up after Mom started needing surgeries and four hours of sleep in the middle of the day.

Anyway, I took the bottle and smashed it against the wall. I hadn't planned any further than that, so I picked up all the shards and put them back in the grave I'd robbed them from. All except one. It was a big piece of glass, narrowing out to an impossibly sharp tip. What I did was I brought it to my feet, bare, dirt clinging to the bottoms of them, and I started jabbing little pricks into my ankles. I was careful not to go above where my socks would be able to hide what I'd done. I don't know how long I sat there, alone, in the dark, on the dirt, poking little constellations and swirling galaxies into my ankles.

I never said anything to those kids after that. I took all of their taunts, their laughter, their following me home every day. I didn't throw any stones, didn't yell back. Just took it. All the while, here I was, in my room, unrolling my sock and adding a little bit more to my painting every day. I'd work in sections, letting one part heal before circling back. I always had something to work on.

I guess it all came back to that creek for me. I'd go there day after day, hopping from one stone to the next, taking those leaps of faith, and inevitably I'd fall in about halfway through. The water would soak my shoes, and I'd get home to see that the individual pinpricked bloodstains on my socks had bled together and faded to a light pink. I let the creek launder my socks, hiding them from the rest of the laundry so that the parentals would never find out.

Until this one day.

This one day, I walked straight from the school bus to the creek. I went without hesitating, jumped from one stone to the next as if I was born to do it. Reached the halfway point, the creek rushing a little faster that day, the water lapping the stone's edges, turning it a darker color. All around me, things were moving even though I wasn't. Things were carrying on. So I jumped. And when I reached one stone, I jumped to the next. And the next and the next, until I made it to the other side. When I got there, I plopped myself down on the grass, on my back, and watched the clouds slice through the sky, watched the planes slice through the clouds. And it was like that for who-knows-how-long. But eventually, I left. Eventually, I went home.

72. Summer Smoke

It's funny what procrastination does. What it takes from you, *who* it takes from you. As I write this, I'm sitting in a motel. There's a mattress in the back alley with a bloodstain that looks like a face. I'm looking at a wall that's been puttied in a fist-sized spot. The mirror's cracked, so when I drink tap water out of little paper cups, I see my face splintered into hundreds of different faces, eyes insectile. I haven't seen Mona in five years. Haven't spoken to her in longer. She doesn't know I'm coming, doesn't even know I'm here. There are those who will tell you that family is how people treat you, that even though someone shares your blood, that doesn't force you to be in their lives forever. You might tell yourself this. I might. And that's fine. But no one can help when that lizard part of your brain needs something more. When that child inside you wants to be there for his mother. With his mother. I don't know the answer to that. You can eat it away, smoke it away, drink it away, write it away, meditate it away, but it'll still be there. Like trying to run away from your own shadow.

I've been here for a month now. I'm taking a break from my internet writing gigs. Taking a break from everything, I guess. Everything except writing this. When I'm not roaming the streets of unincorporated Des Plaines, I'm in here writing for hours on end. Trying to get the beginning and middle down before I can write the ending, happy or not. Whichever it'll be, it's in sight now. We're almost there.

So how can I write about Drew's death in a way that'll make sense? In a way that's real? I don't know what I mean. So let's start with what I do know. I do know that I was home when they came, crisp suits and boots scuffed up by blacktop, gravel stuck to the toes of them. They were solemn and ready to deliver the news, but Mona and Roger weren't home. Mom and Dad weren't home, I mean. So I let them in. And they could sit wherever they wanted, and I put on the TV, but the news was on, and I'm sure they saw enough of that, so off went the TV.

You guys want something to drink? Something to eat? Can I take your jackets? Is that even allowed? How long have you been in the service? Do you agree with the war? Who'd you vote for? Where are you from originally? You guys play video games? Wanna play *GoldenEye* or something? Sure you're not hungry? You can wait till they get back, right? Is there a set amount of time you're allowed to wait for? Do you have to be somewhere else soon? Somewhere in Bay Colony, maybe? Do you know Drew? Did you know Drew? Coke, maybe? Orange juice? Water with ice in it? You mind waiting for the ice to freeze? I bet I look like I just came back from war all wrapped up like this, huh? You wanna know what happened? You guys feeling okay? Can you please just not tell me? Can you just go? Maybe hug me first? Would you hug me? Are you guys allowed to hug people? Is that okay? Can you please not say it? Can you just leave and tell them you told me? Told us?

I remember holding onto one of the soldier's boots. Smelling its leather. Crying. He wanted to step back, but I wouldn't let him. It was my boot, my floor, my apartment.

Hurt connotes ownership. I didn't think they'd tell me. Didn't want them to. Part of me still wishes I could go back, not answer the door, shut the blinds, turn off the TV, crouch into the couch and shush Reb until they took the hint. That if they couldn't tell me he'd been killed, it would make it untrue. They'd go back to base and see him alive and well. I'd see him alive and well. Speak to him again. Tell him I'm fucking sorry, I love you so much, I was an idiot. And how I swayed on the way back up, the whole room spinning in circles, junk-covered carpet beneath me pulsing, and the men were helping me into the kitchen where there was a chair and a perspiring glass of water, where there was a dog who would clean my hand till I was happy again.

When I could think again, I was asking them what happened, how, why, when, where. They were stalling, offering up the story they'd been given, and I was insisting. I was yelling. I was picking up a carving knife and telling them I'd kill myself if they didn't tell me, and they were talking me down, making me drop it, acting like it never happened, sweating now, both of them, just like my glass of water. Your brother stepped on an IED. IED. Improvised explosive device. The acronym came back to me from all those news reports. All those makeup-caked faces reading from teleprompters, changing to practiced concern when they needed to, practiced pity. Getting through it, then ending on something cheery. And I wondered why they couldn't tell our story. Why they couldn't tell the story of Drew, of his real father and the father we shared, of the pictures under the bed and the football games I'd spend collecting wasps in plastic bottles instead of watching Drew play, have a half dozen in there and throw spirals to other football-players-in-the-making, or so our parents thought, lights overhead throwing the field into false daylight, leaving spots in my eyes when I'd look up to catch the spiral, the wasps angry and trying to sting through a layer of plastic that was too thick for them to penetrate, and the smell of hundreds of hot dogs in the trash can as we'd toss the bottle out, cap closed, nacho cheese on everything, the chips meant to be dipped in it crunching underfoot as we ran from the scene of the crime. Not seeing any of the game, really, only the aftermaths of big hits, when the crowd's oohs and aahs drew our attention, then back to running around underneath the bleachers, hurdling and dodging its metal skeleton. Collecting chunky cell phones, loose change, condoms before we knew what condoms were. That's what it was like: running for no reason, collecting the trash of others, sticking something in a plastic bottle before being stuck in one yourself. Feeling the heat punish you as the air got thin, wasn't recycled.

I have a hundred of these stories. Days spent in the arcade, sipping big gulps that'd spill on *Mortal Kombat* joysticks, tossing balls into Big Bertha's mouth, the big cloth carnival game, the inevitable sexual jokes from Drew that I wouldn't get "till my balls dropped," and even writing it there feels like a lifetime ago. Like swimming into the dark.

I remember one of the soldiers started smoking in the house, hands shaking. You could tell he was green. Not to combat—he'd definitely killed a man before. Green to dealing with grief. To being helpless while someone else suffered on the inside. If I were underneath the rubble ruins of my apartment, he could manage. If I'd gotten a leg blown off, he could deal. But what do you do with this? Pat the kid on the shoulder and say "there, there"? He inhaled deeply over the sink, ash dropping from the cigarette, already more than half of it smoked in less than a minute. The other soldier looked embarrassed, passive.

Mona came home first. I don't know when Roger came back from circling Bay Colony, because by then I was gone. In my hideaway, of course. Where else? I dialed Lula beforehand and told her she needed to come. She didn't even ask why, just said she was on her way. I guess she could tell from my voice how serious it was. I couldn't be there with Mona. Call me terrible, but I couldn't do it. So I slipped out the patio door with the faulty lock and crept quietly away, Mona's screams now right behind me, now in the background, now fading into the wind and dissipating like so much summer smoke.

73. Coming Apart Together

I waited by the pond for her to come. Not a ripple on the surface. A second sun glaring back at me. No swans, no people. It was as if everyone agreed that I needed time alone. The only person I wanted to see was Tallulah Belyst. The only person I *could* see was Tallulah Belyst.

I don't know how long it took her to get there. I didn't tell her I was at the pond, but she found me there anyway. She came over and sat on the bench next to me. Didn't say anything. Just sat with me. I got up at some point and walked away. Not away from her, just away. She followed behind me quietly, carefully. We got to Meadow Lane, and she helped me haul up the storm drain cover in silence. I went down first and helped her on the rungs even though she didn't need it. I showed her to my "room," the notebooks not yet flooded out but still threatened judging by the brown stains on the concrete walls. Pens so old you'd have to lick the nib and scrape a spiral on the page before any ink would come out, but they'd work.

We took a seat on the cold, damp floor, avoiding the miniature stalagmites blossoming like calcified flowers in the dark, drips from cracks in the ceiling the culprit. I could watch these drips instead of looking at Lula. Instead of saying anything. I could put out the lightning bug lamps and let the darkness swallow me up. But Lula wouldn't let me, so I turned to her.

"I don't really have any friends besides you. Maybe Wallace. Probably not Topher anymore. I've only had one real friend before. Rodhi Boshi. He died. LC... Mario did it. My bully. He killed my friend. Beat him and put him in a coma. I was there at the hospital, but I didn't see him die. After that, I was supposed to get confirmed, but I didn't. I went to his funeral instead, and I caught a ride from his mom, and we went home, to her home, and we had sex. We had sex a few times after that. I haven't seen her in a while, but I still think about it. About her. I have a brother and his name is Drew and he's dead now. He's a pain in the ass and he's a jock and I love him and I think he was gay but didn't want to tell anyone. I think I might be a little gay. I think everyone might be. I have a grandpa who's dead too. I watched him shrivel up because he was sick, really sick, and I couldn't say anything the last time I saw him. My parents hate each other. They're probably going to get a divorce, and I don't want to be with either of them. I think my dad molested me, but I don't know. I can't remember. It's all fuzzy. I watch a lot of porn and fight videos and gore videos and I don't know if I can stop. I still watch them. After we're done here, I'll probably go watch them. What else? I don't know what I believe anymore. I fucking hate OLPHS, but it's not like I can leave. I'm scared I'm gonna go to hell. I want to be a good person, but I don't think I am. Sometimes I feel like I'm wandering through empty space, like I'm lost, and no matter where I turn there's no way out. I want to love you, but I don't know if I know how."

So here's a new one: Lula was at a loss for words. So we sat together on the cold, damp floor and listened to the droplets hit the ground. I imagined myself at the scale of a mite, each little stalagmite a tower stretching toward a ceiling that was so high up it might as well not even exist. What did I know about love and loss and pain at this scale? What did I know about suffering? Each dimple in the floor's concrete was a canyon, each crack a chasm. Lula was at the scale of a galaxy, so I only ever saw parts of her. The mountain range of her Converse heels. Laces like brilliant white tree trunks lifting up forever high. I never saw the full picture.

"Come here."

I did.

Lula held me in the dark, lightning bugs shining Morse code. They left spots in my eyes. I turned and held Lula's cheek. Kissed her, and she kissed back. My fingers over her clothing, Lula completely still but letting it happen. My hand sliding under, finding warmth, her no longer kissing me. Saying Waldo. Waldo Waldo. My fingers finding their rhythm and her teeth on my shoulder, moisture spreading on my shirt. The buckle and the button and the zipper. These are meant to hold together, but we're coming apart now. Coming apart together. Bug light shining through her panties as they slide around her ankles and she says we don't have to do this, as if there's any other choice. Her hand is in my hair, and she's saying we shouldn't. She's kissing me and finding me down there.

The bugs know nothing of this. Rodhi doesn't know, or Maya, or anyone but us down here, under the city. She says pull out, and I'm putting those words away. She's reaching back to hold my hips and going limp in front of me, sounds cut short, and it's time for me too. Even the droplets don't fall when it's over, even the bugs don't shine their light in the dark. We're breathing in the scent of ourselves.

When we can say something, we say oh no, or oh Waldo, or oh God, and we sit next to each other against the wall and cry in turns, alternating between who comforts whom, the bugs still not lighting up, the droplets still not falling.

74. Into the Labyrinth

We wake and stretch and find ourselves together. Lula takes my pages and reads them before I can tell her not to, by bug light, and when she's done she doesn't say anything. She puts them away, stands, walks to the far wall, and says Jesus even though I'm pretty sure she doesn't believe. I'm pretending I'm more in a stupor than I actually am. She comes over. I get up and hand her a bug lamp, grab one for myself too. She takes it and walks down the hallway, past the endless procession of identical concrete cube rooms, lightning bugs blinking spots on the wall to light the way. I reach her and touch her arm. I say:

"I'm sorry."

"This is kind of like how it was underneath the Center. Maybe a little spookier, but pretty much the same."

"The Center?"

"We had matches, though. All we could sneak in. The light would go out, and you'd get your fingers burned if you weren't careful. I always was, but some of the other girls weren't.

"They'd sneak cigarettes because that's the only way I'd let them come with me. I knew my way around underneath the Center, and they didn't. We called it the labyrinth. I called it that, anyway. I don't know what they called it.

"Anyway, after a while I figured I'd smoke the cigs instead of using the matches since the matches always went out. Cigarettes lasted longer.

"They weren't all cutters. I mean, I was, but some of them were like bulimic or anorexic or something like that. We had this doctor. Dr. Charon, and he'd lead us in what he liked to call Allegorical. He'd tell us to speak our Hurt in one word. He told us it was capital H Hurt. He had a bunch of weird games like that. I don't think any of it helped. I remember one day he asked for my one word and I just left and went under the Center, into the labyrinth, and I smoked my cig, and I pulled out the bobby pin I took from one of the RNs and sharpened it on the concrete and started stabbing it into my ankle. I had thick socks that hid the blood, is why I chose the ankle. In case you're wondering.

"Anyway, I made like little constellations with the pin, in my ankle. No one knew about it. I'd come up and Charon wouldn't ask. He just welcomed me back into the group.

"The other girls always talked about boy problems, friends who were dicks to them, that kind of shit. I was there 'cause my mom had cancer and so I cut myself. There were other reasons, but that was mostly it.

"Anyway, when I'd feel really shitty, there was this one girl. Liza. We were roommates. She was there because when she was four and five and six her dad molested her. He had her wear dresses and sit on his lap when her mom wasn't home, and he'd say he had to adjust her clothes for her, under her dress. She told me all of this. Well it went on for a few years and then just stopped. For a little while after that she could be a normal kid. Or about as normal as you *can* be after something like that. Her dad drank for a while, then didn't, then drank again. Her mom wouldn't leave him alone with her. She never said anything about it, but she didn't have to.

Liza's words, mind you. So anyway, it was okay for a few years. Until Liza started developing. Keep in mind, when I knew her, she was gorgeous. Liza would never admit it, of course. She'd say she just looked normal. I knew her when I was fourteen and she was fifteen. She started developing around twelve or so. Becoming a woman and all that. Meanwhile, her mom and dad's marriage was pretty much nonexistent. Her dad would 'work late' till like ten p.m. At first, he'd call and say he'd be late. Then the calls dropped off. Then he didn't even bother giving excuses. So her mom started 'working late' too.

"Anyway, eventually Liza's mom was out more than her dad was, and Liza was developing, and he started hanging around the house, after work, reeking of booze. He started conveniently doing the laundry across the hall when Liza was in the shower. Their bathroom door had one of those old timey keyholes you could peek through if you wanted to. When Liza realized this, it'd already been like weeks of this going on, but then she started hanging her towel over the knob to cover up the hole.

"So then her dad said she couldn't lock the door anymore. He said it was a fire hazard, or that she could pass out, and what would he do then, just let his own daughter die? She left it unlocked.

"Liza was thirteen the first time her father raped her. Thirteen, and in the shower, and singing some song by Christina Aguilera, and he pushed her against the wall. Stopped her singing. Left the shower running. Got his clothes all wet. And she grabbed at the curtain and pulled half of it down, but he wouldn't stop.

"This went on for a year, like clockwork. When Liza locked the door, he busted the door open and fixed the lock before her mom got home. When she stopped showering, he went into her room at night and did it while she was sleeping.

Woke her up. When she locked her bedroom door, he jimmied it open with a screwdriver.

"It got so death was preferable to life. She fantasized about killing herself. Tried a few times. Or at least said she tried. I think that fighter part of her refused to let her do it, no matter how bad it got. Finally, it was either she'd die or she'd tell someone. She was resourceful. She found a hotline. Told them everything. Gave the cops the whole story when they came. Detailed everything. Her dad was arrested. Tried. Convicted. And so she went to the Center and her dad went away.

"When I met her, she was doing pretty well. Really well, actually, considering the kind of shit she went through. You couldn't meet a more positive chick. The whole time her father had been raping her, she'd gotten super skinny. Scary skinny. But when she came to the Center, she ate healthy, drank a lot of water, went on walks around the grounds and told her Hurt in one word, spoke at every Allegorical. She was like the model resident, but none of us were jealous or anything. She was the kind of person you wanted to see succeed no matter what. No matter who you were. Everyone loved her.

"But she went out on a belt anyway.

"I found her first. Her toes were purple, and she was swaying back and forth like she was on a swing or something. She wasn't on restriction, which is why they let her have a belt. In case you were wondering. 'Cause I was wondering. I was wondering how come they didn't take away her belt and her laces and her sheets and tie her hands behind her back if this is what she was capable of. If this is what she'd do to herself. I hit Charon in the face and I punched a window out and I clawed the wallpaper and knocked over everything I could knock over and I cried till I couldn't cry anymore and could only sleep, right where I was crying, on the floor. I've never cried like that in my life. I don't cry.

"I didn't know why she did it. Still don't. But nothing will change what happened. Nothing will bring her back. And I was hurt for a long time after that. I couldn't deal. And I hated Liza, wished I'd never met her, all that.

"But then I stopped hating her. I stopped trying to blot out the memories we had, and I saw her how she was, before she went out on a belt. In her stories and her smile and the way her eyes lit up when the sun came in just right and it looked like they went from green to blue, just like that.

"Okay.

"Okay, I'm done."

75. A Soldier's Stone

Sitting in class became sitting in class and waiting for Lula to text me saying she got her period. Writing at home became waiting for a call. Every task I performed was done to waste time till Lula confirmed she wasn't pregnant. We didn't bring this up when we hung out, of course. We took walks and watched free movies and I smoked but Lula refused to just in case. She didn't have to say this, and I didn't have to ask her why she wasn't smoking.

That wasn't the only elephant in the room, either. Drew was coming home.

Mona actually came into my room to tell me. That was the first time we'd spoken in weeks, unless you count her screaming obscenities at me, but I tend not to count that. Her eyes were glassy when she told me. Nail polish chipped. Flaking off. Her nails were always impeccably kept, but not now. Hair like straw and dyed an unnatural red, the blonde roots still fighting through. Little scars and pockmarks I'd never seen before on her cheeks, now, in the spots the concealer always hid—a magic trick suddenly revealed. Red pushed into her cheeks. She was bundled in a shawl, two blankets, a sweater she'd only had the energy to get one arm

267

into. She was shivering. She motioned me over with her arm and hugged me like she'd do whenever it seemed she knew I was on the verge of leaving for good. Times she'd remind me that she was my mother, that she'd do anything for me, that she loved me so much. She only said these things when I was latched onto her, holding me there as she said it so I couldn't see her face, her eyes.

"He's coming home" were her exact words, and until she said those words I was strong. Until she said them, I could resist the effects of the lizard part of my brain, the part that insisted that we were blood, that she brought me into this world, that my life only existed because of her, despite all the other shit. Biology doesn't care what we think.

There's a practiced way you hug someone like that. Your body stays stiff, but stiff on the inside. You imitate what an embrace would seem like, and it's a decent simulacrum, but it's not the real thing. Maybe only you know this. Maybe the other party does too. It doesn't matter. What's important is to feel this moment, like clutching a brick wall to yourself, and with your eyes open, staring out behind this person, their perfume stinging your nose, their hair brushing against same, hands closed into fists but only recognizable to you. To the other party, you've wrapped them up completely.

Anyway, that was the plan until the words were said. My fists went limp. Shoulders loosened. Head went into her shoulder. And she held me closer, like a shark smelling blood, cooing words at me she didn't mean, couldn't mean, because she'd have to feel them to mean them. Things like I love you, I'll take care of you, it's okay. Especially that last one. Who are you to tell me "it's okay"? But I hugged. She hugged. And when it was done, I went into the bathroom and washed my mouth out with mouthwash till I could feel the burn deep in my gums, rinse and spit and rinse and spit till I might start bleeding, then actually did, red mixing with Listerine's blue to make some sort of purple in the drain, and she was knocking on the door asking if I was okay, probably worried I was freshening up or else trying to get me out of there so she could do the same. I don't know.

*

Drew came back on a Friday. I remember because I took the weekend off from the theater. Dave didn't ask any questions, didn't offer up any cliché words of condolence, and for that I was grateful. By then, Topher was back to work too, so it was for the best that Drew came home when he did.

There's a flag they give to the family, folded up in what's supposed to be a solemn triangle, but all I could think of was a paper football—the kind Drew and I might've made together when I was just a kid, paper tumbled end over end till it got to the part where you had to rip a little off and tuck the rest neatly inside. The kind you'd flick with thumb and forefinger, with the other person standing a couple feet away, their arms up as mock goalposts, smiling impishly and trying not to blink when you'd go to flick it, trying not to flinch.

Drew caught me flinching every time, but I never got him. Not even once.

I didn't know where to put my feet, my hands, my eyes. Couldn't look at the rigid faces on the rigid bodies stuffed into rigid uniforms who carried his casket, with the red white and blue blurring at the edges in the rain, or else my tears when it finally let up, miraculously so, when he was going to be lowered into the ground, and I couldn't believe this was for my brother, in that box, a box that would stay closed for reasons they couldn't disclose, or rather wouldn't, for our sake. I wouldn't have wanted it open anyway. Wouldn't want to see Drew's crew cut, or his athletic form molded into something even more extreme. Wouldn't want to see him in that fucking uniform if that's what he'd be buried in. I had no idea.

I remember the scent of beer and urine coming from my father, in the field, in the same cemetery PGN was buried in, only a couple plots over, and how Roger spoke of the men who came from the sky, the Grays, who'd show themselves at any moment. How an envelope containing anthrax had been mailed to him. How he'd opened it and didn't know how much time he had left. How I couldn't tell a fucking soul, not even my mother. How they had ways of finding out if this information had leaked. How it was a risk even telling me. How my grandpa was the first target, and Roger didn't kill him, I was to trust him on that, and how they'd try to frame him for what happened to Drew too. That he hadn't had intercourse with my mother for two months because they'd detect the decrease in bodily fluids and catch him that way. Trace it all back. When I cried, I was able to use the funeral as my excuse, and he finally stopped and left me alone, to sit by the stone they'd made—a stone that was way too formal for someone like Drew. Too serious, too stuffy. PGN would like it, though, I think. "A man's stone," he might say. "A soldier's stone."

I sat till the other guests left. Sat through Mona's insistence that I get up, that I get in the car. Sat till I could see our beater pulling away and off to Bay Colony. Not a far walk, is how Mona would justify it to herself. And that was fine.

I cried, then remembered that Drew would say that made me a little bitch, so I laughed instead. Laughed as the snot came pouring out of me and threatened my proper funeral clothes—the same I'd worn to see Rodhi for the last time, just a little tighter from growing. In our household, you had one set of fancy clothes, and you wore that set till the buttons popped off or the zipper broke, and even then you could always get by with like a paperclip or something. You'd have to be resourceful, because if you messed them up you were fucked. I reminisced with Drew about that fact. About how many times our *Space Jam* blanket had been sewn up over the years, about how even after I shit the bed that one time when I was sick, Mona just cut out the affected area and transplanted in a section from our tattered old *Power Rangers* blanket, so that Michael Jordan's smiling head was grafted onto the red ranger's body and was forever destined to be both mighty and morphin'.

I reminded him of days spent feeding quarters into machines at the arcade, of taking Reb home and jousting with sticks and playing baseball as a kid, even when I thought he was a pain in the ass. *Especially* when I thought that. He didn't reply. It wasn't that he couldn't, but that he chose not to. And that was okay. The wind would pick up and rattle the leaves of the tree that gave me shade, the one that would forever give Drew shade, and I could take it as laughter if I wanted to. I could listen to the screaming of the cicadas and almost hear Drew calling me a little bitch, with the love in his eyes that he always had, even when he said it, like he was saying these things against his will and would say how he really felt if he could.

Why did I want to take everything and mash it between my teeth? Why did I want to tear myself into little pieces and scatter them over the creek that fed into Good Lake? What the fuck was so "good" about it anyway? Rodhi lost a shoe in there one winter. It was either his life or the shoe after LC forced him onto the ice with a knife, and Rodhi told himself the ice was thick enough, and I hoped he was right. How it just gave out with no warning, nothing like what you'd see in the movies. Clouds collided, bald tree branches dipped in the chilly wind, and Rodhi thrashed in the water. That's all there was to it. And how I went out there, on the ice, slipping, sliding the rest of the way, pulling him out and almost going in myself. Taking off his wet coat and my dry one once we'd gotten away. Giving him my coat so he could warm up. Prying the manhole cover up, ice flaking off of it as we went into the hideaway. And something else. Something I'd forgotten. The way Rodhi looked into my eyes, in the bug light, then at my lips, and how he kissed me there, in the dark, with the light blinking past my closed eyelids because I was kissing him too, and when we were done we were through, and I held him till he warmed up, against my chest, and we went home, and never spoke of it again. I didn't think of it again, at least not consciously, until now.

I thought about these things until I couldn't think anymore, and then I went to sleep, right there, propped up against Drew's stone.

76. Ethics and Morality

A couple days later, I was officially in my senior year at OLPHS. As I walked in and shouldered past the two-backpack-strap freshies congregating at the Pietà knockoff, the reality of four years hit me like the Oklahoma drill back in my Junior Red Devil days. It could've been yesterday that I was loitering around that creepy statue, unable to fit in. Maybe last week I was calculating the Baby Bottle Pop to Pokémon card exchange rate, plying my trade in the blacktop corner of Mark Twain Elementary's bazaar, not doing too hot at avoiding LC and crew. Yet here I was, eighteen, in my senior year of high school, with a friend and a brother and a grandpa gone, and a girlfriend maybe pregnant, still no period after three weeks, and last I told her, I was broke and waiting for the next theater paycheck to pay for the test, and she knew that wasn't true but went with it anyway.

I got my schedule the day of. Could've gotten it earlier, but going back to school was the last thing on my mind. First period had me in Honors Ethics and Morality II with (you guessed it) Mr. Felter. Only, he wasn't there the first day. Or the day after. Or the rest of the week. Dean Boyle fulfilled Felter's duties, giving us packets and "study time" that amounted to notebook doodling, penis-graffiti-drawing, or coke snorting for the I-seriously-don't-give-a-fuck-anymore variety.

It was the week after that Boyle told us. Seniors first, and we were not to tell anyone else: Mr. Felter's services would no longer be required at Our Lady of Piety High School for Boys. He had allegedly been engaging in... lewd acts in front of an elementary school when the kids got out at the end of the day. These... lewd acts had allegedly been going on for quite some time, and the students' parents alleged they'd nearly caught him before and only succeeded this time when they allegedly boxed his car in and phoned the police. Allegedly. Dean Boyle was well aware of how much of a shock this must be, hearing such things about one of our own, and counseling services would be put in place for those who would require them. I didn't go, of course, but the "services" quickly became a Get Out of Class Free card, with kids blubbering and going on about their "betrayed trust" as much as they needed to to string the counselors along. The packets continued for the next couple weeks, then dwindled, then disappeared entirely. Honors Ethics and Morality II became a study hall, then an optional study hall when half of us decided we'd rather sleep in late than come in. Boyle didn't do anything in the way of punishment, surprisingly.

*

I caught the report by chance, flipping through channels at night and settling on the ten o'clock news. Felter covered his face with a newspaper while a newscaster provided the details. I was about to change the channel when they laid it out—a religion teacher whose older brother was a man of the cloth, Felter alleged (again with that word) that as a boy in CCD, his catechist had frequently molested him when the other children weren't around. The catechist in question, a

Mr. Harold Grissel, could not be reached for comments.

77. One Last Look

Lula peed on a stick, at night, outside, in the lagoon, on a Friday, next to me. I wanted to find out right when she did, so she waited to take it, let it sit in her backpack to be either heeded or ignored every time she reached in for homework or a change of clothes.

After she took the test, Lula tossed the plastic strip into the woods, and we sat there on one of the logs, looking up into a sky wiped of color—a palimpsest where you could almost see where the old colors used to be, but only just. The closest thing to color was a deep, all-encompassing blue that drifted into black so gradually you couldn't tell where one ended and the other began, like passed-around childhood stories of frogs in pots boiling alive without ever noticing anything was wrong. Our heads were barely above water, ears below, faces skyward and cold in comparison to the amniotic warmth below us, treading water, tide coming in strong, filling our noses, trickling down our throats, ears now submerged, now free, and so everything's coming in as wah-wah, and there's no light, no sun, not even any stars to guide us. Just the sound of endless water being shaken and poured on a cosmic scale, our struggle against it. Our hands linked together to prove we're there despite the darkness.

"What are you thinking?"

My voice sounded like it was coming from a stranger a million miles away. Like when you watch old VHS tapes and cringe whenever you hear yourself talk.

"What am I thinking? Waldo, what the fuck do you think I'm thinking?"

...

"What the fuck?"

"Look, I know this seems crazy now, but—"

"Fuck."

"Lula."

"Fuck."

"We've got options, okay? And we're in this together, so it's... it's not like you're alone, you know."

"Oh I'm sorry, are you the one who's pregnant?"

"Lula."

"Are you?"

"No."

"No, so you don't know what you're talking about."

...

"Fuck, and I just started at the Art Institute."

"You can still go. You won't show for a while, and... And we have options."

"Just shut up, please. Okay? I love you, but if you're gonna repeat the same bullshit, then just don't."

So I shut up. Looked at her in the dark and tried to will my love into her with my eyes. She sat next to me but was a million miles away, looking at the leaves, the sky, the ground, anything but me, half-muttering, swearing. I put my hand on her back, but she shrunk from it. When I tried a second time, she stood up and stepped away.

"Just stop. I need a second to think."

Her second became five minutes, then ten, in the dark, her standing and me sitting, lightning bugs twinkling in

277

place of stars that weren't there. No animal sounds, no cicadas. You could barely even hear the cars on 294. The breeze rattled leaves, but that was it.

"I can't."

"What do you mean?"

She turned to me:

"I can't have it."

I worked my jaw: first open, then closed. It seemed to be working fine.

"Waldo, we're not—"

"But there are other options."

"Like what?"

"Adoption, for one."

Her look was the look of a person who's had a knife delicately inserted into their chest by the person closest to them.

She didn't say anything, didn't move an inch. I don't think she even breathed. I know I didn't. And then she did something I'd almost never seen her do before—cry. Eyes burning red, lightning bugs flashing green shutter bulbs against her face, the face that was looking at me like I was a husk of a person. I tried to touch her. Tried to un-fuck myself by doing the same shit again, hand on her shoulder, and she revoked the touch from me. Tossed it into the trees with her eyes, maybe to join the pregnancy test, and I could go there too for all she cared. I could drop off the face of the planet. She said this with her eyes before she said it with her mouth, before she wiped the tears and the snot and pushed away another of my hug attempts and said:

"Fuck you."

And then she left.

I watched her till I couldn't make out her shadow against the leaves of the trees. I watched her like I'd never see her again. I didn't know then how right I might be.

78. The Prodigal Son Leaves

There are only so many times you can call. Only so many attempts you can make, hearing the tone repeat, her voice on the voicemail saying, "Tallulah Belyst," and this is the only way you can hear her. Only so many times you can cry yourself to sleep, not getting an answer for the fifth night, the sixth, wondering how she is, locking yourself up with your dog and your books and your stupid fucking stories that don't change anything, that read like shit, that you'd be better off using as fuel for a fire. Only so many times you can ask Dave where she is, why she isn't working this weekend, or the next, him hiding something behind his shrugs. Only so many times you can hear your dad wailing to himself in the tub, screaming like he's being stabbed, at noon, on a day you're both "sick," him maybe not thinking you're home, not knowing, and so drinking in the tub, spilling beer that clouds into bubbly golden whirlpools, and he's howling that they're going to get him, going to flay him from head to toe and dip him in acid. The empty plastic rings that held the six-pack together sit next to the tub, stretched from where he tried to tear them. He's cracking another one open and pouring it straight into the tub. You don't know that this is the day it happens, that today they will sign the papers and be rid of

279

each other for good.

*

   When Mona gets in, Roger is out. Her speech is slurred, lips sluggish and sagging, and you think this is a stroke. You ask her to sit down on the couch, tell her that you're going to call her an ambulance, and she calls you a fucking coward. You pick up the phone, but she grabs it from you, tosses it on the kitchen floor and knocks the battery out, wire dangling from the back of it. You pick up the battery and reach for the phone, but she smashes it beneath her feet into so many pieces. One of them slides under the oven, and Reb tries to get it out with his nose, then his paw. He whines when he can't reach it, sniffs the broken phone pieces, licks one, walks away. You're asking your mother why the fuck she did that, what her problem is, you were just trying to help, and she's telling you to fuck off. To go away. Her speech is even worse now, eyes glazed over, and you're sitting her down on a kitchen chair, one of the ones your dad picked back in the day, when you went with him, before he started ingesting beer through bathwater. The chair creaks and almost gives way beneath your mother. She's rail thin, has been for a while, but she says it's because she's too fat. When you tell her it's the chair, she slaps you in the face. She yells, and there is no yell. There is no sound. There is a vase on the kitchen table where the flowers went when there were flowers, and it's cool to the touch when you pick it up. Cool, and smooth, and heavier than it looks, and when it shatters against the wall, the little pieces of it fall to the ground and mingle with the phone carcass. You tell her you've fucking had it. You grab the old flip phone you bought with theater money and start dialing, and she screams she's not having a stroke. Stop. Don't call. You ask how she knows, and she's silent. When she tries to get up, you hear the rattle in the pocket of her sweater. You run over and reach into her pocket, and she screams like she's being murdered, and there are the pills, bottle half full or empty depending on your perspective. You wonder what your mother would call it. You run with them into the bathroom, and you know you're not supposed to do this. You close the door, and lock it, and she pounds on it till the door cracks. She twists the doorknob as hard as she can, but it won't go anywhere. She's yelling, now crying, saying you'll kill her, that the pain's too much and she can't live without the pills to help. When you don't respond, it's become a prescription. The doctor ordered she take them, open the door and she'll show you the script. When you tell her she's making up the pain to get the pills, it becomes don't you fucking dare talk to your mother like that. Then the crying again. It's a cycle. And you lift up the seat like all those times freshening up, not feeling that way right now but similar, and the pills drop in without a sound. When the toilet flushes, your mother is wailing that you've killed her. You've done it.

You wait till the pounding stops, and you run out. There isn't a single destination in mind, but you go anyway. You leave.

*

You aren't there when it happens. Aren't present when she gives Roger the papers and he chokes her out, only saved from death by a neighbor who heard the whole scuffle and called the cops. When you come back, he's already gone— locked up again. There are purple bruises on Mona's neck, and she hides them with a sweater that's become a scarf. Her way of telling you they've gotten a divorce is saying the asshole's finally gone. She expects you to cry. You expect you to cry. But you don't. Maybe you've used up all the tears you've been allotted. Whatever it is, you don't cry. And this burns her, so she tells you his shit is going out right now. When this fails to get a reaction, she tells you that the dog's going too. She flinches for the hit. Her eyes tell you she wants a reason to call again. But it doesn't happen. You look her in the eye and tell her that if she gets rid of Reb, you will destroy everything she owns, everything she loves. When you are done saying this, you still look at her, but she doesn't look at you. She goes back into her room and closes the door.

*

Life can be a study of accumulations and removals. You can watch as cells multiply, adding rolls you never had, weakening your breath by stages so subtle you can barely tell, the valve being slowly closed, legs now chafing where they never did before, cheeks drifting away from each other. You can see the clothes stack, one article after another, then old newspapers, magazines, garbage, the tampons that Reb will fish out of the pile and tear to shreds, the careful steps you take, practiced to touch the little remaining floor space left, and the smell of urine that will waft from these piles when she stops letting Reb out during the day, then feces, these piles you have to gather into plastic bags and toss into the dumpster you can see from your bedroom window.

The days will accumulate too, clump into weeks and then months, then you're there on the stage in the heat, waiting for your name to be called so you can take this piece of paper they will give you, take it and leave for college—you applied without telling Mona first. Googled how to apply for financial aid, looked up the school's scholarship opportunities and sent in one of your stories for consideration. Actually got half of your tuition knocked off thanks to the story, this one about a protagonist who's processing his brother's death, the loss of his girlfriend, parents' splintering marriage, all that. Not bad.

*

Reb no longer fit in the carrier he came with, so I had to buy a new one from the pet store. I stocked up on treats for him, snacks for me and the journey ahead: a Greyhound to New York City. One-way trip. I had nothing to say to Mona before I left, so I said nothing. I wrote a note for Lula but hoped I wouldn't have to leave it. If I left it, that meant she hadn't answered the phone or the door.

Goodbye didn't feel like an option.

Mind racing, not wanting to do it.

But then, finally, dialing.

The phone rang and rang. Left that familiar voicemail. That was fine. She'd answer the door.

I knocked and knocked. Waited. And then:

Someone standing in the shadows of the living room. Leaning in to get a good look at me through the window. Watching. Waiting.

Retreating to their bedroom. To Lula's bedroom. Closing the door.

So.

I left the note and got on the Greyhound.

PART III

PART III

79. Baggage Be Damned

If I had to sum up those years away from home, it'd be a collage of gain and loss, with the edges bleeding between the two. Stories I'd knock out in a flow state, send to my prof, get read next class. Stories I'd tune up and revise and sweat over, literally, penciling in notes on a printed-out copy in my AC-less dorm room, sweating like this partly because of the heat but mostly because of the pounds I'd put on. Calls I'd place to Lula, get no response except for once, when there was just silence on the other end, like when Drew used to make his late-night calls, but Lula (or whoever) hung up once I said hello, and I stared at the phone for a while, hung up and tightened up some flash fiction piece I'd been honing. I wasn't the only one being call-screened, though. Mona lit my cell up, left increasingly long voicemails, then texts when she got the hint, then emails written in all caps, telling me about her latest health scare, the mess I left her in, how terrible I was to abandon my own mother the way I did, how I could forget about running to daddy since they locked him up and threw away the key.

*

Sometimes it's best to take the *Katamari* approach. You have to start with the little lit mags. The ones no one's ever heard of. The ones that might just turn up a 404 error in a year's time. The ones run by one person, paying you nothing but the pride in knowing that someone who isn't you likes your work. And you roll up that ball, first collecting more small ones, then some of the midsize ones. All the while, of course, collecting enough rejections to wallpaper every room of your tiny, cockroach-infested apartment. You pay your photographer roommate in pizza to take headshots of you in Central Park, vacillating between serious and playful and intelligent. You settle on being you.

When you publish in the ones with acceptance rates in the single digits, you have an impromptu dance party. When one of the mags wants an interview, you spend a week perfecting every word, trying to exude both intelligence and relatability. You start going for the mags that are easily Googled, ones that include author bio pics so that everyone you've left behind can see how and what you're doing. You win contests and scholarships and tell Reb so he can congratulate you with face licks and head nuzzles. You start a novel, finish it, trash it. You become the poster child of the fiction department, the wunderkind. When you get to this point, not even the sky can limit you. You are destined for great things, baggage be damned.

*

There were way more people at the reading than there should've been. It was filled with veterans—just looking at some of these people, you could tell they'd done this dozens of times before. They had the rhythm, the confidence, the stage presence, all of it effortless. They even did that thing where you read a line or two ahead and then look up from the page to engage the audience. I tried that once. Luckily, it was only for the mirror. I totally lost the story the second my eyes left the page. I had to start all over.

The reading's presenter had been published in The New Yorker, Tin House, Every Place I Dreamed of Getting into but Probably Never Would. She drew laughs in all the right places, absolute silence when it was warranted. Garnered a standing ovation with her story as if it were nothing more than putting groceries in a cart.

I wasn't last, but I wasn't first either. I got there a little late, didn't have time to pull my story out of my pocket and unfold it. Instead, I unfolded it at the end of each reading, a little bit at a time, paper crinkling hidden under applause. When they called out Waldo Collins, I looked around to make sure they didn't mean a different one. My hands shook so much I thought I might drop the story on the way over.

I got up to the mic and just froze. All eyes on me. Polite at first but growing impatient by the second. Throat clearings. So I did the first thing I could think of: I told them I was trying to see how long I could stand up there and say nothing before getting heckled. That got plenty of laughs. I could breathe again.

"This is a story called 'The Prodigal Son.' "

There's that unavoidable moment when you're reading in front of strangers where your voice quavers on the first and second lines. Once you get past that second line, though, you reach a fork in the road. Either you collect your courage and pull through, or you stay in that nervous mode and bumble through the rest of your story. I don't know how or why it happened, but I pulled through. Maybe it was not wanting to embarrass myself in front of such luminaries. Maybe it was kidding myself with the dream that an agent was out there in the audience, looking for a bright new client to take on. Whatever it was, I read like this is what I was meant to do. Like all of my (ex) friends and (ex) family were there, sitting in the crowd, listening to everything I had to say and ready to clap at the end of it.

There's a certain silence that accompanies a good reading. It's hard to describe, but the difference between a rapt silence and an impatient one is like the difference between a human and a chimpanzee. It wasn't a particularly funny story, but it drew laughs where appropriate. This was the longest story I'd read, but it held the audience till the end. And I finished, and the audience took a second to process everything, and the applause was way more enthusiastic than I expected or thought I deserved. I looked out into the crowd, almost by instinct, looking for people I knew wouldn't be there. People I wanted (needed) to see but didn't know if I ever would or should.

80. New Person, Same Old Mistakes

I got there fifteen minutes early, because I'm a dork and that's just what I do. Plus, it was a coffee shop/bookstore, so I got to peruse for a bit, look for my professors on the shelves and use that, again, as evidence that some way somehow I was going to Make It.

I was all about fiction, of course. Flash, short stories, novels, didn't matter. Something that came from you but which you could still manipulate. I hadn't yet considered creative nonfiction. This story wasn't even a twinkle in my eye. Funny how things work out.

She came up from behind and startled me, because that's the kind of girl she was. We'd had a Women Writers class together, she a CNF-er and me a fiction writer. We swapped war stories in between readings of *Nightwood* and *To the Lighthouse*, reminisced on the Chicagoland area. She was from Park Ridge, so not quite as quaint (read: ghetto) as my hometown, but still. The actual asking her out was a moment no different from the beginning of a reading, fork in the road, and I chose the more courageous option. I almost asked if she was sure when she said yes and offered to put her number in my phone.

It's fun to navigate boundaries in a first date situation, even for things as simple as getting the other's drink. If I bought hers, would I look antiquated, possibly even chauvinistic? If I didn't, would I look like a cheap ass? I settled for getting it, because it was a damn coffee and I wasn't going to turn that into an all-night mental gymnastics session. She thanked me. My method of doctoring my coffee consisted of dumping cream after cream into the thing. She got one of those fancy ones that ended in "iato," but not in a Starbucky way. She called a large a large, for example. We sipped in awkward silence for a while, until our coffee mustaches broke the ice and we laughed and pointed them out to each other, the gag never getting old no matter how many times we repeated it.

There exists that nigh impermeable barrier when you go on a date with someone you've gotten to know well in a friendly context. You can't ask the small talk-y things, because you already know them, but you don't feel comfortable asking the personal questions either. She shot first:

"Why are you here?"

"Why am I here? Like here here?"

A nod.

"What's my purpose?"

Another nod.

I stalled out. Couldn't speak no matter how hard I tried. I met her eye contact, looked away, sipped my coffee, burned my tongue, started sweating. I looked back at her:

"I'm sorry."

"No, it's fine. Don't worry. I caught you off guard."

"No, it was... It was me."

...

"So, my purpose. Why I'm here."

No nod this time, she just stared at me. I spoke:

"I feel like for years I was dancing around the thing I really wanted to write about. I was barely scraping the surface of the shit I'd dealt with, not wanting to face it, and so all of my work was surface level. Juvenile. I'm only now ready to start writing about what happened to me. About what it was like to grow up in the environment I was raised in. Maybe that's my way of dealing with it. Writing it out. And maybe it can help others. Maybe it can help me. I don't know. But that's the plan. How about you?"

"Kind of the same, actually, funny enough."

...

"I can't remember if I told you before, but I was adopted."

"No, you didn't."

"Okay. So yeah, I was. I never knew my biological parents growing up and didn't really want to, but then my mom got in touch with me my freshman year of college. My biological mother."

...

"And it was one of those situations where I couldn't talk. I had a million things to say, but none of it would come out. So I just listened to her. She asked if I'd want to meet sometime, and for some reason I said yes. She gave me an address and a good time to come over.

"I sat on that scribbled address for a good week before I went. When I got there, someone else greeted me at the door and led me over to this person who gave birth to me, and we looked alike, and she was on a bed in the living room with an IV in her.

"It turns out this was in-home hospice. She didn't have long. Cancer. She conveniently left that part out in the phone conversation.

"I didn't stay long that first visit. I say first, because for some reason I kept going back. She gave me her life story in mini chapters, from childhood to the present day. She didn't skip over my birth and the months leading up to it. Didn't sugarcoat the panic and the hatred and the hopelessness. Didn't skip over having to sell her body to keep a roof over her head, doing it even while she was pregnant with me, doing it till she was showing and then subsisting off of whatever she could buy or steal from the convenience store.

"She found a nice, childless couple from the suburbs.

"When she delivered me, she couldn't look at first, or wouldn't, and it wasn't till they were going to take me away that she had to take one last look, have one last cry.

"They offered to let her keep in touch, even visit from time to time, but she refused. She convinced herself that it was because she didn't want to see me. Finally admitted to herself that it was really because watching me grow up with another family would break her. She knew I'd find out eventually, but she wanted me to have as normal a life as possible.

"She told me she wasted her life. Fucked up everything. But this would be the one good thing she did. The one good thing aside from having me, from giving me away.

"So.

"That's what I want to write about."

*

We sipped drinks at local borough bars, because that's what you do when you're Illinois transplants writing in New York City. We talked some, joked some, flirted some. And then she asked if I wanted to have some coffee at her place. I tried not to blurt out a yes but did anyway.

Her apartment was nothing but art. Bookshelves overflowing. Her paintings on the walls, stacked in corners. Little knit figures representing her fandoms. She had Tame

Impala's *Currents* on vinyl. And did I like Tame Impala? And I loved Tame Impala.

She prepared coffee in the kitchen while I sat and listened to Kevin Parker sing about transitioning into adulthood. She came back into the room right as the song "Eventually" started playing, and we sat in silence for a while and listened to Parker insist that we'd both be happier eventually, whoever "we" was. We sipped our coffees for all of thirty seconds before putting them down and racing to the bedroom.

My shirt ended up on the bed, and she brushed it off as she slipped out of her own. She undid my buckle and turned around, pressed up against me and reached back to hold my hips. She moved against me for a while, and then let go. Made it so we were coming apart together.

I stopped. Stared at her wall adorned with paintings but didn't see it. Didn't see anything. I stepped back and redid my buckle and felt my lungs constrict in my chest. She turned around, went from biting her lip to asking what was wrong. I said "nothing," but I could barely get it out. I grabbed my shirt, got one arm into it, and left the bedroom. Tame Impala still spun on the record player as I slipped on my shoes, Kevin Parker insisting that he feels like a brand new person but keeps making the same old mistakes.

81. I'm Going Home

We didn't talk after that. Deliberately altered paths to classrooms. The whole nine. I tried to just move on with my life, focus on writing and publishing. And it would've all kept going on like that if it weren't for that meddling graduation.

I sent out resumes to publishing houses, literary journals, marketing firms. Their replies, when they did come, were opportunities for me to see how quickly I could find the word "unfortunately" embedded in boilerplate. I got good at it, too. Too bad I couldn't put that on my resume.

I started losing weight not out of a concern for my health, but because I could only afford to eat every other day. I subsisted off of ramen and sugar foods. Walked everywhere—I couldn't afford a metro pass. Did shit like go to Mass at a church I'd never heard of, given in a language I couldn't understand, so I could take and eat a wafer I didn't believe in anymore. I spent whole days lying in the tub, adding in hot water when necessary, writing over the bubbly surface and walking over to the library the next day so I could transcribe/submit. I had no money for internet.

Walking kept my mood up, so soon enough I supplemented it with a little running here and there. Nothing fancy—I was still in no shape to do Dumas suicides, but it was a start. I'd get gassed after a quarter mile, sure, but it was something. Every time I stopped, every time I wanted to quit and walk back home, I'd get this vision. I know it sounds stupid, or crazy, but I'd see Drew standing next to me in workout gear. Barely breaking a sweat, of course. He'd ask if that was it. If I was gonna be a little bitch and just quit. So I kept going. For him. For me. For I-don't-know-who. I just ran. I journaled, too. Poured my thoughts into something other than fiction. Wrote down what I was grateful for. That portion of my daily entries always took the longest to get down, but I'd always make sure to write something.

Somewhere along the way, it didn't feel like the days were dogpiling me anymore, one on top of the other. They were running alongside me, just as spent as I'd be at the end of them—tired but happy. Was that happiness? Could it be trusted? Shit if I knew. But I kept going.

I lost twenty pounds. Thirty. Turned a pair of my old jeans into parachute pants that I hammer-timed in once I hit sixty pounds dropped. I tried to tuck the extra skin into my pants on bad days. Pretended to be Stretch Armstrong on good ones.

Somewhere along the way, I started writing for me. Not to impress Lula, or Mona, or show up Topher, or any of that bullshit. I was digging out my heart and putting it down on the page, one word after another.

I got some sporadic internet writing gigs based on my pub credits. They helped me afford food, but I still kept up the whole moderation thing. I kept the pounds off by running, a now daily habit that just showed up unannounced at my doorstep one day, like most major life changes tend to do.

I considered going back home. No expectations of course, just to face that son of a bitch called the past once and for all.

If I turned into a pillar of salt along the way, so be it.

Then I got the call. Funny how the universe works like that sometimes.

Glioblastoma. Yes, terminal. Yes, it was real. Yes, the doctor recommended I come see her.

So I packed up. Bought another new carrier for Reb, the old man having reached full size. His age showed by the graying whiskers around his eyes, nose, mouth. I bought another Greyhound ticket. Climbed aboard and watched Manhattan skyscrapers segue into cornfields and endless plains, en route to Chicago, where I already had a rental car reserved. I don't remember precisely when it hit me, but when it did, I could think nothing but this, over and over and over again:

Holy shit.

I'm going home.

82. The Prodigal Son Returned

So here I am. Driving down 294 and watching Bay Colony's apartment buildings rise up. Considering the prodigal son story. The biblical nature of good old Des Plaines, IL. And all that.

I took the first exit. Went down Golf, past the old fisherman's lagoon (still just as abandoned as ever), and on down Potter. The road was widened in my absence, a couple of the houses renovated, and more than a few "for sale" signs adorned the lawns, but it was largely just as I'd left it. I took a turn. Went down Meadow Lane. Idled for a while outside Wastoid's place, then onward to the stop sign at the end of the block, still riddled with holes. I turned right, into Bay Colony's entrance, but couldn't go in. At least not yet. Some force field was holding me back. I got out and stood there for a while, taking in the choir of cicadas, the scent of baking blacktop.

When it was time, I parked the rental car, left the window open for Reb, and got out. I surveyed this land that belonged to me, this land that could never be mine. I walked over to my old complex.

The patio blinds Drew and I once knocked down during a game of indoor football had all been fixed, but the faulty lock hadn't. I opened the door and went inside.

I expected mountains of garbage, piles of scattered clothes. But there was nothing. Mona must've cleaned up. Or had someone do it for her. But none of it made sense. The whole place had been rearranged. Furniture swapped out, style decidedly un-Mona. And then the actual owner of the place walked in.

"What the fuck are you doing in my apartment?"

"What? I... I don't—"

"Who are you?"

"Sorry, this was my place. My parents' place. I thought they still lived here."

"Get the hell out before I call the cops."

"Yeah. Okay. Sorry."

So I left. He even made a show of locking the faulty door behind me. Must be new here.

*

I heard "Waldo" while walking back to the rental but refused to turn around because I was done with the old ghosts of Bay Colony. I was done, that is, until I heard it again. And again.

It was Maya.

Our feet were planted on blacktop as we stood and stared. Features changed with age, both of us, but still the same people. Maya had just gotten out of her car, keys still in hand, wearing the same uniform she wore all those years ago, when I used to visit and stay the night.

I approached as if there were a wild animal hiding somewhere out of sight. Our hug was uneven—she hung on too long, I didn't hang on long enough.

"You've come back."

A nod from me.

"Why?

"That's a good question."

Quiet for a while. The cars on 294. Maya looked into my eyes. *That* look.

"Do you want to come inside?"

"I..."

...

"Yes."

New furniture, new bills on the table, but otherwise the same. The same paintings hung from the wall, and she still had lassi ready at a moment's notice. We sat on the couch next to each other, too close, legs almost touching, and sipped our lassis in silence for a while.

"Where did you go?"

"New York. To school. I'm trying to be a writer."

"You always made good stories."

"Thank you."

Sip.

"Waldo, your mother... She's gone. Did you know?"

Nod.

"Gone. Really. Packed nothing. Just gone."

...

"I tell her she can stay here, but she doesn't want to."

...

"She has nowhere to go."

I gulp the rest of the lassi down.

"You've come back to find her?"

"In a way. I mean, I already know where she is. But yeah."

"And what else?"

"Hmm?"

"What else have you come back for?"

She scooted imperceptibly closer to me, legs touching but only just.

"I don't know. I guess I'll see."

Maya leaned over and took my empty glass, rubbed against me both ways. When she saw the tightness in my jeans, she dropped all pretenses and reached over. I closed my eyes—maybe to enjoy it, or maybe to act like it wasn't happening. Like I wasn't there.

"Maya. I can't."

She stopped but kept her hand right where it was.

"Why not?"

"Because... Because I don't know."

She smiled, went back to rubbing me. I took a second, cleared my head, and formed my words.

"Because you're my friend's mother."

She stopped.

"Because you could be my mother."

Removed her hand.

"Because even though I'm old enough now, I wasn't then. I don't judge you. It was... It was what it was. But I can't anymore. I still care about you. Still love you. But I can't anymore. You know what I mean?"

Maya closed her eyes and nodded.

A minute passed, maybe two. No sounds.

"You want aloo palak?"

"Only if you were already going to make it."

"I was."

*

When we finished our meal, Maya hauled out a dusty old box and brought it into the living room. We sat on the floor and sifted through its contents together, mostly photos but some other trinkets as well. I found some old pictures of

Maya first. I guess I shouldn't have been surprised, but she was stunning. Still is. There she was with a young Suddho, his hair combed back and a mustache to replicate the Bollywood action stars of the time. Hell, Bollywood action stars *still* look like that.

Rodhi was a cute baby. Where I was crying in every damn picture taken of me, Rodhi was the exact opposite. Not just smiling, but beaming. As if this picture being taken was the best thing that had ever happened to him. There were more than a few of Rodhi with his abacus, something he still used to use when we were having a study session at his place and he had to make a complicated calculation.

There's that thing that happens when you're looking at photos of a dead person where you realize that there will be no more photos. That however many you have of them are all you're going to get. That if something were to happen to these pictures, that person might as well have not existed. Rodhi only had a handful of years, but Maya made them count with her photos. She kept them here, in this box, away from the sun, to be preserved better than a museum. Maybe he was still alive in these photos.

When we finished with the Rodhi pictures, we found more Suddho ones. Maya lingered on these, don't get me wrong, but not nearly as long as she did with the Rodhi ones. When she set them back in the box, she put them facedown so they could never look at her again.

"Why did you never remarry?"

Maya sorted through a couple more photos as if she hadn't heard me. Shuffled them into order, set them in the box, and then finally looked at me.

"Suddho was... jealous.

"I am a young woman and I look..."

"Beautiful."

"I look beautiful. And he covers me, he takes me away,

303

he tells me to stay at home with our child.

"My friends he sends away. My family he says we have family now. We are a new family.

"So I stay home and I cook and I mind sheets and I cry in the bathroom with water so he does not hear, and he sits in the living room and paints. Only paints.

"I tell him this air is not safe for our child. He is only a baby and it is not safe. I try to take him outside but Suddho grabs me. He sets me down on the couch and tells me I will stay."

I guess something changed on my face, because:

"I know it's bad. But he is not bad. Not all of him. In stories there is sattva and tamas. Sattva light, tamas darkness. Both in everything. Everything you do, both. Same with Suddho. Sometimes sattva, sometimes tamas. I never know which, so I stay. I don't leave him.

"Only thing tamas can't corrupt: breath. So I take Rodhi outside and I slam the door on Suddho so he cannot follow. I run with Rodhi down by the pond and he thinks this is a game. He laughs and smiles and he cannot stop. I stop and we sit under the tree with its branches that hang. Quiet. Still. Swans on the water. They don't make a ripple. You know?

"I think of leaving. Put Rodhi on a bus and we will go far away from here. Don't know where. Don't care. But I stay. You know why?"

I shook my head. Maya:

"I loved Suddho. This is a very stupid thing to do, but I do anyway. I believe he will change. And he does, a little. But still the same. Still needs to control. Control, control.

"And here I am. He is gone and I am alone."

"So why don't you remarry?"

She turned, looked at me.

"I was never Maya before. I was Father's daughter. Mother's daughter. Brother's sister. Uncle's niece. Husband's wife. Son's mother. Now who am I? You know?

"I am Maya."

I helped her pack the rest of the past away in comfortable silence. When we hugged at her door, we wanted it to be forever, but it couldn't be. And that was all right.

*

The next stop on Waldo's Comeback Tour was Dee Park. Reb whined the second we pulled into the parking lot, remembering younger days with Frisbees and tennis balls, times Drew and I would play games of Reb in the Middle, the little pup sprinting back and forth, determined but never quite fast enough, tongue flapping in the wind and him eventually stopping to lie down and pant, barking to tell us to wait for him. We'd have him go up on his hind legs to drink from one of the few working water fountains. Times I'd launch bottle rockets with tiny green soldiers strapped to the business end, Rodhi taking care of the logistics when we'd combine several into one Megarocket, both of us sprinting home when the rent-a-cops came around on their dorky bikes, screaming at us to stop.

I let Reb out but kept him close on the leash, kids in the distance playing on a park that wasn't mine anymore but which once was, some young cricket players way off at one of the diamonds, surprisingly still some little leaguers too.

We stopped in the center of the field. Reb whined, but I tried to coax him back to the car instead. He wasn't having it, so I let him go. I watched him run circles around me and then go full speed one way, turn around and go the other way. Reb was old, but no one bothered to tell him that.

So I ran with him. I ran faster than I did in suicides with Dumas, playing tag. I gassed myself chasing him, but I kept going anyway. I ran till I couldn't breathe but could still laugh. Ran till my eyes burned from the sting of sweat. Ran till Reb and I could do nothing but collapse on the grass with the cicadas screaming in the trees and the flies collecting into a cloud of sex above our heads, trying to blot out the sun but not quite able to.

83. Bridges Burned, Bridges Mended

Technology is amazing, especially when you're the one doing the spying and not the technology itself. Facebook snooping. You know you've done it. Don't judge.

I started with Topher. Found him, but unless I wanted to go back to New York I wouldn't be meeting him face to face anytime soon. Turns out he went to the same school I did, and we didn't even know it. Small world.

Then Wallace. Same deal, but different coast—Los Angeles. From what I could tell, he was busting his ass to get on any set he could, in any capacity available. I pictured him with a new JVC. New in name only, anyway—he'd put it through its paces for sure.

I sent them both messages, the common theme being forgiveness. Granting it to Topher and asking for it from Wallace.

Forgiveness is a funny thing. Like an elephant sitting on your chest, squeezing the life out of you, impossible to budge. Or so you think. The second you want to, it can be done. The second you want to, you can lift it like it's no heavier than a balloon. Like the mothers in stories who lift cars off of their children, it can be done when you need it to be done.

I logged out, turned my phone off. If they were going to answer, I wasn't ready for it yet. I needed to clear my mind.

So I ran. I circled the entirety of unincorporated Des Plaines. Crossed over to Park Ridge. Went past the theater (totally unchanged, by the way), then on to good old Mark Twain Elementary. I took a break on the sunbaked blacktop, the old bazaar back in grade school days. The place where we traded Pokémon cards for Wonder Balls. Warheads for authentic Duncan yo-yos. The surveillance cameras still perched like hungry vultures. I hugged the wall under one of the camera's blind spots, feeling like a secret agent, the same way I did all those years ago. I sprawled out on the ground, eyes on the sky, watching the clouds float lazily past, not knowing that this was the exact spot where I fell after Fernando leveled me in the gut that one time, after LC ripped one of my cards in half. The trailer was still there too, and peeking in one of the windows I could see art projects on display, flat screen monitors where the chunky old PCs used to be.

When I got back, a message was waiting for me. Drumroll, please:

From Wallace. Spoiler alert, but Topher never did message me back. Hey, you can't win 'em all, right?

Anyway, Wallace was Wallace. He said it was a bunch of dumb kid crap, all water under the bridge. He asked if I was still writing fiction, left the door open for future collaboration if I ever wanted one of my stories adapted to the screen. It might be a small, internet-only screen for now, but a screen nonetheless. He caught me up on the years that passed, but with frustratingly little detail about Lula. It turns out he left when I did and didn't know what happened to her either. He linked me to a Facebook page for a short film he'd been shopping around at festivals and asked if I'd help spread the word. Told me he'd do the same if I had anything.

After doing a little social media promotion for him, I sent Wallace a message back. I agreed that working together again would be cool. I meant it, too. Sent him over one of the stories I'd gotten published but still wasn't totally enthused with. Told him to chop it to bits. Then I asked for him to wish me luck.

He was online at the time. He asked me what the luck was for.

I'll need the luck, I told him, if I'm ever going to find Lula.

84. I-N-V-E-T-E-R-A-T-E

So I called her. Got nothing. As usual. I tried using star sixty-seven to catch her off guard, but she'd gotten used to that one too. She refused all calls that came up as private, I guess. But love does funny things to people. It makes them persistent (read: stalkerish). I walked Reb, gave him some food, and headed out in my rental alone. Off to Lula's parents' place.

They basically never saw me when the two of us were together, so I was fairly incognito. Incognito, I guess, until I told them who I was, why I was looking for Lula.

"Waldo? Waldo Collins?"

Her dad. His face: I can't fucking believe this. Luckily, Lula's mom was there too. She held him back. Like physically held him back. I just stood there. Lula's dad:

"I'll fucking kill him."

Lula's mom:

"Stop it. You're being crazy."

"The hell I am. Who does he think he is coming here now?"

"Just stop."

I apologized profusely, and that helped a little. I didn't know exactly what I was apologizing for, but still. And then

310

Lula's mom got serious. She looked at her husband, then back at me.

"We should tell him where she is."

"You can't be serious."

"Look at him."

He did. Lula's mom:

"He doesn't know. He has no idea."

Me:

"Know what?"

"See?"

Lula's dad started sighing instead of punching. He wasn't looking at me.

"Fine."

Lula's mom wrote Lula's address on the back of an old grocery list, the ink bleeding through. I said thank you, and her mom said fine, and her dad said nothing, and I got into my shitty rental before her dad thought twice about the whole killing me thing.

*

Her place was right on the border between Evanston and Chicago, a little townhome nestled between apartment buildings on a tree-lined street maybe a ten minute drive from Lake Michigan. The lake itself is shaped like a U, just like the buildings of Bay Colony. But this cup's been filled and will stay that way for the foreseeable future.

Everything was too quiet. The cicadas were MIA. Sound of traffic being piped in from some tiny speaker a mile down the road. The water a lazy hush in the distance, like a slurred whisper. Leaves wiggled against each other to help, but they were quiet too. I got out of this car that wasn't mine. I moved legs that suddenly *felt* like they weren't mine. I breathed deep breaths, from my diaphragm, like they said to do at the Zen

311

temple I went to back when I hit bottom, when the only way I could go was up.

I stood at the door. I waited. Then I knocked.

Watched the doorknob twist. Saw the door open.

Looked down.

Standing in front of me was a kid no older than seven. A boy. His hair a shaggy, dirty blonde verging on brown. In my day he'd get the bowl cut treatment, but his hair was swept to the side. In his hands a trading card of some sort. Could've been Pokémon, but he was hiding it from me. Eyeing me like I might try to steal it. My heart hurt like it would when I first started running.

"Don't worry, I'm not here to steal your card. Is your mom home? Or dad?"

More chest pain. I remembered to breathe.

"Who are you?"

"I'm an... old friend of your mom's."

"You look sad and happy and weird and how do I know you're not a weirdo?"

I laughed.

"I am a weirdo. You're correct. But so is your mom. That's why we used to be friends."

...

"I'm a good weirdo."

Before he could say anything, she was there. Behind him. Standing at the edge of the light that was coming in through the front door, so I couldn't see her clearly but she could see me just fine. I blinked. Cold drops of sweat trickled down my sides and stopped at my waistband. The kid looked at me, turned around. Back to me. Then his mom.

"I don't know who this guy is, but he's an old friend. He's a good weirdo."

Lula just nodded. He could go inside now, sweetie.

We didn't move at all. We were in a Mexican standoff.

Guns at our hips. Lula sighed, or maybe she just remembered to breathe too. She walked toward me, crossing the doorframe, into the light, and I watched it happen like it was a movie.

We took turns trying to say something, but the words just wouldn't come out, so we stood there and looked at each other instead.

The way she looked was like a promise that'd been fulfilled. I wondered what she thought of me, agonized over it, then tried to blot it from my mind. Everything was blotted from my mind when I looked at her.

"Waldo? What are you doing here?"

The million dollar question. Salt pillars. And all that.

"I wanted to see you. Not in a weird way. I got your address from your parents. Your dad wanted to beat my ass, but your mom ended up giving it to me. I sound really stupid right now. I'm going to let you talk."

"I don't know what to say."

"Is that a good thing or a bad thing?"

"Bad. Maybe good. Or both. I don't know."

"If it's about the kid, I mean, that's fine. I didn't have hopes about you and I or anything. All right, that's not true. But it's okay. We can just see each other, if you're cool with that. Just talk."

"I don't know. Maybe. Sure."

"The kid's dad is at work, right? I'm not gonna get beat up, am I? One potential fight in a day is way over my quota."

"His name's Cal. Calvin if he's in trouble. And his dad..."

Everything in my chest migrated suddenly to the pit of my stomach.

"His dad hasn't been around in a long time."

"So he's... out of the picture?"

"I thought so."

"You thought so?"

"Well, yeah. I mean, he was out of the picture. Until now."

Deep breaths. From the diaphragm. I opened my mouth, closed it, opened it again. Tears formed, and I forced them back.

"Is this real right now?"

A nearly imperceptible nod from Lula.

"But you said... I thought you weren't going to do it."

"I thought so too. And I have nothing against it, you know, but I don't know. Something just told me not to. So I didn't."

"So you didn't."

"So I didn't."

"So what's he like? Can I talk to him?"

"Can we take this a little slower? I mean, you did just show up at my door, unannounced, after seven years."

"I would've come sooner. I mean, I wanted to come sooner."

"And you didn't because..."

"I thought you didn't want anything to do with me. I tried calling, but you never picked up. I took the hint."

"There was no hint. I wanted you to try harder. I wanted you to want it."

"I did want it. I *do* want it."

"If you wanted it that bad, you wouldn't have left."

"That's not fair. I was going to school."

"You were running away. I didn't get to run away."

"If I knew you were keeping it... If I knew you were having him, I never would've left."

"Bullshit. You wanted to give him up for adoption. Wanted me to carry him to term so you wouldn't have to live with the guilt."

"Lula, I was seventeen. I was a kid."

"Don't give me that, 'I didn't know any better' crap."

"No, I did. I did know better. But I wasn't ready to be a father."

...

"You could've told me. I wish I would've known. I would've come back."

"Well, now you know."

"Yeah."

The card had to have been Pokémon. I could hear the theme song carrying from under the door, the singer insisting he wanted to be the very best, like no one ever was.

"So did you at least become a big fancy writer man like you always wanted?"

We smiled at each other through our tears.

"I became something. Not sure what yet, but I became something."

Lula just nodded. Looked me over.

"You look good, by the way. Fit."

I had a hard time maintaining eye contact. No one had ever accused me of being fit before.

"You're a beautiful."

Lula laughed out loud. I could feel the heat in my cheeks:

"'You're a beautiful'? Did I really just say that?"

"I do believe you did, yes. That was a thing that happened."

The wind carried our laughter down the street. The theme song finished, and you could hear a summary of what our protagonists were up to via voiceover.

"So I know I'm pretty cool and all, but there's got to be some other reason you drove all this way, right?"

"Yeah."

"And?"

"My mom's dying of cancer. My dad's I-don't-know-where. Maybe in jail. And I think my old bully might be here too. Could be wrong, though. Probably should've done my research before driving the eight hundred miles to get here, huh?"

Silence.

"How's that for baggage?"

She smiled.

She said I looked hungry, that I should come inside for like a grilled cheese or something. I did that thing where I said I wouldn't want to impose while desperately hoping she'd insist. She did, so I accepted.

Cal was on the couch when I got in, sketching Mewtwo and getting frustrated whenever the camera cut away too soon. He filled in the details he couldn't see from memory. He was really good, too. Line work and shading disciplined for a kid his age. So he was an artist like his mom? He didn't know, he just liked to draw stuff. Mostly Pokémon. And could I watch the episode with him, or would that disturb his creative flow? I could watch it with him if I wanted. I just needed to try not to move too much or it'd shake the paper. I thought I could manage that.

Butter sizzled in the pan, in the kitchen that was only a few feet away from the living room. Cozy would be the glass-half-full way to describe the place. We were close enough that I could see Lula covertly peeking at us, making as if she was looking for a spatula, or a plate, or a slice of cheese every time I'd try to catch her in the act.

"So you're in, like, what? Second grade?"

"Third."

I nodded like an idiot.

"Cool. Very cool."

...

"Got any favorite subjects yet?"

"Art."

"Makes sense."

Butter sizzling. Pikachu Pika-ing.

"I'm guessing you've seen this episode before?"

"You can stop asking me questions."

"What?"

He stopped sketching. Looked up at me.

"You keep asking me questions because you want to know more about me because I'm your son, but I don't want you to. So you can stop asking."

Lula, from the kitchen:

"Calvin."

Me, from the couch:

"How did you...?"

"I'm not stupid. I'm little, but I'm not stupid. Everyone thinks kids are dumb. I look like you. I sound like you. You've been gone for a long time. I figured it out when you guys were talking outside."

QED. Back to sketching Mewtwo. Lula flipped over a sandwich, stirred the tomato soup.

"Yes. Well. Okay. Sorry for underestimating you."

"It's cool."

Lula:

"Cheese has been prepared in grilled fashion."

We sat down to eat. Lula with hers cut into quadrants, both mine and Cal's cut into triangular halves, his with the crusts amputated like I'd always have it as a kid. Strictly ketchup dipping for Lula, but Cal and I did the same thing where we'd soak our sandwich halves in tomato soup till critical soggy mass before eating them. He even crushed up Saltines in his hands and sprinkled them over his soup the same way I always did.

We didn't talk at all, but it wasn't necessarily an awkward silence. A strand of hair pulled loose from Lula's ponytail and dangled over her grilled cheese. My hand reached out of its own will, got as far as the space above the table between us. Cal watched us as he turned soupy crackers into soupy mush with his spoon. Lula pushed the hair back over her ear, looked at me while she did it.

Cal finished first so he could get back to sketching/watching, and I helped Lula with the dishes. When we finished, she hinted that it was time to go, and I was positive that only like two minutes at most had elapsed since I knocked on her door. I had trouble with my laces. Cal asked if I needed Velcro shoes or something, and I called him an inveterate smartypants. He actually went, "Inveterate, I-N-V-E-T-E-R-A-T-E, inveterate," and I couldn't keep up with the deadpan, so I laughed. I told him that was really good.

Lula led me out, closed the door behind her.

"Thanks for the cheese prepared in grilled fashion."

"You're most welcome, kind sir."

I bowed, and she curtsied. The birds were talking very loudly, then not at all. They wanted to eavesdrop.

"I know this sounds cliché before I say it, but it seriously feels like two seconds have passed since I saw you last, tops."

"Waldo."

"Yeah, yeah, I know, slow down, I'm going too fast, I know. It's just, I have a hard time doing that when the love of my life is standing there in front of me."

"Don't do that to me."

"I know. I'm sorry. I can't help it, though. I mean it. I feel it. It's hard enough not to kiss you right now. And I know you can turn me down. I know you can cut your ties and move on with your life and that'll be it. I know you can say no. But that's not going to change how I feel. And it's stupid, and I'm stupid, but I still love you."

Her chest hitched when she told me to stop. Eyes filled.

"Right, but I can't. For seven years I tried to do that. Tried to swallow my feelings for you, swallow Drew dying, Rodhi, all of it. I can't do it anymore. I can't. I've got to be me. I've got to say these things in my brain. I have to let myself feel things."

Lula tried to will the tears back in, but one of them fell anyway. She breathed. She nodded.

"Okay."

"Okay?"

"Okay."

"I'm going to go do what I came here to do. So I'll leave you alone for now. Let you think. Call in a couple days. Would that be cool?"

"Yeah."

"Cool."

"Yeah."

I made the long walk back to my rental. Acted like I was fiddling with my keys when I got in, but I just wanted to see her there some more, outside my window, across the street, the shadows of branches dancing on her face, hair, hands.

I didn't make a noise the whole drive back to the motel. I listened to cars displacing air all around me. I watched things move from one location to another.

85. Well, that was fun.

The palliative care place puts me on hold before they get my name. On the line, there's a soulful instrumental version of "Careless Whisper," all saxophone, and I'm smiling even though I feel like I'm going to throw up. Sorry, PGN, get sick. The song's cut right in the middle of a sax solo, and there's a nurse on the other end who's trying to sound cheery despite the nature of her job. She asks for my name, and I say well. She asks Earl? I say um. She insists she didn't catch that, and can I say it again please. So I hang up.

I take Reb out for a walk, let him pee on all the things. We come back, but he didn't shit, so we go out again. I try to take him out for a third walk a couple minutes later, but he whines. I look at him:

"Fine. I'll do it."

*

They have these little paper cups inside with smiling baby animals on them. The nurse at the front asks for my name, and when I tell her, she asks if I was the weirdo who hung up on her. I tell her yes, that was me. She asks if I'm here to see Mona. I say that I am. She insists she understands why I might've had second thoughts. No offense, of course. I assure her none is taken.

She leads me down the hallway and to the door of Mona's room, which is closed. When she goes to turn the knob, I tell her no. That will not be necessary. I extend my hand for a handshake. She looks at me like I have mental problems. Asks why I want a handshake.

"Look, I'm nervous and I haven't seen my mom in seven years and would you just shake my damn hand?"

She does. I tell her she can go now. She does. I tell myself I can open the door now. I do.

"I told you I'm not getting any more fucking lines put in today. You can wait till—"

And then she sees me. Everything comes in slow and wavy like the air above a summertime grill.

I can hardly recognize her. Her face is bloated, scarred, worn. Her eyes look dead, like there's no one home. The bags underneath them are grayish pillows for tiny people. I can't help myself:

"Oh, you are sick."

Her face changes slowly, then all at once. Her eyes fill with tears that she quickly squeezes down her cheeks. She holds her IVed arms out to me.

"My baby."

I'm not sure she ever called me her baby, even when I *was* a baby. I stand right there.

"Come here. It's okay. Come here."

I shuffle over, ignore the scent of urine in the air, and bend over her, let her grab me and hold me close. When I pull away, I catch a glimpse of her face for just a second. It's empty—wiped of emotion. She could be waiting for the bus or something. When she knows I'm looking, though, it turns back to a sad smile, fresh tears brimming at the edges of her eyes. She looks at me:

"I can't believe you're here."

"I know. Me neither."

"You're silly."

She laughs. I guess my wince is visible, because:

"What's wrong? What is it?"

"Why aren't you yelling? Calling me a fat fuck or something?"

"First of all, you're not fat. You look good."

I feel like I've been punched. She goes on:

"I've changed. I'm a new person. These years have given me a long time to think. To figure out what's important."

"That's pretty convenient."

Her right eye twitches, but just barely. Blink and you'd miss it.

"Look, I know you're mad at me. And you have every reason to be. Every right to be. But I'm a new person."

She's staring wide-eyed, like I just said I was the one with glioblastoma. The thought crosses my mind that she's trying to will my belief into existence.

"Waldo, I'm dying. Please believe me. Can't you give that to your mother? The person who raised you?"

"No. You don't get to say that. You don't get to make me feel guilty. You didn't raise me. Pokémon raised me. N64 raised me. Cartoons and shitty stories I wrote as a kid. Those things raised me. You didn't raise me."

"Waldo—"

"No. And you know what, I said I wouldn't be angry or bitter, but fuck that for like five minutes. For five minutes, that Waldo can go to hell.

"All my life, you either tried to make me into something I wasn't or else treated me like I was some unwanted lump. And I know it sounds like 'oh, poor me,' but I need to fucking get this out, so don't. Every parent has their day of reckoning, when they need to face their kids and all the shit they've done to them. I'll have mine, I'm sure. So here's yours. It wasn't my fault Grandpa died. Or Drew. And the worst fucking thing, the *worst* thing you can do to your kid is make him feel like it *is* his fault. Do you know what that does to a person? Do you know the kind of gnawing, keep-you-up-all-night-every-night guilt that gives you? And I know you were projecting your own shit onto me, I know you never dealt with your issues and so you made me deal with them instead. I know all that. But it doesn't make it any less shitty.

"But even as I'm saying this, even now I don't hate you. I want to with every fucking fiber of my being, but I don't. I refuse to."

Her eye twitches again:

"Are you done being a crybaby?"

I laugh, but when it comes out it sounds more like leaking air. I look up at one of the room's corners and shake my head. She goes on:

"You think it's all about you, don't you? Even when I'm dying."

"I should've known you'd pull the 'I'm dying' card every chance you got. God knows you always wished for something like this."

"How dare you talk to me like that? Show some respect."

"I'll show you respect when you've earned it. Until then, maybe I'm just better off leaving."

"Yeah, quit. Walk away. It's what you're good at. Just like your father."

"You know, a part of me... A naïve part of me really did think you'd change. That you couldn't be that awful when the end was staring you right in the face. That we could have that cliché forgiveness before you slipped away, and it'd all mean something. But I was wrong. Should've stuck with my gut."

"And I thought you'd do something other than run away from your family when they needed you. Your grandfather would be ashamed, God rest his soul."

"Oh yeah? And what would he say about you? About how you treated your own son like absolute shit? Or how about when you siphoned Drew's Army money? Or when you got addicted to pills? Or what about you fucking a married man?"

It's right about here she picks up the phone next to her many beeping machines and throws it at my head. It misses and catches the door handle behind me instead, phone guts spilling out, but there's no oven for them to slide under, no Reb to paw at them.

"Get out!"

She's red in the face, forehead vein throbbing. I'm calm.

"Don't worry. I'm going."

I step over the broken phone pieces on my way out and close the door quietly behind me.

86. And that's all right.

So I go home. Sorry, to the motel. It's the closest thing I have to a home at this point, and that's all right. That's okay. I stand by the wall and stare at the puttied-over, fist-sized mark that was there when I got here, consider adding one of my own. But I don't. I sit down on the motel room's sole, wobbly chair and pull out my laptop. I start it up and work on a manuscript. *This manuscript*. I'm almost done with it, too.

Reb whines, so I feed him and put more water in his dish, but that's not it. He nudges his nose under my hand and practically forces me to pet him. It's for your own good, he's telling me. So I comply. When his affection meter's full, I get back to writing. I make the mistake of reading what I put down months (and hundreds of pages) ago. There are whole chapters I want to cut, events I want to scrub out and make a happy palimpsest of instead. But I can't.

So I call my mother. It rings and rings, and when the nurse hears I want to talk to her again, she asks if I'm sure. I say I am, and she asks if I'm sure I'm sure. I insist that I'm sure I'm sure. She puts her on.

"Look. You're not going to hang up on me. You're going

to hear me out. I don't give a shit what you did, what I did, what was said yesterday or seven years ago. I'm going to visit again, and I'm going to keep visiting, and you're going to go along with it because you have a soul. Because you're not as terrible as I make you out to be. Because I need answers, and you know I should have them. So that's it. That's all. I'll be back. You can hang up now."

Click. Dial tone.

*

I find LC the way I found Wallace and Topher—through Facebook. Most of his info is guarded from prying eyes. All I basically have to go on is his American flag profile picture, his hometown of Des Plaines, IL, and what he has listed as his current city—also Des Plaines, IL. So I message him. None of the forgiveness-offering I sent before. I just say I want to meet. That I'm in Des Plaines, and if he wants to meet too, he can name the time and place. I click send.

His reply comes less than an hour later. All he sends is an address and a time. Noon tomorrow, and the address ends up being the townhouse that that kid with the pellet gun used to live in, on Meadow Lane.

*

I open the car door right after turning off the engine, because if I don't then I might never do it. I might just leave. My legs go numb the closer I get to his front door, stomach drops out like I just sped over a hill. I feel cold all over, so I take deep breaths from my diaphragm and close my eyes till the feeling goes away. I knock and wait.

I don't hear any steps. I consider leaving. He could've been bullshitting about wanting to meet up. This could be an ambush. But then the door opens. And almost closes. He stops it with one of his front wheels.

I'm supposed to believe that the wasted man sitting in the wheelchair in front of me is Mario Scalveretti III. I'm not supposed to stare. But there you go.

His left leg ends at shin-level, and he's left the smooth nub exposed. His left hand's missing both ring finger and pinky, so he could perpetually be giving a peace sign. The place where his left ear once was is now a whirl of scarred flesh, the scar not so fresh that it'd be bright red (like my car-dragging scars were for a while), but not so old that it's become faded and white either. His nose is largely missing, lips grafted from what I guess must be ass flesh. He looks up at me from his burn-scarred face, expressionless, and it's only when he passes his eyes over me that I realize his left eye isn't following his right one.

"Bwaldo."

I could laugh at the way his lips render my name, push him out of his chair. I could do these things if I wanted to.

There's 294 again, beyond us. Cars whooshing past because there's always somewhere to go, someone to see.

"Mario."

He motions for me to come in. I do.

Mountains of dirt have ascended in all the corners of all the rooms. Dust tumbleweeds roll down rubber-scarred hardwood, some scrapes in the wood where I figure his brakes must've locked up on him once or twice. Garbage overflows from the kitchen's can, and there's some older trash gathered at the can's edge, some of it worked into the tile where his wheels must've run it over endlessly on his way back and forth. On the whole, Mona could've been his interior decorator. Other than a single giant American flag draped across the wall, his place is pretty bare. Other than that, his place could be a rarely cleaned hospital room. He squeaks up to me before I can complete my visual tour.

"Dhyou bwant someding do drink?"

My lips are dry. Throat is cracking.

"No, I'm good."

"Byou sure? I got sub PBR."

"I'm good."

So he wheels into the kitchen and brings back two cans. I'm about to refuse, but then I realize they're both for him. He drinks with his right hand and wipes away the beer that trickles down his incomplete mouth with his left. He finishes the first beer before I can decide who should or will talk first. It'll be him, apparently:

"Dhyou know I bwas like this? Is at bwhy you came?"

I shake my head. He cracks open the second beer and finishes it in half the time it took him to finish the first.

"Bwhat are you dinking?"

I make my eyes catch his.

"There's what I'm thinking and then there's what I want to be thinking."

He nods for me to go on.

"I want to say you deserve it. Want to laugh in your face. If I'm being honest, I want to push you out of your chair right now and beat the shit out of you. Maybe kill you. If I'm being honest."

"Bease do."

"I want to do these things, and maybe I'd even be justified doing them, but I can't."

Silence.

"Maybe can't's not a good word. Maybe won't's better. I won't do them."

"Bwhy not?"

"Because... I don't know. Maybe because I've earned the chance to be better. Maybe you have too. And this could change two minutes from now. Don't get me wrong. Two minutes from now, I could want to choke you to death. But I'm trying, Mario. I'm trying really fucking hard not to. Because I know... Because I know Rodhi wouldn't want me to. Because I know I'm better than that. I know I *can* be better than that. You know what I mean?"

He just looks at me. I can't tell if the tears in his eyes are the result of injured tear ducts or what.

"I bwould undershand. I killed your frien."

Deep breaths. Deep and deeper still.

"Ish it 'cause you're scared do?"

"It's 'cause I'm scared I would. It'd be too easy."

And we sit like that, in silence, till Mario wheels over to get more beer. On his way, he disembowels one of the empty cans, knocks over the other. He stops before he reaches the kitchen, though. Opens the basement door and looks down into the dark for a while. Turns his chair to face me.

"It *could* be eashy. It could be an acciden."

The wind picks up outside, knocking around leaves that have jumped the autumnal gun. It whistles in the cracks of Mario's door, the cracks he can't or won't fill in. When Mario blinks, his right eye resets but his left one doesn't, like it's the point upon which everything else in the house orbits. So I get up. Accidentally kick one of the cans across the room, where it clatters against a trunk Mario must've brought back from Afghanistan. So I walk over to him, behind his chair. So I rest my hands on the handles. Mario doesn't inhale sharply. Doesn't wince. None of that.

My knuckles whiten. On my hands, there are blue-green veins.

The cicadas outside protest the wind. Birds, too.

I let go of the handles. Walk over to the fridge and take out a PBR. Drink it without breathing, till it's empty. Take another and another, only drawing breath between them, coming up for air after a deep dive. Mario watches me finish his six-pack and doesn't say a word.

*

When Mario gets out of his chair, he becomes a hermit crab leaving its shell—arms grasping, movements awkward, shifting weight. I slur that I can give him a hand, but he's fine. He can manage. Dust clings to him as he army crawls over to the trunk. It mixes with his sweat and stains his clothes.

In the trunk, there's a uniform, some personal effects, a medal. Some papers that mean nothing to me but which must mean something to Mario. He's propped up against the wall, sifting through what's inside, making arbitrary piles. He pulls out a picture and stares at it for a while. Passes it over to me with a lopsided grin.

"He had doe idea."

It's a picture of Mario in full uniform, before his injury, posed in front of an immaculately kept American flag. Crew cut on full display. Barely an ounce of fat on him. All sharp lines and angles. Not a hint of emotion on his face. Eyes hardened. You know the kind of picture I'm talking about.

He finds another picture, scrutinizes it before passing it to me. He's a little more relaxed in this one, letting a hint of a smile show on his face as he stands in front of an armored personnel carrier.

He passes me the next one a second later. It's Mario and what must be the rest of his unit, all of them with rifles equipped, their digital camo approximating the sand behind them decently well. All of the faces looking like... All of the faces...

It's Drew. Standing there next to Mario, sporting his practiced tough guy look. A bit more muscle mass, a more angled face, but it's him. It's Drew. Mario just nods. Smiles.

He takes his time to say it right:

"Your brother."

He watches the way I smile too, even against the tears. He says: "Our brother."

I can't cry about this one. Rather, I could, but I won't. I choose not to. So I laugh instead. Mario joins me when he realizes it's not a malicious laugh or anything. And in time, he'll tell me all about how Drew saved his life, how he took point when he didn't need to, how if Drew wasn't right there at the exact moment the IED detonated, Mario would've been the one in the pictures, unable to explain away the look on his face, unable to reminisce. But for right now, we're laughing. For right now, we're sitting on the floor, being here, the both of us, in this moment. And that's all right.

87. I found it.

My father's room in the group home he's staying at is remarkably similar to the one my mother occupies over at the palliative place. He's not supposed to smoke inside, but he does anyway, blowing his smoke into the open window. There are little pinhole burns on his sheets from where he must've dropped his cig while smoking in bed. Someone's taken my dad's skin, stretched it out about two sizes too big, and then put it back over the frame of his body. His mustache is gone, and I consider that this might be the first time I've seen him without it. He's starting to gray. He's got an old fishing pole in the corner of his room, what I can see is one of the few possessions he brought here with him. When he's done ashing his cigarette, he sits at the edge of his bed and feeds line through the spool, reels in and watches potential tangles straighten themselves out before disappearing back into the fishing pole's innards. When he looks at me, he smiles like I've just walked in and we're making our introduction, even after the fifth or sixth time. I pepper our intro convo with a couple of duplicate questions, but he looks at me funny and asks why I keep asking the same thing. No memory loss, I guess.

"How long have you been here?"

He reels in. Doesn't look at me, but says this:

"You remember when I used to take you down to Busse?"

"Yeah."

"And that time you caught the largemouth, and we went down to the bait shop to get our picture taken, and how you held the bass up like it was a piece of poo?"

I nod.

"And the look on your face. Priceless."

He reels in all the way. Opens up the spool and gives it some slack so he can do it all over again.

"The one you caught was bigger than mine. Those were some good fish, too. You remember that?"

"I do."

"I remember the way you picked out the bones from the flesh and stuck them into your mashed potatoes like little flags. Little fish flags, you called them."

"There'd be like a dozen fish flags by the end."

"That's right. At least."

Just the wind-click-stop of the reel.

"How long have you been here, Dad?"

"I remember when you were still inside your mother and we went out to a bar one night and she wanted to play this one pinball game there. What was it called?"

"Dad."

"Super Mario. You remember Super Mario?"

"I remember Super Mario."

"Good. Well it had a picture of Mario up top. He was in the air, just hovering there, like he was always jumping. I remember I gave her some of my Jack and Coke. She didn't want to take it, but I told her it'd be fine. So she had a sip. I said another couldn't hurt, right? Then she'd take a sip every time she got a point bonus. Then when she got multiball. By the end of it, I was carrying her in my arms out of the bar like a baby. She didn't get sick, though. I remember that.

Your mother was never one to get sick after drinking."

...

"You didn't cry at all when you came out. We thought you might be dead. Born dead. You know. But you weren't. There you were."

"Yeah. Yeah, right."

"There you were."

"How long have you been here?"

"Since you left. They had me in this other room at first, but I had them move me."

"Why'd you move?"

"You look good, Wally. I'm proud of you."

My voice fails me for a second, but then it comes back:

"Why'd you move?"

My dad stares at me with bulging eyes that appear out of nowhere. His veins stick out.

"Those bastards were trying to kill me. All of them. They had everything down to a science. They were trying to destroy me. They bugged my pillow. I have it."

I sigh.

"What?"

"Nothing."

"I've got the bug if you want to see it. Come here, I'll show you."

"Dad, you don't have to..."

But he's already searching, first the scant dresser they've given him, then under his bed, his mattress. When he starts trying to pry up floorboards, I ask him to stop. He does.

"I know it's here somewhere. I found it, Wally. I found it."

...

"You've got to believe me. I *found* it."

"Dad, you—"

Breath leaves me.

"What?"

"Nothing, Dad."

"I *found* it, Waldo. I really did."

"Okay, Dad."

"Okay?"

"Okay."

I walk over and put my arm around him. He latches onto me like he never wants to let go. Like he's found something precious and doesn't want it to ever leave.

88. I tolerate you.

Weeks pass like days. I keep up with running, with writing, with submitting, with visiting, with everything. I keep up. I've taken the *Katamari* approach to it all—start small and keep rolling till you've rolled up an entire city. It's a decent strategy, too. I've been getting more short stories published, landing more freelance gigs. I'm saving up. My mother calls me on the good days and tells me it's safe to visit. Safe, like she's a werewolf and we're avoiding the full moon. Even her good days are fading, though. Days when she'll call me Drew, or Roger, or even Joe. Mario Joseph Scalveretti, Jr. would take too long to say, I guess.

On these good days, I feed her ice chips and stories, watch shitty soap operas, and we call each other fucking assholes till we've tired ourselves out and both end up needing ice chips to cool down. The nurses have learned not to interrupt when we're in a yelling binge. It'll end eventually anyway, and then we'll be back to where we started—making fun of crappy daytime TV and acting like these good days will last long enough. Long enough for what, I don't know. Or maybe I know but don't want to say.

She says she loves me at first, but I call BS, and after a few yelling binges on that she switches over to, "I tolerate you." And that's how our good days end, with one of the nurses telling me visiting hours are over, and Mom looking out the window, her eyes sometimes lucid, sometimes gone, and us going:

"I tolerate you."

"I tolerate you too."

*

I get a call from a nurse one day, her tone all put-on somber and necessary professionalism. "Hello, Mr. Collins," etc. I cut to the chase:

"She's dead, isn't she?"

"She, uh. No. No, she's not dead."

"But she will be soon?"

"We're not entirely—"

"I should visit? Pay my last respects? Speak now or forever hold my peace?"

"Yes. Yes, basically."

"Okay. Okay, thank you."

*

Outside, the trees are just starting to lose their leaves, some of them dropping before they're ready, before they've even changed color. I walk over these scattered green leaves, these un-crunchy discards, and I am okay with this. This is okay exactly because it isn't. Because nothing ever is, and why would we even want it to be?

So I walk into the palliative place and fill two cartoon animal paper cups with ice chips. So I sign in and ignore the looks of pity from all the nurses I come in contact with, these looks they must've given a thousand times before. So I walk into Mom's room.

The only way to describe it is to say she's done the best she can to hold on till I've gotten here. Her eyes wander over the pockmarked ceiling, through and past her TV, settling on the beeps and blips of her machine before finding me in all that fog. When she talks, it's like she's speaking from the bottom of a well that's been filled with noxious fumes, holding her breath in between words and trying not to succumb to the poison that's all around her. When she's not talking, her mouth hangs slack, eyes lost and faraway. The chemo has left her a wasted shell of herself. Her eye sockets bulge from her skull. Nose looks like it's melting off her face. Arms held together by hollow bird bones. Not a hair on her, like she's suddenly become a newborn. Like she's been wiped clean to start all over. It's beautiful outside. It's perfect outside. I hold a cup out to her.

"Ice chips. Eat them."

"Fuck you too."

"Yeah yeah yeah."

She takes her cup and balances it on her chest, because to hold it would require strength she doesn't have. She doesn't take any chips, though.

"I'm not above force-feeding you ice chips, you know."

"Oh, shut up."

She brings the cup to her mouth with a shaky hand. Jostles it till a few chips slide in and puts the cup back on her chest.

"Happy?"

And it's this word, this one little word that brings it all out. I don't know why. It just happens. I laugh so I won't cry and then cry because I can't laugh anymore and then laugh just to see what it feels like, and she laughs too, but it sounds like it's coming through PVC pipe lined with broken glass, so she stops, at least audibly, her laughter now silent, and the tears roll down both of our cheeks, and I'm silent now too, and it's just our lungs fighting to breathe, fighting for different reasons but fighting still, and when I know it's over, when I know I can speak again, and we've caught our breath, and the only sounds are the steady beeps of her machine, I tell her:

"Yes. Yes, I am."

And then we say it, both of us, so perfectly synchronized I can't even tell who said it first, a definite jinx-you-owe-me-a-Coke moment for sure:

"I tolerate you."

And I stay with her there, without a word, because all of them have been said, and there's no sound except the rhythmic beeps, and in time even those fade, and I watch the way the leaves fall outside in utter silence, in a perfect void, fluttering safely to the ground.

89. Here's Waldo

When we leave the car and close our doors and come out into this night that's like being scrubbed clean after a long run, it's just the three of us, out here, navigating grass that leads us to a hill. The way the three of us are lined up we could be Orion's belt, with me at the front, Lula in back, and Cal there between us, holding it all together. I walk this ground that I've walked a thousand times before, mount the hill and stop at the top so I can admire the way the light pollution gave up just for today, the way it let the universe have its turn so we could see the stars that we're mimicking now, or at least were mimicking until our constellation shifted so we could stand there, together, at the top of the hill.

Everything's in place. Everything is as it should be.

The willows dip their fronds over water too tired to move, too tired to do anything but rest and reflect, with the rocks at the boundaries of this old pond set to glimmer in the night and shine with the lightning bugs who own this place now and forever, little green flickers under their wings and the way the red dots on their heads look like eyes forever staring.

We make our way down to the water, us three, and I take

off my shoes, sit down on the grass, and dip my toes in. The water is cool and still. Cal wants to do this too, and Lula lets him. After a while, she takes her shoes off and joins us. And there's a swan, paddling in so slowly it doesn't even send up a ripple, gliding right toward us even though we have no food. It stops there, angling its neck just so. Watching us. I take out the jar I've brought with. I open it up and poke little air holes at the top of the lid. I hand it to Cal and tell him to catch every lightning bug he can find. To fill his jar with the stars. Lula and I watch the way he runs off into the night, with the lights and the sounds and the things that are all, all of them, all right.

About Atmosphere Press

Atmosphere Press is an independent, full-service publisher for excellent books in all genres and for all audiences. Learn more about what we do at atmospherepress.com.

We encourage you to check out some of Atmosphere's latest releases, which are available at Amazon.com and via order from your local bookstore:

An Expectation of Plenty, a novel by Thomas Bazar
Sink or Swim, Brooklyn, a novel by Ron Kemper
Lost and Found, a novel by Kevin Gardner
Skinny Vanilla Crisis, a novel by Colleen Alles
The Mommy Clique, a novel by Barbara Altamirano
Eaten Alive, a novel by Tim Galati
The Sacrifice Zone, a novel by Roger S. Gottlieb
Olive, a novel by Barbara Braendlein
Itsuki, a novel by Zach MacDonald
A Surprising Measure of Subliminal Sadness,
    short stories by Sue Powers
Saint Lazarus Day, short stories by R. Conrad Speer
The Lower Canyons, a novel by John Manuel
Shiftless, a novel by Anthony C. Murphy
Connie Undone, a novel by Kristine Brown
A Cage Called Freedom, a novel by Paul P.S. Berg
The Escapist, a novel by Karahn Washington
Buildings Without Murders, a novel by Dan Gutstein

About the Author

Nick Olson is an author and editor from Chicagoland now living in North Carolina. He was a finalist for *Glimmer Train*'s Very Short Fiction Award, and he's been published in *SmokeLong Quarterly, Hobart, decomP,* and other fine places. When he's not writing his own work, he's sharing the wonderful work of others over at *(mac)ro(mic)*. Here's Waldo is his first novel. You can keep up with Nick at nickolsonbooks.com or tweet him @nickolsonbooks.